Who are you, Joy Donnelly?
Doug asked silently.

Where did you come from, with your big dreams and your heartbreaking smile and your eyes full of hope? And what did they see, those eyes, that you're so afraid to tell me? Why won't you trust me?

Trust me. Doug pressed his fingers against his burning eyelids. He was beginning to wonder if she ever would. Damn—she was just so…so bottled up. So full of pain. It was driving him crazy, not being able to reach her, not being able to get at what was eating her alive.

The thing was, he kept wanting to reach for her, touch her, hold her in his arms and make it all go away. And that was driving him crazy, too. He was afraid he was getting too close to this case.

Too close to *her.*

Dear Reader,

Talk about starting the new year off with a bang! Look at the Intimate Moments lineup we have for you this month.

First up is Rachel Lee's newest entry in her top-selling Conard County miniseries, *A Question of Justice*. This tale of two hearts that seem too badly broken ever to mend (but of course are about to heal each other) will stay in your mind—and your heart—long after you've turned the last page.

Follow it up with Beverly Barton's *The Outcast*, a Romantic Traditions title featuring a bad-boy hero—and who doesn't love a hero who's so bad, he's just got to be good? This one comes personally recommended by #1-selling author Linda Howard, so don't miss it! In *Sam's World*, Ann Williams takes us forward into a future where love is unknown—until the heroine makes her appearance. Kathleen Creighton is a multiple winner of the Romance Writers of America's RITA Award. If you've never read her work before, start this month with *Eyewitness* and you'll know right away why she's so highly regarded by her peers—and by readers around the world. Many of you have been reading Maura Seger's Belle Haven Saga in Harlequin Historicals. Now read *The Surrender of Nora* to see what Belle Haven—and the lovers who live there—is like today. Finally there's Leann Harris's *Angel at Risk*, a story about small-town secrets and the lengths to which people will go to protect them. It's a fittingly emotional—and suspenseful—close to a month of nonstop fabulous reading.

Enjoy!

Leslie Wainger
Senior Editor and Editorial Coordinator

Please address questions and book requests to:
Silhouette Reader Service
U.S.: 3010 Walden Ave., P.O. Box 1325, Buffalo, NY 14269
Canadian: P.O. Box 609, Fort Erie, Ont. L2A 5X3

EYEWITNESS

KATHLEEN CREIGHTON

Silhouette®
INTIMATE™MOMENTS®

Published by Silhouette Books

America's Publisher of Contemporary Romance

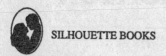

SILHOUETTE BOOKS

ISBN 0-373-07616-9

EYEWITNESS

Copyright © 1995 by Kathleen Modrovich

This edition published by arrangement with Harlequin Enterprises B.V.

® and TM are trademarks of Harlequin Enterprises B.V., used under
license. Trademarks indicated with ® are registered in the United States
Patent and Trademark Office, the Canadian Trade Marks Office and in
other countries.

Printed in U.S.A.

Books by Kathleen Creighton

Silhouette Intimate Moments

Demon Lover #84
Double Dealings #157
Gypsy Dancer #196
In Defense of Love #216
Rogue's Valley #240
Tiger Dawn #289
Love and Other Surprises #322
Wolf and the Angel #417
A Wanted Man #547
Eyewitness #616

Silhouette Desire

The Heart Mender #584
In From the Cold #654

Silhouette Books

Silhouette Christmas Stories 1990
"The Mysterious Gift"

KATHLEEN CREIGHTON

has roots deep in the California soil but has recently relocated to South Carolina. As a child, she enjoyed listening to old-timers' tales, and her fascination with the past only deepened as she grew older. Today, she says she is interested in everything—art, music, gardening, zoology, anthropology and history, but people are at the top of her list. She also has a lifelong passion for writing, and now combines her two loves in romance novels.

To Gary, for all the best reasons

Chapter 1

The blonde lay sprawled in the tumbled sheets like a bride on her wedding night, one arm flung out and back with the hand resting seductively on the pillow beside her head. The nails were a soft seashell pink, the fingers almost white and delicately curled, like the petals of a water lily. The other hand, gently fisted, nestled in the V of her rib cage just below her breasts, betraying a self-consciousness somehow the more poignant for falling short of full modesty.

Viewed from above, her eyes appeared to be closed, as if she were sleeping. Or, perhaps, from the slight upward curve of her lips, simply anticipating her lover's touch. But from Detective Sergeant Justin Tyler MacDougal's position near the foot of the bed he could see that they were only half closed, and that they had the unmistakable flat sheen of eyes that would never look upon a lover's face, or anything else, again.

Another one, he thought, feeling every one of his thirty-seven years and then some. And then, as almost always happened when the victim was young, female and beautiful, he had an instant's flashback to a different scene entirely, a scene from long ago but one he knew he wouldn't forget if he lived to be 137.

"Shot once in the head, looks like—right here." Careful not to touch anything, his partner, Burnside, leaned over the body, squinting in concentration. "Barrel impression, no powder burns around the entry wound. Small caliber, maybe even a .22. Wow." He made a clicking sound with his tongue and shook his head.

MacDougal grunted softly in agreement. A .22 slug could do a lot of damage rattling around inside a human skull.

Burnside, who hadn't been his partner very long, glanced at him to see if the grunt required a response, then turned his attention back to his examination. He peered closely at a pillow, cautiously sniffed it.

"Powder residue here, too. Looks like he put the pillow over her face to muffle the shot. That plus the small caliber—explains why nobody heard it."

MacDougal nodded his approval. It was beginning to look as if the kid might have the makings of a good homicide detective.

"Doesn't look like she put up a fight, either, does it?" said Burnside as he came to join MacDougal at the foot of the bed. "No bruises..." His voice trailed off and the two men stood together for the space of a moment too full of mutual understanding for words.

Burnside cleared his throat. "Whoever did it, looks like he, uh, made love to her and then shot her. Just like that. Before he even got..."

"Ain't love grand," MacDougal drawled, deliberately keeping his tone dry. Emotions like anger and outrage had no place in a homicide investigation.

Meanwhile, his gaze was traveling a familiar route around the bedroom, searching, cataloging. No sign of the weapon, but he hadn't expected it to be here. He'd been wrong before, but he was pretty sure he already knew how this one was going to go down.

"Stay with her until forensics gets here," he said, tucking his notebook into his shirt pocket. "I'm going to check around outside, see what the lady's neighbors have to say about her love life."

Carefully retracing his steps back through the apartment, he detoured long enough for a quick check of the contents of a purse he'd spotted earlier on the floor beside the couch. Balanced on the ball of one foot, he carefully withdrew a wallet of burgundy leather—not an expensive one—and flipped it open to the driver's license. He stared at the photograph encased in cloudy plastic for a long moment, then closed the wallet again. Before he slipped it back into the purse he poked once more through the accumulation of odds and ends in the bottom, just to make sure that what he hadn't found really wasn't there. He rose, then, and let his eyes make a brief but thorough survey of the living room. Nope—not here, either.

Two steps to the right gave him a good view of the tiny kitchen through a pass-through opening lined with wooden swivel-type bar stools. He gave it the same once-over, paying special attention to the countertops and the small pile of items beside the phone, all the places a woman might be expected to drop a set of car keys. Like the gun, he didn't really expect to find them.

He stepped outside onto the sunbaked landing. Milton Stanislowski, the medical examiner, was toiling up the concrete stairway from the courtyard below, sweating in the October heatwave in spite of a relative humidity that had to be near zero.

When the ME saw MacDougal he reared back in mock surprise and growled, "What the hell are you doing here? Oh, Lord, it must be a homicide. Can't think of anything else that'd tear MacDougal away from The Big Game."

MacDougal acknowledged that with a wry snort; it was common knowledge around the precinct that, having grown up in the shadow of Chavez Ravine, he took his baseball seriously—if you could apply a word like "serious" to someone whose favorite team was the Los Angeles Dodgers. This year, for example, after several grim seasons spent languishing in the bottom half of the Western Division, the Dodgers had defied all the odds-makers' predictions and

streaked to the lead after the All-Star break. Then, in typi-
cal Dodger fashion, with pennant fever in L.A. approaching epidemic levels, they'd gone into an equally dazzling
tailspin. They'd just barely managed to hold off a season-
ending charge by, of all the teams in the league, the lowly
San Diego Padres!

In the end, as it seemed to so often when the Dodgers were
involved, the unimaginable had happened. The two bitter
rivals from opposite ends of the 405 Freeway had finished
the regular season in a dead heat. A one-game play-off
would decide the Western Division winner, to be played, by
virtue of a coin toss, which the Dodgers had of course lost,
in San Diego. That game was being played this evening.
Right this very moment, in fact.

MacDougal had pulled every string he knew how to pull,
but he still hadn't been able to wrangle a ticket to the game.

The ME, having at last achieved the landing, elbowed him
in the ribs and grinned. "Hey, one helluva game, too. I was
listening to it on the radio on the way over here. Listen to
this—top of the second, and Sanchez leads off—"

MacDougal planted a good hard grip at the join of Stanislowski's neck and shoulder and proceeded to explain in a
good-natured and friendly way exactly what part of the
ME's anatomy he planned to cut off and feed to him if he
finished that sentence.

Stanislowski gave an admiring chuckle followed by a
grunt of sympathy. "Taping it, are you?"

"I sure hope so." MacDougal flattened himself against
the railing to get out of the way of the arriving swarm of
forensics experts, then jerked a thumb toward the open door
and muttered, "Bedroom—Burnside's in charge." He
started down the stairs. "I've got a six-hour tape in my
VCR. First guy that tells me how that game comes out's going to wish he hadn't."

"Good luck," the medical examiner wheezed cheerfully,
and heaved himself through the door after the photographer.

Yeah, right, good luck, thought MacDougal as he made
his way down the stairs and along a concrete walkway

shaded by overgrown banana plants and made perilous with
bird-of-paradise spikes and tendrils of creeping lantana.
Tonight that broadcast, featuring the golden voice of Vin
Scully, was going to be leaking through every wall and
booming from every car window in the city. He'd need to be
damn lucky, as well as deaf and blind, to avoid it.

Out in front, the uniformed officers who'd been first on
the scene were busy securing the area and interviewing possible witnesses. MacDougal always liked to keep up with the
new faces on the force, but he didn't recognize either the
Hispanic male unreeling the yellow crime scene tape or the
black female he could see talking to a a cluster of neighbors
on the apartment building's tiny rectangle of lawn. There
sure were a lot of new faces these days, he thought. Lot of
shaking up going on throughout the department, too, all
part of getting a new chief, he supposed—kind of a trickle-
down effect.

He'd been feeling a few of those trickles himself, pressure from some people who meant him well. But he had no
desire for a lieutenant's job and the desk that went with it,
not yet, not for a few years yet. He liked the streets, and he
liked partnering the rookies. He'd been around a long time,
and liked to think there were still a few things he could teach
these gung ho kids.

The officer on the lawn stopped scribbling in her note-
pad as he approached. MacDougal nodded at her while he
took careful note of the neighbors, who seemed a little edgy
and excited but not terribly broken up—about normal for
L.A. He glanced at the officer's name tag.

"Officer Cook? Sergeant MacDougal—homicide.
What've you got?" He looked at his watch. Almost nine-
thirty. It was going to be a long night. He wondered briefly
if the game was over yet, and who was winning.

Mary, JoJo, Daisy Pepper and Preacher threaded their
way together through the maze of parked cars in the Jack
Murphy Stadium parking lot. They were quiet but not
gloomy, simply subdued, like exhausted children after a long

day at Disneyland. That is, until JoJo hunched his massive shoulders and ventured, "It was a good game. Exciting."

"Hah," snapped Daisy Pepper. She was still sore about the bet she'd lost to Preacher; two bits was a lot of money to Daisy.

Mary heaved a sigh and shook her head. "I still can't believe the Dodgers scored *four runs*. And with two out in the ninth. Goes to show you." She looked around the half-empty parking lot. "I bet a lot of people are going to be surprised tomorrow morning."

"Teach 'em to leave in the seventh inning," Daisy scoffed. "You'd never catch anybody doin' that at Wrigley. Anybody did that, he'd never live it down." Daisy was an ex-bleacher bum from Chicago and didn't have much respect for West Coast fans.

"Seven to six," groaned Preacher. "What kind of score is that? That's not a baseball score, that's a football score."

"Well, the Dodgers got a good team," JoJo rumbled, lumbering along in their wake. "Score lotta runs. Makes it exciting. I like that."

"Exciting? You call that game exciting? Children, you don't kno-o-ow about exciting," Preacher intoned in the voice that had earned him his nickname. "You call these prima donnas the Dodgers got now a good team? The 1963 Dodgers—now *there* was a team. One-nothing, that's how they won games in those days. Won the pennant, and took the series from the Yankees in four straight, too, just like that. One-nothing. Koufax or Drysdale on the mound, Wills leads off with a walk, steals second, takes third on a sacrifice by Gilliam, comes home on a long fly ball off the bat of Frank Howard. Bingo—all she wrote. Give those guys one run and it was all over. Ten, twelve strikeouts a game, easy. Now, *that* was exciting."

"Sounds boring as a day in church to me," said Daisy. "Me, I like to see some runs. Give me a day in Chicago with the wind blowin' out, and I'll show you excitement. Balls flyin' outta there like they was made of rubber. Kids used to chase 'em in the street. That's the way baseball oughtta be. Fun."

Preacher snorted. "Sloppy. No finesse."

"Sports snob!"

It was an old debate and probably would have gone on a good bit longer, except they'd reached the car by that time and there was something new to argue about, like who got to sit up front this time. Mary left them going at it while she got out her keys and unlocked the Bronco, stepping over a pile of trash to do it.

"Unbelievable," she muttered under her breath. She got so tired of litter. She gathered up a crumpled cigarette pack, a paper cup and grease-stained bag from McDonald's, and a newspaper that was just beginning to scatter in the late evening breeze. Out-of-towners, she thought scornfully, when she saw that the paper was today's *L.A. Times.*

"Hey," she said as she tossed the trash into the back of the Bronco, "any of you guys want this paper?"

"Mine," yelped Daisy, giving Preacher a smug look. She was probably figuring it made up a little for the two bits she'd lost; newspaper was a valuable commodity on the streets. It was clean bedding, toilet paper, protection from the rain and insulation against the cold. Nobody was forgetting that it was October and that there'd be some nippy nights ahead, even in San Diego.

"It's yours," Mary said, but her voice trailed off, and instead of handing the newspaper over to Daisy she went on holding it in both hands while she stared down at the front page. The faces of three men gazed back at her with the fatuous self-confidence of political candidates. Beneath the faces was the headline, Search for New Police Chief Narrows. And below that, Three Final Choices for Head of LAPD to Come from Rank and File.

"Give it here," Daisy prompted from the back seat, wiggling outstretched fingers.

"In a minute..." Two of the faces were blurred and faded. The third stood out stark and clear in the artificial twilight. As stark and clear as a memory. "Oh, God," Mary whispered. "I don't believe it."

"What'sa matter?" JoJo asked, looking worried.

Daisy snaked a scrawny arm over the back of the seat and snatched the newspaper. She scooted back, folding it and tucking it jealously away inside her sweater.

"The world is the matter," Preacher said with a sorrowful sigh. "A mean and dangerous place. Filled with selfish people, hostility and distrust." He glared meaningfully along his shoulder at Daisy Pepper, who squinted up her eyes and stuck her tongue out at him.

Mary started the Bronco and edged cautiously into the line of vehicles winding slowly out of the parking lot.

"Mary?"

"Yeah, JoJo?"

The huge black man turned his head toward her and smiled, revealing missing teeth. Under the right circumstances, JoJo's smile could be a fearsome sight. "Thanks. You know—for the game and everything."

"Yes, indeed," Preacher drawled from the back seat, "we've all been remiss. Thank you, m'dear, thank you. Except for the, uh, unfortunate and completely unnecessary edict regarding alcoholic beverages, it has been a most enjoyable evening."

"You're welcome," Mary said, "but I can't take the credit. We should all thank the guy who donated the tickets."

"Yeah, but you picked us," said JoJo.

"Hey," said Mary, "sure I picked you. You guys are my friends." She glanced in the rearview mirror. Daisy Pepper was already snoring away with her head on Preacher's shoulder.

Preacher nodded, bumping her frowsy gray-blond curls with his beard. "That we are. That we are."

"Friends," said JoJo solemnly.

Friends. Mary shivered and reached to turn on the heater. It was a mild night, but she felt cold and frightened. Like a child walking home in the dark, suddenly aware of the silence and emptiness around her.

It was nearly one-thirty when Doug finally climbed the long flight of stone steps that led to his front door. He could have taken the inside stairs from the garage on the street level to the kitchen, and sometimes did when it was raining and the steps were slippery with bougainvillea blossoms. Most of the time, though, he took the long way. He needed the exercise.

As he inserted his key in the lock he could hear what sounded like a telephone ringing. "Stupid bird," he muttered. He pushed the door open, dropped the keys into his pocket and threw his jacket onto the back of the couch. "Okay, knock it off, Maurice."

The ringing sounded again. Doug yawned and regarded the occupant of a large wire cage on the table in front of the living room windows with distaste. "Cut it out, dammit. It's too late for this crap. You'll wake the neighbors."

Maurice the mynah bird cocked his head, fixed Doug with one beady black eye and uttered a breathtakingly obscene remark just as the telephone rang again.

"Hey, Maurice, that's really—" Doug began in genuine admiration. Then realizing belatedly that ventriloquism was probably beyond even a mynah bird's capabilities, he dived for the phone and snatched up the receiver, swearing under his breath.

"MacDougal," he barked, then listened for a while, asking a question now and then. After he hung it up he stood for a minute with his eyes closed, rubbing the back of his neck.

"Dammit to hell," offered Maurice. Doug snorted. The mynah bird added something impressively foul in tones of sympathy.

Which summed up Doug's sentiments pretty well. The murdered blonde's car had just been found, parked in a turnout up on Angeles Crest Highway. The missing boyfriend had been found, too. Sitting in the driver's seat, dead of a single small-caliber gunshot wound to the head. The lab work wasn't completed yet, but the gun found in the young man's hand was almost certainly the one that had killed his girlfriend. Nice kids, both of them. The boy had been a premed student at UCLA.

What was it about love, anyway, Doug wondered, that it could turn into such a force of destruction?

Dammit to hell, indeed. Sometimes there was no joy in being right.

He covered Maurice's cage, then picked up the VCR remote control and punched the power button. It was late; he hadn't planned to watch the game tonight, but after that phone call he knew he wouldn't be sleeping for a while, anyway. He figured he might as well turn it on, see how it went, see if he could manage to lose himself in the intricacies of the national pastime. If nothing else, the Dodgers could probably be depended on to give him something else besides the case to get irritated about.

The tape had run out and automatically rewound to its beginning, so he didn't have to resist the temptation to check the end to see how the game had turned out. He switched the TV on, fast-forwarded through the opening hype, a dozen or so commercials, "The Star-Spangled Banner" and the San Diego pitcher's warm-up tosses. When the next set of commercials came on, he went out to the kitchen to get himself a beer, which he sipped standing up while he watched the Dodger's lead-off batter ground out to the third baseman on the first pitch. He set the beer down on the coffee table, using the latest copy of *Reader's Digest* as a coaster, and pulled off his tie. The second batter went three and two, then popped up to short. Doug swore softly and went off to his bedroom to change into sweats and a T-shirt.

When he came back the Padres were batting. The Dodger pitcher had a bad case of first-inning jitters. He'd hit the first batter and thrown three straight balls to the second, so he was taking his time about things, rubbing up the ball, playing with the resin bag and generally fidgeting around up there on the mound. Vin Scully, the Dodger announcer, was filling in the dead time with his usual grace, setting the stage, talking up the grand old game while the cameramen took turns focusing on close-ups of fans taking in the action—or lack of it—from the box seats just behind the dugouts. Kids, mostly. Sleeping babies or some little kid with a glove big-ger than he was, hoping for a foul ball to come his way. Pretty girls in sun tops.

Muttering in annoyance, Doug hit the pause button and headed for the kitchen to get himself something to eat.

He was halfway there when a strange little frisson of awareness suddenly shivered down his spine; he could feel the fine hairs on the back of his neck lifting; his scalp prickled. He turned and walked slowly back toward the TV set.

On the screen, a woman's image was frozen into flat immobility, her face half turned, as if she'd been about to speak to the person next to her. Doug reached for the remote and thumbed the picture into action, and an instant later the woman's face vanished, to be replaced by the Dodger pitcher, delivering a fastball for a strike. He stabbed at the buttons, rewound too far and had to fast-forward, then rewind again. And finally he had her.

She was a cameraman's dream, no doubt about it. And she wasn't even wearing a sun top. Short brown hair, sun-streaked and tousled, like a very small boy's...doe-soft eyes and a smile that would light up the stadium. Unforgettable eyes. Unforgettable smile.

Doug stared at the woman's face until his eyes burned, rewinding and playing it over and over again. The cold, shocky feeling was wearing off, and he could feel his heart thumping away, going like a jackhammer. He couldn't be wrong. He couldn't be. The hair was different, but those eyes, that smile... After so many years it was incredible how little they'd changed, and how vivid and clear they still were in his memory. Like a brand new print of an old Technicolor movie.

Still, he had to be sure. Once more he froze the image, rendering it flat and grainy as old newsprint. He went into his bedroom, into the closet, where he took down a box from the top shelf and placed it on his bed in the middle of the unmade tumble of sheets that made him think briefly, just briefly, of that other bed, and another murdered blonde.

The box had been taped shut. He ripped at the tape, tearing it apart down the center seam, and opened the flaps.

The photograph was right there, on top of an untidy stack of notes, clippings and files, just as he'd remembered. A black-and-white studio head shot, eight-by-ten glossy, the kind aspiring actors send by the thousands to agents and casting directors, each and every one of them a ticket to someone's dream. He lifted it out of the box and held it, looking at it as he'd looked at it so many times before. There it was, that incredible smile, and those big brown eyes with the wistful, hungry look of a waif gazing through a candy store window. There, too, was the long, graceful neck, the tumble of hair. Soap opera hair, someone—his partner, probably—had called it. Light brown, they'd said. The rich red-brown of sage honey.

From the living room came a sudden burst of music and gunfire; the pause mechanism had released automatically, reverting the system to regular network programming, a vintage western, by the sound of it. Taking the photograph with him, Doug went into the room and picked up the remote. Then he carefully laid the photo down on the coffee table, placed the remote on top of it, picked up his beer and took a long swig of it, then a couple of deep breaths. His chest hurt, as if he'd been holding his breath without realizing it.

He got comfortable on the couch, sitting way up on the edge of the cushions, with the remote control in one hand and the photograph in the other. Finally, frowning intently at the set, he turned the VCR on and found the right place on the tape. "Oh, my—now I ask you, isn't that a beautiful sight?" the voice of the Dodger announcer was crooning. "What a smile..."

What a smile. Yes, indeed. It was a smile he hadn't been able to forget in almost ten years. And it still didn't seem possible that it could be the smile of a murderer.

He reached for the phone without taking his eyes from the TV screen and punched a preprogrammed key. The number sang in his ear, then one brrr, and a click. A sleepy voice mumbled, "Yeah...Shannon."

"Hey, Jim? It's Doug."

"Hey, partner . . ." The voice on the other end of the line suddenly got more alert. "What's up? What's wrong?"

"Nothing's wrong. Listen—"

"Doug, it's two o'clock in the friggin' a.m. Something sure as hell better be wrong."

Doug laughed softly. "Jim, you're not going to believe this."

"Try me, dammit."

"I've found her."

"Found who?" There was a suspicious pause. "Are you drunk?"

"What? No, I'm not drunk. Will you shut up and listen? I've found her, partner, and you're not going to believe where. It's like some kind of miracle. If I hadn't—"

"*Who?* Dammit—"

Doug took a patient breath. "The Rhinestone Collar case. Remember?"

There was dead silence. And then, in a completely different tone, Jim answered, "Yeah, of course I remember. How could I forget?"

"Well, I've found her, Jim. Our missing witness."

There was another, longer silence. "My God. You don't mean *Joy Donnelly?*"

"That's who I mean. I'm going down to check it out—"

"Going down? Down where?"

"San Diego. At least to start. I'm not sure—"

"Jeez, you mean you haven't seen her yet? Talked to her?" Jim Shannon's voice sounded tense, almost testy. "Look, man, how can you even be sure it's her? You've always been obsessed with that case. Especially that damn roommate. It's been a long time—how many years?"

"I'm sure," Doug said with a low chuckle. "There's nobody else in the world with a face like that. She's cut her hair, that's all—everything else is just the same." He waited, and finally prompted, "Hey, partner, you haven't got much to say."

Some soft swearing drifted down the line. "Well, hell, it's kind of a shock."

"Yeah, isn't it? I know what you mean. I couldn't believe it myself."

"You're sure you're not just—" Doug heard the long hiss of an exhalation. "Jeez, I thought she must be dead." There was another long silence, which Doug didn't interrupt; he thought he knew exactly how his ex-partner must be feeling. Finally Jim said, "When are you going?"

"Tomorrow. Today. As soon as I shower and grab a bite to eat. Might as well—won't be sleeping, anyway. That way I'll miss the traffic." Funny how he didn't feel tired anymore. He felt keyed up, exhilarated, like he was on some kind of potent drug. And he'd even forgotten all about the game. Well, okay, not quite. But it didn't seem all that important to him now.

"Keep me posted," his ex-partner said tersely. "I want to know the minute you find her."

"You bet." Doug started to hang up, then snatched the receiver back and said, "Oh, hey—almost forgot. Congratulations, *Chief*."

Shannon snorted, but Doug could hear a smile in his voice. "Well, it's a little soon for that. There's a couple other guys in the running, you know. Good men, both of them."

"Yeah, yeah, I know," said Doug with another chuckle. "They have to make it look good. But we're all betting on you. There's nobody in this world deserves it more, partner. Nobody."

Chapter 2

Mary always remembered that night as if she was watching a movie, one that had been carelessly edited, so some of the scenes were indistinct or had been cut altogether while others stood out as if they'd been augmented with special effects, like lighting and sound and slow motion.

She saw the body fall; that always came first. It fell with a slithering, rustling sound, like silk sliding over nylon stockings, coming to rest at her feet with a curiously flat and final *thump*. The arms and legs were all twisted awry like a broken doll flung down by a careless child, and the hair flowed away from the face in a silvery stream to lap over the toe of Mary's shoe. She could feel the weight of it, still warm and alive and smelling of perfume. Belle's perfume, a naughty, spicy scent that suited her so well . . . rapidly mingling now with the nauseating stench of death.

It was strange. In that memory the body was always alone, isolated, as if there had been nothing and no one else in the room at all. Even though Mary knew very well that *he* was there, not quite in the scene but just outside it, awaiting his entrance. And though it must have lasted only a second, maybe two, in her memory the scene was frozen in that

one particular frame for what seemed like forever, giving her
time to record every detail with nightmare clarity. Except
that these were waking memories, not nightmares. She was
afraid to sleep, because the nightmares were worse, far
worse.

So she spent the night huddled in one corner of the couch,
arms wrapped around her drawn-up legs, waiting for the
dawn to come, while the Siamese cat Moki lay like a sphinx
along the back of the couch and watched her with unblinking intensity, curious, perhaps, about the sounds she was
making—soft, animal sounds, the breathy whimpers of a
frightened child. She didn't close her eyes, but it didn't
matter. The images came, anyway. She saw it all again, as
if it had been yesterday...the wide, bulging eyes that seemed
to stare right into hers, and the mouth, opened in a horri-
ble travesty of a smile, lipstick all smeared. Funny how that
still bothered her, that small thing; Belle had been so particular about her makeup—an artist, really.

And the red satin dress, twisted half around and completely baring one white breast, its nakedness seeming in-
decent, a shocking violation. More shocking, oddly, than
the slash of crimson across the pale, arched throat...a slash
of crimson that glittered like diamonds.

Doug thought every cop probably had one—the unsolved case he couldn't let go. The one that haunted his
sleepless nights. For Doug it was the one the L.A. newspapers had nicknamed "The Rhinestone Collar Murder."

Oh, how they'd loved it, the press and the town both, the
case of beautiful saloon singer and party girl Belle Landon,
strangled with the rhinestone-studded strap of her own
cocktail dress. And why not? Doug had always thought it
was a case made for Hollywood. It had everything, sleaze
and glamour, alleged ties to the mob, rumors of connec-
tions to various well-known and influential people—and
best of all, an intriguing little mystery. A missing key witness, the murdered woman's roommate, a sometime singer-
dancer-cocktail waitress named Joy Donnelly, who'd disappeared without a trace on the night of the murder.

The local press had speculated wildly, of course, the consensus of opinion being that Donnelly had been killed, too, to silence the crime's only witness. But most of the LAPD, those directly involved in the investigation, anyway, were convinced Donnelly had killed her roommate, most likely in a fit of jealousy over some man. A classic lover's triangle. It was a theory that fit all the facts, but for some reason it had never made Doug happy.

He and Jim Shannon had been part of the team of investigators handling the case right from the word go. And from the word go it had been a nightmare. Nothing seemed to go right. There'd been so much evidence, at first—too much, almost. But lab results had been lost, tests botched, evidence turned up missing, and all the clues seemed to lead to dead ends.

Doug had been a newcomer to the homicide bureau back then, which might have had something to do with the way he'd let that particular case get under his skin. Whatever the reason, he never had forgotten his first glimpse of that apartment. The body . . . that cascade of silver hair and that blood-red dress. What a waste, he'd thought, not for the first or the last time; in fact, it was almost always the first thing in his mind when he viewed the scene of a homicide. He wasn't sure what it was that made that one seem especially poignant. *What a waste.*

But it was the missing roommate, Joy Donnelly, who'd kept him awake nights. Photographs in the apartment she'd shared with Belle had given him a face to haunt his dreams, a sweet, vulnerable face, a smile of heart-stopping radiance, eyes full of optimism and hope. It was the face of a small town girl with a head full of dreams, dreams of finding fame and fortune in the big city, and amazingly unmarked by the disillusionment and disappointment she'd found there instead. The question he kept asking himself was whether such a face could also mask the heart of a cold-blooded killer. That was what most of his fellow investigators, including his own partner, believed. And if it wasn't so, why didn't she come forward with what she knew?

The only answer seemed to be the one he could never bring himself to accept: Joy Donnelly was dead.

But now he knew that Joy Donnelly was very much alive.

While he was driving along the San Diego Freeway in his ancient Mercedes diesel, heading south through the well-lighted loneliness of a big city's predawn, that thought played over and over in his mind like a remnant of song. As he drove past the airport, the oil refineries of Signal Hill and the shopping malls and subdivisions of Orange County, the excitement was like a low-voltage current thrumming inside his chest. *Joy Donnelly is alive. Alive!*

Not only alive, damn her, but enjoying the hell out of herself, by the looks of it. Laughing with friends, munching hot dogs and peanuts salted in the shell, taking in a ball game—one *he* couldn't even get tickets to. Ironic, wasn't it?

After all these years, he finally knew that Joy Donnelly was alive. Now all he had to do was find her.

He hadn't thought it would be so easy.

Just past Del Mar traffic started to pick up, but he was early enough, and pushing it, so that he was able to squeeze between Old Town and Lindbergh Field and slip on into downtown before it got too bad. He headed for the San Diego PD's central station first, both as a courtesy and because Jerry Delgado, the homicide bureau chief there, owed him a favor. He figured Lieutenant Delgado was good for the loan of a phone book and a phone, at the very least, and if he was lucky, maybe a cup of coffee and a couple of doughnuts in the bargain. Doug's stomach was beginning to remind him that he never had made it to the kitchen for that snack he'd been about to fix himself just before he'd paused his VCR on the laughing face of Joy Donnelly.

Half an hour later he was back in traffic, with a maple bar and two cups of black coffee under his belt and a San Diego street map spread out on the seat beside him. More important, he had the SDPD's promise of full cooperation, just in case things got interesting.

The telephone hadn't helped much. Dialing the television station had got him one of those automated operators—"If you are calling for program information, press one, *now*." He'd worked his way through all the options in hopes of eventually speaking to a live human voice, and instead was rewarded with a recording explaining that the switchboard was closed and he'd have to call back after nine o'clock. God, how he hated those things. He'd decided he'd rather fight traffic and drive out to the station than go through all that again.

Actually, finding the TV station was the easy part; finding somebody who could tell him what part of Jack Murphy Stadium that particular camera had been pointing at took a bit longer. It was close to noon before he got it narrowed down to probably the first twelve rows above the dugout on the third base side.

By that time he was starving to death, so before he took the information and his videotape out to the Padres ballpark in Mission Valley, he stopped off at a taco stand for a couple of chicken burritos. Not bad for fast food—they did something interesting with rice instead of the usual beans and cheese, which made him a little happier about his cholesterol and calorie intake, and a little less guilty about the maple bar.

He drove to Mission Valley with his diet soda wedged between his knees, Mercedes-Benz's being short on the little amenities, like cup holders. It seemed strange to him to be driving across the vast, empty stadium parking lot, and it occurred to him suddenly that he still didn't know who'd won last night's game. He hadn't turned the radio on, still hoping he'd have a chance to watch his tape someday, he supposed, although it felt like old news to him, now. For what it was worth, though, he didn't think the Padres' home ballpark looked like a place that was about to host a League Championship Series, so maybe that was a good sign.

The person in charge of the Padres' season ticket sales didn't care much for the idea of giving out information about his best customers. Doug politely reminded him that he was conducting a murder investigation, and that he'd get the information sooner or later, anyway, and that the more help and cooperation he got, the less mess and turmoil there was going to be. Secretly, he was cheered by the guy's surly attitude, and took it as another good omen for the Dodgers.

The holders of most of the seats above the dugouts, Doug discovered, were businesses—small corporations, car dealerships, real estate and insurance companies, who handed the tickets out as employee bonuses or used them to entertain important clients. He'd figured it might take him several days to track them all down, but he got lucky on the third try.

"Why, I gave those tickets away," the round, cherubic owner of a chain of fish and chips restaurants told him, beaming through the clutter of an office that overlooked Mission Bay. "I usually do, actually."

"Uh-huh," said Doug. "Makes a nice tax write-off. Who'd you give 'em to?"

"Oh, it isn't that." When the cherub smiled, his eyes made little upside-down crescent moons above his round, rosy cheeks. Doug thought he looked like a clean-shaven Santa Claus. "I give them to one of the homeless shelters, when I can." He shrugged, looking almost apologetic. "I know what it's like, you see—been there myself, believe it or not, thanks to a little problem with the, uh, bottle, if you know what I mean."

Which explained the rosy cheeks—and nose, thought Doug, looking at the little guy in a whole new light.

"Yesterday... let me see now. I took those tickets down to Saint Vincent's," Benny went on, beaming anew at the recollection. "You know, down on Imperial? Woman who runs the place—just the sweetest, prettiest little thing you ever saw. Mary, I believe her name is. I gave them to her, told her to pick three of her best customers and take them out to the ball game. Oh, she was just so tickled—has a smile that makes you feel warm all over. A smile like that means a lot to you when you're down and out. Believe me, I know."

Doug nodded and managed to keep his face under control, but he was getting that high-voltage thrumming feeling in his chest again. He took the black-and-white photo out of a manila envelope and handed it to Benny. "This the woman?"

"Why, yes—yes, it is, that's her. My, my, isn't she pretty? Isn't she...hmm. Hair's different, though. Seems to me it's a lot shorter now." Benny looked up, his smile changing to a look of alarm. "She's not in any trouble, is she? Oh, I just can't believe she'd do anything wrong. She's just the loveliest—"

"No trouble," said Doug, retrieving the photograph and tucking it away. "I just want to ask her some questions. Saint Vincent's, you say?"

"That's right, down on Imperial—can't miss it. Saint Vincent's Rescue Mission." Benny still looked unhappy, as if he didn't believe a word of Doug's assurances. He called him back just as he was heading out the door. "Oh—detective?" When Doug looked around, he saw that the little man was smiling again, almost wistfully, he thought. "It's Wednesday—that's chili day at Saint Vincent's. Make 'em a nice donation, won't you? They have very good chili...."

"Bear alert," said Daisy Pepper when she came through the chow line, speaking out of one side of her mouth, like a character in a bad spy movie. Daisy had done some trucking in her younger days, and still liked to speak the lingo now and then.

Inside, Mary felt a cold little zap of fear, like a mild electric shock, but she went on smiling as she spooned chili into a bowl and set it on Daisy's tray. "What are you talking about? I haven't seen any cops."

"Yeah? See that big guy over there—*no, don't look!*— kind of off by himself? There's a bear if ever I saw one." Daisy sniffed. "In a plain brown wrapper, but that don't fool me. He's got cop's eyes. And he's been watchin' you like a hawk."

"Maybe he's just new," said Mary carefully, covering a sudden shortness of breath. "I don't think I've ever seen him in here before." That, at least, was the truth; her cheeks were burning with a hot flush of pure relief. He wasn't the one. Not *that* one. She'd have known *him,* even after all these years.

"He sure don't look like he belongs here," Daisy grumbled, scowling from under the bill of her baseball cap.

"Nobody belongs here," said Mary. "Hey, he's probably hungry. Don't you think maybe he just came for a bowl of chili?"

Daisy snorted to show she wasn't convinced and went off to find Preacher.

He does look hungry, Mary thought, but not necessarily for chili. She went on mechanically filling bowls, and smiled and chatted with her "regulars" as she set the bowls on proffered trays, but her mind wasn't on it. Because now that Daisy had pointed him out, the stranger stood out like a sore thumb, and she was conscious of him all the time, there, just on the edges of her vision, a presence as real but intangible as a shadow. She could feel his eyes on her, watching her, but when she did look straight at him, he was always looking someplace else. She began to feel a whole new kind of fear, an itchy unease that was wholly feminine. It nibbled away at her nerves and self-confidence.

It was strange, but in all the time she'd worked at Saint Vincent's, located right in the heart of San Diego's skid row, she'd never once worried about her personal safety. Oh, sure, there had been a few incidents, and she knew how to protect herself if it came to that, but in a strange way she'd always felt a kind of kinship with the street people who came to the mission for meals and occasional shelter. They might not have believed it to look at her, but she knew, if they didn't, that she was one of them. They were displaced and disenfranchised, and so was she. She might have a job and a place to live, but she had no home, not in the true sense of that word. Like most of them she had no family, no past, and no future that she could see beyond today. The shelter was the only place where she felt safe, and the street people were her only friends. She was comfortable with them, probably because they asked her no questions, and she trusted them because she knew what to expect from them, and what not to expect. They were who they were and never pretended to be what they were not.

Oh, but this man, this stranger—he was definitely something else entirely. She didn't know what to make of him. What was he doing here, and what did he want? Who was he, that just his presence could make her feel hunted and vulnerable again?

Maybe Daisy was right, maybe he was a cop. But if he was, why *now?* Could it possibly be just a coincidence? And how in the world could they have found her, after so long?

In any case, Mary thought, Daisy was right about one thing—he didn't look as if he belonged in a skid row shelter, regardless of the rumpled clothes and a couple days' growth of beard. It was more a matter of attitude than anything. He just didn't have that beaten-down, defeated look homeless people get—that air of hopelessness, as if they carried the whole world around on their shoulders. This man's dark eyes were clear and intelligent, his jaw rock-hard and pugnacious. The combination gave him a look of authority, the kind a man is born to and that doesn't need trumpeting. Add to that the fact that he was big and looked very fit, and you just knew that, cop or not, this would be a bad man to cross.

But not a cruel man, she thought. Tough, but not *mean*.

Her hand jerked suddenly, slopping chili over the side of a crockery bowl. Oh, God, the man was coming toward her. He'd taken a tray and was moving unhurriedly down the line, collecting plate, napkin, silverware, rolls. Moving inexorably closer. Mary knew a moment of unreasoning, heart-pounding panic, heard the clamor of alarm bells inside her head, voices screaming, *Run!* But then it was too late and he was there right in front of her, a shadow no longer. And, oh yes, he was big. Big as a mountain.

"Oops, sorry—guess I kind of made a mess of that one," she said with a husky laugh, and made a swipe at the spilled chili with her finger. Oh, God, she could feel herself losing control; any moment now her mask would slip and he'd see her fear, and know she had something to hide. Nervously, she popped the finger into her mouth and lifted her eyes to the stranger's face.

That was when her body seemed to go numb, impaled by a thousand cold prickles, while her mind slipped into some sort of overdrive, instantly recording...oh, so many impressions, so many thoughts, on so many different levels.

Could I be wrong? He's not the one, but he looks so familiar. Where have I seen him before?

His eyes are blue, dark blue. And he's not so tall, after all. Just big... big and broad, and strong.

He has a nice face...an honest face. Attractive, too. Very attractive.

I think...I would feel safe with him. Safe! A cop? How can that be?

And overriding every other thought, like an air-raid siren going off during a party: *Oh, God, he knows me. It's in his eyes. He knows....*

The man was speaking to her. He had a good voice, she noticed, not too deep, not loud, but with power behind it. He said, "Somebody told me you had good chili."

Mary felt her stiff lips stretching with her smile. "Oh, yeah? Who told you that?" At least, thank God, her voice was okay—raspy, but okay.

"Friend of mine—Benny Gregg. You know him?"

"Benny? Oh, yeah—Mr. Gregg. Sure—he's a nice guy." That was wrong. She sounded too breathless, like she was trying too hard. She had to relax. Maybe flirt a little.

"Heard he gave you some baseball tickets."

Big smile. "Oh, yeah, yeah, he did. For the game last night. He told you about that, huh?"

"Yeah, and I have to tell you, I was pretty jealous. Heard it was a great game."

It wasn't difficult to make a wry face. "Yeah, but the Padres lost."

The man smiled. He had an unexpectedly charming smile. "Well, since I'm a Dodger fan..."

She groaned. "Oh, no, don't tell me. Are you from L.A.?"

"Yeah, I am, as a matter of fact."

There was the tiniest of pauses—would he notice?—before Mary freshened her smile and inquired brightly, "What brings you down this way?"

"Business."

"Oh." Damn—she'd gone breathless again. "Well, I didn't think you looked like . . . you know. Like you needed a hot meal and a place to sleep."

It was all so light and casual on the surface, the words the usual polite give-and-take of strangers, with perhaps just a hint of unanticipated sexual awareness thrown in to add a touch of tension. But, Mary thought, there was definitely something in his eyes that unnerved her. They never lost that searching intensity, not even when he smiled.

He knows.

Something brushed her fingers where they curled, white-knuckled, around the handle of the chili ladle. Looking down, Mary saw the man's hand, a wrist with a black-banded watch and a light furring of coarse brown hair, an arm in heathery-gray suit material, reaching across the serving table. She uttered a soft gasp and her fingers opened reflexively, letting go of the ladle so that it clanged against the side of the pot. But before she could jerk her hand away, he had caught it and deftly tucked something inside her palm. Something warm, permeated with the moist, intimate heat of his body.

She gave a little squawk of surprise and dropped the thing as if it had been a cockroach, then watched, stunned, as a folded twenty-dollar bill fluttered like a single errant leaf onto the table beside the big stainless-steel chili pot.

The man chuckled softly. "For the meal," he said, and abruptly turned, taking his tray with him.

Mary whispered, "Thanks," to his broad back, then watched in bemusement as it moved away across the dining room, weaving between rows of tables that were quickly filling up with the usual assortment of shelter regulars—stubble-jawed old men in dusty jackets, hunched like buzzards over their trays; younger men, too, quick-eyed and twitchy; old women with their limp hair and layers of clothing, brightened unexpectedly with poignant splashes of

color; and more and more often, now, the families, hag-
gard mothers, old before their time, and children with
pinched faces and quick, irrepressible smiles.

As she gazed at the man, her fingers moved, of their own
volition, it seemed, to retrieve the twenty and tuck it into the
pocket of her chili-splashed apron.

Daisy Pepper used a broken-off piece of bread to wipe up
the last of the chili in her bowl, then popped it into her
mouth and licked her fingers with a satisfied smacking
sound. She nodded her head toward the man in the rumpled, blue-gray suit. "JoJo, tell me that ain't a cop."

JoJo nodded in solemn agreement. "Got a cop walk—
kinda slow and bossy, always lookin' around, checkin'
things out."

"Not undercover, though," mused Daisy, as if he hadn't
spoken, regarding the object of conjecture with thoughtfully narrowed eyes. "Not scuzzy enough. So he ain't a
narc. What do you think, Preacher? Missing persons? Private dick, maybe—lookin' for some runaway kid."

"I'm not the expert on the, uh, various species of law enforcement personnel," Preacher drawled in an undertone,
"but whoever he may be, he seems to have upset our Miss
Mary. Check it out."

Daisy and JoJo followed Preacher's gaze with an elabo-
rate show of nonchalance.

"What's she starin' at?" asked JoJo, looking perplexed.

"Looks like she seen a ghost," said Daisy.

Preacher nodded. "Scared."

Daisy hitched forward and picked up her coffee mug.
"Think that cop could be after *Mary?*" she asked in a
gravelly growl that was meant to be a whisper.

JoJo looked profoundly shocked. Preacher shook his
head. "I would personally find that very hard to believe."
He stroked his beard thoughtfully for a few moments.
"Unless... I would be more inclined to think...
information."

Daisy grunted agreement. "Knows something. Seen
something, maybe. She's afraid to talk, hidin' out. I knew

it," she said morosely into her coffee mug. "Had to be a reason why a pretty girl like that wants to hang out in a place like this. Spend all her time with losers like us."

"We her friends," JoJo protested in an injured tone. "She don't think we're losers."

"That," said Preacher with a belch and a sigh, "is what makes our Mary a unique and special human being. It does not speak well for her judgment."

"What's she doing?" JoJo asked suddenly. "Where's she going?"

"Splittin'," said Daisy. "Good for her. She don't want to talk to that cop. Don't blame her."

"Uh-oh," said Preacher. JoJo sat up straight and opened his mouth in mute alarm. "Bear on the move," Daisy muttered.

"He's goin' after her," JoJo squeaked. "He's gonna stop her."

"That," said Preacher grimly, "would appear to be his intention."

"What we gonna do?" JoJo looked as if he might cry.

"We gotta do something." Daisy picked up her tray and shoved back her chair. "She'd do the same for us. Come on, you guys, follow me."

"What we gonna do?" JoJo protested as he heaved himself to his feet. "You said he's a cop. We ain't gonna mess with no cop."

"I believe," Preacher murmured, panting a little, "the play she has in mind is called 'running interference.' Or 'setting a screen.' Depending on your sport."

JoJo brightened. "Oh, yeah," he said, just as a loud crash echoed through the dining room.

Daisy Pepper had just plowed full tilt into the guy in the blue-gray suit.

Chapter 3

Doug never saw it coming.

He blamed himself, having broken one of his own cardinal rules of self-defense, which was never, ever, to lose track of where you are and what's going on around you. But...oh man, *Joy Donnelly*. That was all he could think about. He was having trouble just believing it, that it was really her, in the flesh. And although his training and common sense told him she was a fugitive and a homicide suspect, all he could think of when she turned that megawatt smile on him was that this had to be the most beautiful woman he'd ever seen in his life.

He didn't quite know what had happened to him at that moment, except that everything inside him seemed to shift and resettle, as if it was something he'd been working toward, not just for the last ten years, but maybe even his whole life. And something had gone wrong with his breathing. He kept having to remind himself to be cool, just like when he was in junior high school and trying to get up enough nerve to ask Carol Ann Tuttle to go to the movies with him.

Even so, he had enough cop sense left not to do or say anything that might spook the target until he was ready to make his move. He didn't care much for the idea of confronting her over the chili pot, maybe causing a big scene in a room full of people that ranged from small children to dope addicts and the mentally unbalanced. No, he thought, better just to hang around for a while, keep an eye on her and wait for a chance to catch her alone, maybe when she left for the night. There wasn't any hurry, he told himself, since he was pretty sure she hadn't made him yet. She'd seemed a little nervous, sure, but the nervousness had a familiar feel to him, the kind of warm, flustered awareness that had more to do with chemistry than fear. The kind of awareness that quickens the pulse and kindles a fire in the loins and awakens the mind to all sorts of intriguing possibilities....

So he really wasn't prepared when, out of the corner of his eye, he saw his fugitive witness suddenly cast a quick look in his direction, then shuck off her apron and head for the kitchen with obvious intent.

At that point there was only one thought in his mind, and that was to head her off before she got to the back door. It was a good safe bet she had her car parked out there somewhere, and his own vehicle was off in the opposite direction and not exactly built for high-speed chases. So he'd come up out of his chair like a dog flushing a covey of quail, and started after her as if she'd had him on a long leash. Which was the best explanation he could think of for why a fifteen-year veteran of the LAPD let himself be blindsided by a little old woman in a baseball cap.

Her dinner tray caught him in the side, just below his ribs. As he doubled over, he said *owuff*, which was the approximate sound the air made as it exploded from his lungs.

"Whyn't yah watch where yer goin', yah big galoot!" the woman screeched, and, to add injury to insult, began whacking him in the shoulder with the tray.

In spite of it all, Doug thought at first that he was doing okay. He grabbed the old harridan's arm to prevent further mayhem and was just about to regain his balance when

somebody's foot somehow got tangled up with his. Down
they all went together, Doug, the woman and the owner of
the foot, who turned out to be a tall, thin, hawk-nosed fellow with gray hair and a silvery beard who bore a striking
resemblance to Moses—as played by Charlton Heston.

The tray landed with a clatter, Doug devoutly hoped
somewhere safely out of the woman's reach.

"Ow, get offa me, lemme up, yah big clumsy ox!" The
woman was yelling and pounding on Doug with her fists, to
the apparent dismay of the gray-bearded guy, who was trying without much success to restrain her.

Doug managed to get a good grip on those skinny, flail-
ing arms and set the woman firmly to one side, then scrambled to his feet, swearing, breathing hard, pumped full of
adrenaline and ready to resume pursuit. He caught a
glimpse, just a glimpse, of his quarry in the kitchen doorway, her brown eyes wide with consternation and something he'd have sworn was blank terror. And then she was
gone. Doug vaulted the two struggling bodies at his feet and
started after her, but found that his way was inexplicably
blocked, the aisle barricaded by a body the size of a small
Volkswagen. Looking up, and up, he saw a chocolate-
colored face with droopy cheeks and large, sorrowful eyes.

"You okay, mister?" the VW asked in the thick, heavy
speech of the brain-injured or simple-minded. "You ain't
hurt, are you? Daisy didn't mean no harm. We didn't mean
no harm, we was just—"

"Shut up, JoJo," the old woman said with a note of af-
fection and familiarity that wasn't lost on Doug.

He hunkered down to the level of the pair on the floor and
said patiently, "Now, look here, I don't think you understand. This isn't—wasn't—what it looks like. I wasn't trying to hurt your friend—what's her name?"

"Mary," supplied JoJo helpfully, while the gray-haired
man hissed sharply at him to be quiet.

"Mary..." Doug scrubbed a hand over his own un-
shaven jaws, then reached inside his jacket and reluctantly
pulled out his badge. "Look, I just want to ask her some

questions about a case I'm working on. You don't happen
to know where she lives, do you?''

JoJo shook his head slowly, as if he was really sorry he
couldn't help.

"Nope, sure don't," said the woman, obviously not sorry
at all.

"We don't ask questions of one another," the bearded
man added in a sonorous voice, as if he were about to
launch into the Lord's Prayer. "First names is all...only the
good Lord knows the rest."

"Yeah, right," said Doug. He let his breath go in a long,
frustrated sigh and tucked his badge away. Gone again, just
like that. He couldn't believe it. After ten years, he'd been
close enough to touch her—he *had* touched her—and he'd
let her get away from him.

Not for long, though, he told himself with grim resolve.
If this was where she worked, she must get a paycheck. Her
address would have to be on record. Couple phone calls and
he'd have her. He figured he'd better be quick about it,
though, because he had a pretty good idea "Mary" Joy
Donnelly wasn't going to be coming back to Saint Vincent's anytime soon.

One thing he knew for sure. He wouldn't underestimate
her next time. When he found her again he was going to take
her in, in cuffs, if necessary.

It was a day she'd always known would have to come. The
day of reckoning. The day she'd finally have to face the
consequences of the secret she'd carried for so long. But
even though her whole life had been on hold now for—oh,
God, had it been ten years?—she still didn't think she was
ready. Not yet, she wanted to cry. Oh, please, not yet. Let
me have a little more time.

She knew what she had to do. There had been so many
times, especially when the nightmares were bad, when she'd
thought she'd have to find the courage to put an end to
them, no matter what the cost. But then ... the sun would
come up one more time and life would seem so sweet, so

precious, that she just couldn't bear to think of losing it. *Not yet . . . not yet.*

But yesterday . . . yesterday she'd known that the time had come. She couldn't wait any longer, it had to be now. If she could just stay alive long enough. That cop at Saint Vincent's—he'd said he was from L.A. How on earth had they found her? And why *now,* after so many years?

She'd have to leave, of course. She'd known that from the moment she'd seen that look in the cop's eyes—the look of recognition. It wasn't that big a deal, she could lose herself again easily enough—God knows she'd done it many times before, and this time it wouldn't have to be for very long. She just needed a little time to figure out exactly how to go about this so there was at least a chance she might come out of it alive.

She wished she could just *leave*—right now, just keep driving until it felt safe to stop. But she couldn't. In the past she'd always lived from one day to the next, ready to pack up and go at a moment's notice, but in the last few years she'd begun to feel safer, more settled. She'd even begun to put down a few tentative roots. She'd acquired a house, a cat. She couldn't very well leave Moki behind.

Mary first noticed the other car when she turned off of Imperial. She made the left turn after the light turned yellow, and the car behind her did, too, snugged right up on the bumper of her Bronco so that she glanced automatically in her rearview mirror to see why the lights were so close and bright. Right after that, though, the car dropped back, way back, which struck her as just a little odd.

She knew she was probably feeling paranoid after what had happened at the shelter, but just as an experiment, she tried slowing down. Then she slowed down some more. Strangely, the headlights in her mirror didn't seem to get any closer.

Something cold raced up her spine and clutched at her shoulders. Her breathing quickened, hurting deep inside her chest like a freezing wind. She flexed her fingers on the steering wheel, waiting . . . waiting . . . and at the next corner, jerked the wheel to the right without signaling. Then she watched her mirror with her heart hammering in her throat until she saw a car pull slowly, slowly, into the dark street behind her. She could see that it was a tan car, nothing special, probably American. A Ford, maybe.

Panic exploded through her in a single starry burst, then sifted away like embers in a night sky, leaving her mind clear. Clear and cold and dark. Oh, she thought with a grim little smile, she knew what it was to be hunted. But this was her turf, she knew it like the back of her hand, and by God, before she'd allow herself to be tracked down like a helpless doe she'd lead those hounds on a chase they'd remember!

She knew the next intersection was a four-way stop, and she could see that there wasn't anybody at the cross street's stop sign. She ran the stop without touching her brakes. Halfway down the next block she cut her lights, slowed without braking and at the corner, made a hard right. Now, several long blocks ahead, she could see the bright lights and traffic on Imperial. It was a long sprint—could she make it? She gripped the steering wheel and gunned it, roaring down the quiet residential street at freeway speed. In her mirror she could make out a set of headlights, tiny and far behind.

Half a block from Imperial she turned her headlights on, made a quick stop and then turned right, pulling in front of a red Toyota, which screeched and honked in indignation. Mary ignored it, and two blocks farther on, lurched into a supermarket parking lot, zipped into a space between a minivan and a two-toned station wagon, and once more cut her lights. She sat there, holding on to the wheel, shaking, tense and wide-eyed with dread, but her pounding heart ticked off seconds, then minutes, and no tan Ford pulled after her into the parking lot.

Gradually, the shaking subsided and her breathing slowed. She slid down on her spine and leaned her head back against the seat, swallowing repeatedly, tasting the brassy tang of her own fear. She realized that she was sweating, that her forehead was clammy and cold. No more, she thought, clenching her teeth in bitter fury. I can't live like this anymore. I can't.

She waited fifteen minutes, then drove home by a long and roundabout route, watching her rearview mirror every inch of the way.

Moki was waiting for her, as usual, crouched on the table beside the front door in eager anticipation of his nightly prowl.

"Not tonight," Mary muttered, and closed the door firmly behind her. If she let him out he might be gone for hours, and she couldn't risk the delay. "Sorry..."

She tried to scoop the cat into her arms, hoping to mollify him with a cuddle and a chin rub, but he eluded her with a graceful leap to the back of the couch, vocalizing his displeasure as only a Siamese can. She left him there, furiously pacing, and went to throw the few things she needed into her only suitcase.

When she came back into the living room with the suitcase in hand and a jacket over her arm, Moki was lying along the back of the couch like a panther on a tree limb, staring intently out the front windows. She knew he was still miffed, because the end of his long, almost prehensile tail was twitching back and forth...back and forth.

"Hey, look, I said I'm sorry, okay?" She picked the cat up and tried to tuck him under her arm, but his body felt like a bundle of springs wound up too tight. A singsong feline growl issued from his throat. "All right, so you're ticked off at me. I can't help it, okay? I swear I'll make it up to you."

Damn. This wasn't going to be easy. Where in the dickens had she left the cat carrier after the last trip to the vet, anyway?

She didn't have time to look for it now. "We're going for a ride—I know you're going to just love that," she told the cat under her breath, getting a good grip on him before she opened the door. On the front steps she paused, set the suitcase down beside her feet and took one quick look back at the tiny duplex she'd called home for more than two years. Then she pulled the door shut and heard it lock with a firm and final *click.*

From that moment on, things happened in slow motion.

From somewhere nearby she dimly heard a car's engine fire, heard it roar to life. She turned, slowly, slowly, and saw the tan Ford across the street. She felt the cold shock of recognition numb her body even as Moki's body went rigid in her arms.

She opened her mouth, but wasn't sure what she shouted. Some instinctive rejection of what she knew was going to happen, perhaps. Or maybe it was Moki's name as she felt him catapult from her grasp. In any case, she remembered grabbing for the cat in one desperate lunge, and then she was falling, falling, while the night exploded all around her.

She felt pain—all over her arms and body, like a thousand tiny hot knives. She thought, Strange—I never expected bullets to feel like this.

And then she was lying in damp earth and prickly leaves, while over the dying echoes of gunfire she could hear screeching tires, revved engines, door slams and running footsteps. Survival instincts whispered warnings that resounded in her stunned brain like Klaxons: *Don't move. Don't breathe. Play dead.*

She lay in the darkness with the smell of earth and decaying leaves in her nostrils and heard the thud of footsteps on thick grass, harsh breathing, muttered swearing. Something heavy jarred the ground nearby and the bushes around her began to thrash and shake. In spite of her resolve, she nearly screamed when she felt the hands touching her. It took every ounce of control she had left to lie still and let them roam as they pleased, first over her legs, then groping rapidly on up her body—accompanied by more shaking of shrubbery and a muttered "Ouch!"—to press finally and firmly against the side of her throat. She lay still, so still, wishing she could somehow stop the rhythmic surge of her blood against the weight of those fingers. *Now,* she thought. Now he'll finish it. Please, make it quick. I don't want to know...

She heard the soft hiss of an exhalation, and then, to her utter bewilderment, in a voice gravelly with emotion, "Thank God. Thank God, you're *alive.*"

Doug didn't think it was possible to feel any worse than when he saw the object of his ten-year search take a dive off her front steps in a burst of automatic weapon fire. If it was, he didn't ever want to know about it. However, now that he knew his worst fears hadn't been realized, that Joy Donnelly was still a living witness—and judging from that pulse of hers, not even badly hurt—he was beginning to be damn mad. What the hell was going on here, anyway?

Lights were coming on all over the neighborhood, and somewhere a dog was going crazy. It was a pretty safe bet somebody'd already called 911, so it was only a question of how long before he started hearing sirens. And before the local authorities arrived there were one or two questions *he* wanted answered.

First things first. With some difficulty he took his hand from Joy Donnelly's neck, eased himself back away from those damned thorns and asked, "Are you all right? Can you hear me?"

After a brief hesitation she answered grudgingly, "Yeah, I hear you."

"Have you been shot?"

Another pause. "I don't think so."

"Are you hurt? Can you move?"

"Yeah, I'm hurt." Her voice was stronger now and sounded reassuringly indignant. "I hurt like hell, I hurt all over. And I don't think I want to move. Dammit, this stuff has *thorns.*"

Doug gave a sympathetic grunt; he was nursing a puncture wound on the heel of his own hand. "Yeah, it's pyracantha, I think. You've got to get out of there somehow, though. See if you can roll over on your stomach and crawl through here."

There was another, slightly longer pause before she said in a flat, suspicious voice, "Before I do that, there's something I want to know."

That surprised him, but he said, "Shoot."

"Don't say that."

To his greater surprise, he felt a rising bubble of laughter, which he firmly squelched. "Sorry. What do you want to know?"

"You're the guy who came into Saint Vincent's tonight, right?"

"That's right."

He could hear a quick, tense breath. "Are you a cop?"

"Yeah, I am. LAPD."

There was another, curiously vibrant pause before she said, "I knew it," and expelled her breath slowly, in what was almost a sigh.

"And," he went on, any lingering impulses to laugh extinguished by the renewed realization of disaster miraculously avoided, "I have one or two questions of my own, lady. However, in a very few minutes we're going to have a lot of official company, and I'd like to be the one to handle things, if you don't mind. Let me do the talking. But first, for God's sake, let's get out of these damn bushes—do you mind?"

He could hear her muttering furiously under her breath, but there were also various grunts and scufflings, and in a minute or so she came worming out from under the bushes, practically under his feet. He grasped her elbows and pulled her the rest of the way, ignoring her efforts to avoid his help. Once upright, however, she pulled out of his grasp like a contrary child.

"Leave me alone, okay? Jeez, I'm all right." She turned away from him and set about brushing herself off and picking leaves and twigs out of her hair.

Doug said, "Yeah, right," but his voice had gone gravelly all of a sudden. In the darkness she seemed unreal to him again, ephemeral as a puff of smoke, and he had to tuck his hands in his pockets to keep himself from reaching for her, just to assure himself that she wasn't a figment of his imagination. "Hey, tell me something. This neighborhood—you got a lot of gang bangers around here?"

She paused in her grooming to glance at him, the streetlights reflecting in the dark pools of her eyes. "No! It's mostly old people."

"That's what I figured. Any ideas why somebody might want to shoot at you?"

"Not a clue," she said instantly. Too quickly. "Guess they must have mistaken me for somebody else."

Her voice was trying hard to be flippant, but he heard a quiver in it. That made him wonder if she thought maybe *he'd* been the one doing the shooting. Then he thought about shock, and the fact that he really needed to get her inside, get her warm, see if those dark splotches on her pale face were blood or just dirt. Odd how much it bothered him to think of her injured, that incredible face damaged.

The sirens were very close now. He could hear them howling through the quiet streets, then saw a black-and-white turn onto this one a block or so farther down, splashing red-and-blue light across blind windows and parked cars. Neighbors were beginning to peer cautiously out their front doors, stepping bravely onto their porches, sweaters and bathrobes hugged close with crossed arms. Doug took off his jacket and put it around Joy's shoulders, then went to greet the car that was just pulling up to the curb.

Left standing there alone, suddenly and unexpectedly enveloped in warmth, Mary found that she was shaking. To add to her confusion, she also had a terrible, demoralizing urge to cry.

Why had he done that, anyway—given her his jacket? The guy was a cop. And what was worse, he'd said he was from L.A., although it didn't look as if he was there to kill her. At any rate, he hadn't been the one in the tan Ford, which seemed to have disappeared. But if he wasn't here to kill her, then what did he want with her? Oh, God—she was so confused. So scared. And so fed up with being scared.

She gave a violent shiver, then hunched her shoulders inside the jacket, snuggling into the warmth of it. It was so big, and it smelled like…like what? Like all sorts of things. Like *him,* she supposed. His very own personal and unique man-smell. How strange it felt to be sharing that warmth and that smell when they belonged to someone she didn't know at all. The intimacy of it was unsettling, and yet—and this was the strangest thing of all—she didn't want to take

the coat off. In it she felt comforted, somehow. She felt . . .
safe.

Safe. She was suddenly remembering the notion that had
come to her tonight at Saint Vincent's, when she'd first seen
the guy face to face. Oh, God, *could* she trust this guy? Did
she dare? The seductiveness of the idea was awful, close to
physical pain. *Oh, if only I could.* A wave of longing almost swamped her. How wonderful it would be, not to be
alone anymore.

No. As powerful as the wave was, the backwash, when it
hit her, was even stronger, rejection and denial so violent it
was almost revulsion. It had been too long, the habit of
distrust was too deeply ingrained, so much a part of her now
that she didn't think she would ever be free of it. No—no
matter what sorts of weird, cozy feelings this man might stir
in her, she couldn't trust *anyone,* least of all a cop. She'd
learned that the hard way.

And speak of the devil, there he was now, coming up the
walk toward her with a uniformed San Diego policeman at
his side. The San Diego cop was young, slim and blond, and
almost militarily tidy—a real contrast with the rumpled
plainclothes cop from L.A. Funny, though. In spite of the
fact that he hadn't shaved in a while and looked as though
he'd slept in his clothes, Mary decided it was the L.A. cop
who drew the eye and commanded the attention. There was
just something about him, something indefinable—call it
charisma, call it presence—but even the San Diego cop
glanced at him first, almost as if asking for his permission,
before he planted himself in front of Mary in an official-type
stance and muttered, "Evening, ma'am."

Mary nodded mutely back at him and tried to shrink
deeper inside the enveloping jacket, while her eyes sought
the confident blue gaze of the man from the LAPD.

She's scared to death, thought Doug. And no wonder,
what with people taking potshots at her. What the hell was
going on, here, anyway?

He listened to the routine questions and mumbled calm
and lucid replies, trying hard not to show impatience or un-
due concern, nothing that might snag the suspicions of the

officer or impede the smooth flow of the investigation. Just
let him finish the job and get the hell out of here, he prayed
silently, with the mental grinding of teeth. He had a few
questions for the lady himself, questions he meant to ask her
in private, if possible.

"I don't *know*," she was saying for maybe the third time,
sounding as tense as he was, as if she was clenching her jaws
to keep her teeth from chattering. "I just think they thought
I was somebody else. What else can it be? Jeez, I don't even
know anybody with a machine gun."

And again, from out of nowhere, Doug felt a quick little
lift of laughter.

"She works at Saint Vincent's," he offered in a low voice,
because he could see this young hotshot was the stubborn
type and not apt to let it go until he had something to chew
on.

The San Diego cop was up on the steps, hunkered down
with his flashlight trained on the bullet holes in the door. He
looked over at Doug in surprise. "The homeless shelter?"
He rose and shifted his attention back to Mary like a dog
sniffing a new scent. "There's a lot goes down in that
neighborhood—maybe you saw something there you
shouldn't have."

Her head moved, a sharp little shake of denial. "No—
nothing—I swear."

"Maybe...something you didn't know you saw. Think
hard," Doug urged.

"I haven't seen anything," she whispered. And then,
much more forcefully, almost defiantly, "And anyhow, the
people down there wouldn't hurt me." She threw Doug a
look that said she didn't appreciate his butting in. "They
wouldn't."

There was a long pause while they just looked at her,
Doug and the San Diego cop both. She stood there gazing
back at them, with eyes like dark blotches in her pale face,
lovely as a wild fawn, vulnerable as an abandoned waif. A
man would have to be made of stone not to be affected by
the sight, and the cop from the SDPD was definitely flesh
and blood.

"Well," he said, abruptly clearing his throat, blustering a little to make up for his momentary lapse. He came back down the steps, pulling on his gloves. "You think about it, okay? Give us a call if you remember anything—anything at all. Right now, why don't you try and get some rest. You might want to have a doctor take a look at those cuts, too. You got a neighbor, a friend, somebody that could stay with you tonight?"

"I'll stay with her," said Doug, turning the cop with a subtle hand to the elbow before he could see the look of shock and dismay that had just flashed across Mary-Joy's face. "My wife would insist on it," he confided in a smooth undertone as the two of them walked together back to the patrol car. "She's her baby sister, you understand? Kind of the family black sheep, but . . . well, you know how it is."

The San Diego cop chuckled. "Yeah, sure do. Appreciate your help, Detective . . ."

"MacDougal," said Doug. "Hey—just glad I showed up when I did." He leaned down to the open window of the patrol car and spoke to the young officer's partner, an older, heavy-set Hispanic man who was jotting things on a clipboard and muttering sporadically into the radio mike. "Anything yet on that partial plate number?"

The cop gave him a glance. "Nothing yet. We'll let you know when we have something."

At that moment a new call came over the radio. The young cop lifted a hand as the other responded. Doug stood back and watched the patrol car ease away from the curb and accelerate down the street. In the quiet that came with its departure he heard mutters of distant conversation, footsteps, the sounds of doors closing as neighbors retreated once more into the relative safety of their homes.

He turned and walked slowly back to the house, to the lonely figure he'd left waiting at the foot of her bullet-pocked steps. She was standing exactly as he'd left her, very straight and still, almost as if she'd taken root. His jacket hung loosely on her now, its shoulders making a ridiculously wide base for the slender column of her neck. There was something almost noble about her, Doug thought—

noble, but resigned. So might Anne Boleyn have awaited the
approach of the headsman.

He didn't know what to say to her. He'd waited, hoped
for this moment, for almost ten years, but now that it had
come, it wasn't anything like he'd imagined it. He'd never
felt less like a police officer, a fifteen-year veteran of one of
the finest law enforcement agencies in the country. What he
felt like was a rookie—no, worse, a high school kid. His
hands were clammy, his heart was beating way too fast, and
there was a curious, high-pitched ringing in his head that he
hoped was only a bad case of nerves and not something potentially lethal, like high blood pressure. For what seemed
like a long time he stood there, face-to-face with her, so close
he could hear the sounds of her breathing—quick and shallow, like that of a pursued animal. He could see the yellow
orb of a street lamp reflected in her eyes.

"Joy Donnelly," he said at last, letting go of the breath
he'd been holding, "I presume..."

Chapter 4

Her eyes met his without flinching. "My name is Mary Jo Delinsky." She said it in a clear and sullen voice, and even though he knew better, Doug had the strangest sense that she might be telling him the truth.

Taking himself in hand—as well as a no-nonsense grip on her arm—he growled, "Come on, let's get inside."

She went without protest until they reached the top of the steps. There she turned on him and in a low, stricken voice said, "Uh-oh. It's locked."

"So unlock it. Where are your keys?"

"I, um . . . I left 'em inside."

"You *what?*"

"Well," she returned in a bright little flare of anger, "I wasn't planning on coming *back.*"

He was beginning to recognize that quicksilver temper of hers. He noticed, too, that it came and went as spontaneously as her smile.

"Burning your bridges?" he asked softly. "Why was that, Mary-*Joy?*"

She didn't answer. "I don't believe this," he muttered, and led her around to the side of the house, swearing under his breath.

"I don't believe it, either," she remarked sarcastically a few minutes later, pacing in annoyance behind him while he picked the lock on her kitchen door. "A cop, breaking into my house."

Doug just grunted and pushed the door open. He hesitated for a moment, listening, but the house had a cold, unoccupied feel he found reassuring. "You ought to have dead bolts," he remarked as he moved into the dark kitchen.

She made a soft, derisive sound and hit the light switch, revealing a room that was utterly devoid of personal touches, like a hotel room. There were no photos that Doug could see, no plants or knickknacks, no notes stuck to the refrigerator door with cute plastic magnets.

He told her to stay where she was while he went down the short hallway to the living room. He scanned it quickly without turning on the lights, then crossed to the window and drew the curtains. He was glad that at least the glass wasn't broken. He'd already taken note of the splintered door and the downward arc of bullet holes across the stuccoed wall where they'd followed their intended target into the pyracantha bushes. He thought again what a miracle it was she hadn't been hit.

When he went back to the kitchen, he found the target in question standing at the kitchen sink, right in front of a nice, big, unshaded window.

"What in the hell are you doing?" he yelled as he took her by both arms and jerked her to one side, out of range. "You haven't been shot at enough for one night?" He leaned across the sink to peer out the window, trying to penetrate the darkness beyond. "What's out there?"

She gave him a withering look and rubbed at her arms as if she wanted to erase his touch. "Garbage cans. Fence. My neighbor's yard. They have a Doberman. Do you *mind?*"

She nudged Doug out of the way with an insolent elbow and went back to what she'd been doing when he walked in, which, he now realized, was using the dark window glass as a mirror. He watched for a moment while she scrubbed at a dirt smudge, then gingerly touched a bloody scratch near the corner of her mouth, pushing her tongue against the inside of her cheek in an experimental sort of way.

"Ooh," she said. *"Ouch.* Damn."

He winced along with her, a fact he observed but didn't try to analyze.

"Here, let me see." Once more he put his hands on her, conscious this time, as he turned her to face him, of the way the rounded bones in her shoulders fit the palms of his hands, the way her flesh felt—warm, resilient and alive. His fingers were much more gentle when they touched her chin and tilted her face toward the light. "That's a bad one," he murmured, suddenly feeling as if a truckload of gravel had been dumped in his chest. "Got any peroxide?"

"What?" Her eyes were gazing straight into his, luminous and transparent as amber. In their depths he could see pain, confusion and fear. The edges of his vision caught just the slightest movement of her mouth, while his fingertips recorded its tiny quiver, like the practice stirrings of a hatchling bird's wings.

"Hydrogen peroxide," he repeated, lightly brushing the cut near the corner of her mouth with his thumb. "You know—disinfectant?" God...she did have the most incredible mouth.

"I don't know...." When she spoke he felt the movement of her lips, the moist heat of her breath, humid and intimate as body-warmed silk. "Under the bathroom sink, maybe."

"Stay right there." He gripped her shoulders hard and backed her up against the kitchen sink. "Don't move—you understand me?"

Just to make sure she did understand he gave her one more shake, then dived out of the room. He managed to wait until he was halfway to the bathroom to let go of the breath he'd been holding and grab for a fresh one like a drowning man going down for the last time.

"You're the bossiest person I ever met!" Mary yelled down the hall after him.

Alone, she pressed her clasped hands to her lips and looked around the room—her own kitchen—like a wild animal newly caged.

What am I going to do? The question kept ricocheting in her mind without hitting upon any answers. Oh, how badly she wanted to run—desperate instincts told her to run—but common sense told her it would probably be only a classic case of hopping out of the frying pan and into the fire. Whatever this cop's game plan was, at least he didn't seem to want her immediately and irrevocably *dead*. Whereas, she had to believe the people in the tan Ford were still out there somewhere, probably just waiting for another chance.

No, she told herself, for the time being she was definitely safer where she was. She just had to be careful, that's all. Watch her step and bide her time.

And please, God, she prayed as she heard the sound of returning footsteps, don't let him see how scared I am.

The cop had paused in the doorway with a brown plastic bottle in one hand and a box of tissues in the other. He was frowning. He looked large and slightly uncomfortable. "No cotton balls?"

"What would I want with cotton balls?" Mary shot back. "What do you think this is, a pharmacy?"

"Don't get testy, I just thought women always had cotton balls." He placed the bottle and tissues on the countertop as if it were a difficult and delicate operation. "You know—for makeup and ... things."

"Yeah, well, in case you hadn't noticed, I don't wear makeup." She watched warily as he unscrewed the cap to the brown bottle and saturated a tissue with clear liquid. When he reached for her, she hissed sharply and leaned away from him. "Hey, what do you think you're doing?"

"Hold still." His hand closed firmly on the back of her neck. "This isn't going to hurt...."

For so big and strong a hand, it was surprisingly gentle. So were the fingers that held the tissue and began to dab oh-so-carefully at the cut on her cheek.

Mary held herself very still, not because *he'd* told her to, but because all at once she didn't trust herself to move, or even to breathe. It was so quiet in that room she could hear the faint stirrings of his breath, and the sizzle of peroxide on her own raw flesh. And although he was right, and it didn't hurt at all, for reasons she couldn't begin to fathom she felt the hot sting of tears behind her eyelids, and a worrisome pressure in her throat.

"So," she said, rapidly blinking to fend off disaster, "I suppose your wife uses cotton balls?"

His voice was preoccupied. "I'm not married."

"You mean, you lied to a cop?" She "tsk-tsked" facetiously.

He stopped his doctoring long enough to give her a quick, hard look, which she met with somewhat dogged defiance. "Would you rather I'd told him the truth?"

She coughed and turned her face away, but with the pressure of just one knuckle against her chin he brought it right back to where he wanted it, which was helplessly pinioned under that penetrating blue stare. She opened her mouth to protest, but all he said was a quiet, authoritative, "Hold still."

And instead of the denials she'd primed herself with she surprised herself by obeying the command, and then by asking gruffly, "Hey, have you got a name? Or something?"

Evidently she'd surprised him a little bit, too. His steady gaze flickered, then slid away. He cleared his throat and went to work on a new scratch, this one on the side of her neck, far down, near her collarbone. "Sorry. It's MacDougal. J. T. MacDougal. Most people call me Doug."

"Yeah?" His loss of composure fascinated her. She hadn't thought cops ever felt unsure, or embarrassed, and the mounting evidence that this one did made her look at him in a whole new light.

It occurred to her that his face was very close to hers. She could see the little lines around his eyes, a tiny muscle quivering high up on his cheek, the way the whisker stubble bracketed his lips. There came to her suddenly a clear and unexpected memory of what he looked like when he smiled.

She shifted, mentally shaking herself, and said, "What's the J.T. stand for?"

"None of your business. Turn around."

Once again she found herself obeying him, moving under the firm but gentle guidance of his hands. She tilted her head forward automatically when she felt the kiss of cool liquid on the nape of her neck.

"Must be something really awful," she murmured after a moment. "You wouldn't have to abbreviate it if it was just plain old John, or Tom...." Her eyelids felt so heavy; it was all she could do to keep them from closing. There was something about the way he was touching her, almost as if he were massaging her neck, she thought. But... oh, how gently.

"Yow," she exclaimed, straightening as if he'd jabbed her. "What was *that?*"

"A bad one," he muttered, sounding so grim she wondered if he was angry about something. "You picked the wrong top to wear for a romp in the bushes, lady, that's for sure."

"Oh, yeah? What's wrong with it?" Actually, it was one of her favorite tops, a long-sleeved cotton knit in horizontal pink, blue and lavender stripes, cut wide and short so that it barely reached the waistband of her jeans. Now, though, she could see that it was pretty well ruined, snagged in at least a dozen places and speckled with bloodstains. A little shiver ran through her.

"Well," she said dryly, looking away and flinching as she encountered her own reflection in the window glass, "I wasn't exactly planning on 'romping in the bushes,' now, was I?"

"Just out of curiosity," he countered in a tone as dry as hers, "where were you planning on going with that suitcase?"

She hitched one shoulder in an offhand shrug. "Nowhere special. Just taking a little trip, that's all."

"Yeah, right... Hold still, dammit."

Mary's temper flared. "Yeah, that's *right*, Mac-Dougal," she snapped at him over her shoulder. "A vacation. You ever hear of vacations?"

"Vacation..." Without stopping what he was doing, he murmured, "Gotcha, Mary-Joy. You shouldn't lie—you're not very good at it." She cast one wild, guilty look toward the unwashed dishes she'd left in the sink, the half loaf of bread and three yellow bananas in the basket on the countertop, but before she could begin an explanation, or even think of one, he went on in that same soft, expressionless voice, "You told me you weren't planning on coming back—remember?"

She couldn't think of anything to say to that. For a few minutes—a few dangerous minutes—she'd actually forgotten she was talking to a cop. Once again tears prickled her nose and burned hot behind her eyes, but this time she could readily identify the causes of them as fury and frustration. *What am I going to do?* Cops—oh, how she hated them. Especially this one.

"Hold it up," the cop said, so abruptly it made her jump.

She gave a small, distracted gasp. "What?"

He spoke softly, patiently, as if to a not-very-bright child. "Your shirt is in the way. Hold it up, please, so I can see what I'm doing."

She twisted around to give him an "over my dead body" glare just as he straightened slightly from his bent-over position, and thus found herself suddenly within point-blank range of his dark, much-too-perceptive gaze. For the space of several seconds they stared at each other, breathing in quick, syncopated rhythms, and then, with a rasp of amusement she hadn't heard in his voice before, he said, "If I wanted to ravish your body, I don't think I'd need to be this creative, do you?"

I really do hate him, she told herself again, but this time it was without as much conviction. She gave a sigh and looked up at the ceiling—hoping, perhaps, for divine intervention—then hitched the back of her top up to her shoulder blades. The rest of it she gathered into a tight knot which she crushed in her fists and pressed against the apex of her rib cage, just below her breasts. Cool air shivered her skin into gooseflesh and hardened her nipples so that she was uncomfortably conscious of them, and the way they chafed against the soft knit fabric of her shirt.

"That's better—thank you," MacDougal said pleasantly, and a moment later her skin quivered and flinched under his feathery touch.

"Tickles," she murmured. He didn't reply.

After a few minutes, curiosity overcame embarrassment and she peered down over her clasped hands, trying to steal a look at her bare midriff.

"Holy sh—sheepskins," she exclaimed.

"No kidding," Doug said in a strangled voice.

Damn—the last thing he wanted to do right now was laugh. He didn't want things getting relaxed and friendly here, at least, not yet. He still wanted answers from this woman, and to get them he needed her scared and vulnerable awhile longer, and thinking hard about who the hell wanted her dead.

"Here—I've done what I can back here. You can reach the rest." He thrust the peroxide bottle and a fresh tissue at her and went to lean against the counter a short distance away, arms folded across his chest, the picture of calm authority, patience and self-control.

The truth was, he was keeping his distance because he'd about reached the limits of his self-control, and he didn't think it would be a good idea if the woman in his tenuous custody felt his hands shake. He hadn't known it was going to affect him like that—almost but not quite touching her, scrutinizing that fine-grained skin at such close range he could actually see her pores, and the almost invisible golden down that dusted the bumps of her spine. He knew that she had a small brown mole just about where her bra clasp would be, if she'd been wearing one. He knew that she smelled of soap and baby powder, and very faintly and unexpectedly of strawberries.

Although, he thought, it wasn't much better this way, watching her doctor the scratches on her bare stomach, seeing the way that soft concavity moved in and out with her breathing, then flinched and tightened when she touched it. He could feel his own muscles tense up in automatic response, and had to keep making a conscious effort to unclench his jaws.

He could see that she was conscious of him, too. And understandably embarrassed, which actually he didn't mind at all. He knew he could have said something to make it easier for her, made light conversation to take her mind off things. But he didn't. Instead he deliberately watched her while he let the silence stretch and grow heavy. And still heavier. It was a tactic he'd used before when questioning suspects and witnesses alike, usually to very good effect. Because the fact is, silence makes people nervous. Most people don't like silences; sooner or later they have to try to fill them up. And in Doug's experience, there was no one who hated silence more than someone with a guilty secret.

This woman was no different; it was only a matter of time. He could see that it was getting to her by the way she carefully avoided looking at him, by the tiny frown that had formed between her eyebrows, the sheen of sweat on her upper lip and the bridge of her nose. She kept making small, throat-clearing noises and not saying anything. Then she did look at him—quickly—and away again, while the faintest tinge of pink crept across her cheekbones. And still Doug waited, letting the seconds go by while the tension grew almost audible, like a ticking clock.

When they finally came, the words were too loud and sounded rusty. "That name you called me by... what was it again?"

"Joy Donnelly," Doug supplied, without inflection.

"Yeah, that's right." She was trying so hard to be casual about it. She'd finished with the scratches on her stomach now, and was going after the ones she could reach on her arms and the backs of her hands with great concentration. Her features were composed and utterly still, but her mouth had a bruised look. Her eyes flicked upward, met his briefly, then dropped again. "I was telling you the truth, you know. That's not me."

"Suppose we take your fingerprints," said Doug placidly. "Compare them with the ones we found in Joy's apartment."

A tiny muscle high on her cheek betrayed her. It flinched, as if in expectation of a blow. She reached out slowly with both hands, like a blind person groping for something solid, and placed the bottle and tissue on the table. Then she carefully smoothed her shirt down where it belonged, rubbing distractedly at the wrinkles she'd made in it with her hands while she looked around once, quickly, as if she thought there might be some miraculous hope of escape. She swallowed several times, took a deep breath and opened her mouth...

Doug's beeper went off.

In his opinion, which was shared by pretty much everybody he knew, there is no such thing as a good time for a beeper to go off. But then and there he decided that if anyone ever compiled a list of the all-time worst possible moments, this one would have to be right at the top.

The effect it had on Joy was both predictable and instantaneous. Her mouth snapped shut as if it had a spring lock on it. Doug snatched at the beeper, checked the number, then let his breath out in a gust of sheer exasperation and growled, "Can I use your phone?"

She nodded and gulped, "In the living room."

He thanked her and went. Inside he was swearing passionately, making good use of what he could remember of Maurice the Mynah's vocabulary. Damn—he'd had her. He was sure of it. Now he was back at square one, and he had a bad feeling that time might be running out on him. And on Joy Donnelly.

Much as he hated to, he had to risk the light. He turned it on and found the phone, quickly dialed a number he knew by heart.

It was picked up on the first ring. "Shannon."

"Yeah, it's me," said Doug just as tersely. "What's up?"

"What do you mean, 'What's up?' Talk to me, partner. Have you got her or not? Last I heard from you, you had her tracked to some rescue mission—what's the name?"

"Saint Vincent's. Yeah, I've got her."

"Oh, man." Doug heard the rush of an exhalation. "So it's really her? You're sure?"

"I'm sure."

"So... tell me what's going on. I'm dyin' here. This is as much my case as it is yours, you know."

Doug let go of his own breath and briefly closed his eyes. "Yeah, partner, I know. It's just that there's been a lot going on down here. There've been some, uh, developments."

Alarm crackled through the line. "What developments? What's going—"

"Somebody took a shot at her a little while ago."

"At Donnelly? You're kidding me. She's not—"

"She's fine. Pure luck, though. They meant business. Automatic rifle, something pretty heavy-duty. I got there just in time to keep 'em from finishing the job."

There was the briefest of pauses before Shannon asked with a hard edge in his voice, "So you got the perps?"

Doug almost smiled. Cut to the chase—that was the Jim Shannon he knew. Even after riding a PR desk in the chief's office for so many years, for Jim the bottom line would always be simply, "Did you get the perps?" That was what was going to make him a damn fine chief of police.

"No," he said with a sigh, the admission coming with the same reluctance he'd felt when he was a rookie, and newly partnered with the best detective on the force. Shannon had already won the first of his two medals of valor by that time; the second he'd earned saving Doug's life. "Just a partial plate number. Nothing on that yet."

"Good Lord." There was a longer, significant pause; the implications didn't need spelling out. "What about Donnelly? You get anything out of her?"

"Not yet. She's not real anxious to talk." Doug gave a tired chuckle. "You couldn't have beeped me at a less opportune time, buddy. Another five minutes...who knows?"

"You're kidding—oh, man, I'm sorry. This sure makes me wish I was back in the thick of things. This case—I'm going nuts here, know what I mean?"

"I know. Forget it. This is one we both want. But sooner or later she's got to talk, and I think she knows it."

"So... what now? You bringing her in?"

Doug propped an elbow on one knee and let his forehead drop into the support of his hand. He pressed hard on his temples, massaging slowly.

"Doug?"

"Yeah." He took a deep breath, feeling as if he were walking a beat through a rough neighborhood in a pea-soup fog. "Jim, I don't like what's going on down here. Something doesn't feel right. Remember how it was before with this damn case? Seemed like somebody was always just one friggin' jump ahead of us? Well, it's like it's happening all over again." His voice had started to rise, and he hastily lowered it. "It's taken me too damn long to find this girl, and I'm for damn sure not ready to let her slip out of my hands again."

"So what are we talking about?" His former partner's voice had gone soft, too. Soft and wary. "Stashing her someplace?"

He hesitated. Beyond the living room doorway he was acutely conscious of another presence, intently listening. He cupped a hand around the receiver, the decision sliding firmly into his mind even as the words took shape on his lips. "Look—Jim. You've got a lot at stake right now. If I tell you what I'm up to, either you're going to have to try and stop me, or you're going to put your whole future on the line."

"Don't worry about it. What are friends for?"

"Don't joke, partner."

"Who's joking? Doug, you know you can trust me. You always could."

Memory rolled over Doug like a cold ocean wave. Turbulence and confusion, darkness and brilliance, the roar of traffic, shouts, gunshots, the shock of a body hurtling through space, knocking him to the ground. The heavy weight of that body on top of him, the sticky warmth of blood that wasn't his.

He laughed softly, painfully. "Forget it. How's it going to look for the new chief of L.A.'s finest if he's implicated in a conspiracy to withhold evidence in a homicide investigation? Look..." He spoke rapidly now, urgently, rolling over Shannon's protests. "Right now I just need to get her out of here—fast. I'll keep you posted. The minute I find out anything, believe me, you'll be the first to know."

He hung up on the tinny squawks of protest, just as Mary-Joy Donnelly stepped through the doorway and into the light. She came that far and no farther, leaned against the door frame and folded her arms upon her chest. He regarded her with hard eyes and clenched jaw, knowing how important it was to maintain absolute control of the situation and trying hard to hold on to his purpose and resolve. But God, it was hard, when her mouth had that waif look again, vulnerable but defiant. When her hair was tousled, completely artless, so that she looked like a little kid just waking from a nap. When her eyes were so huge and hurt, and accusing. Looking at her made something strange happen inside him, something painful and, in a vague sort of way, frightening.

"So," she said, just a shade too loudly, "are you going to arrest me, or what? Aren't you supposed to read me my rights or something?"

"Probably," said Doug. He rubbed a hand over his face, noting with surprise the length of the beard stubble on his jaw. He leaned back, laced his hands behind his head and studied the woman in the doorway thoughtfully. "What is it I'm supposed to arrest you for, Joy?"

Her chin came up one brave notch, but she couldn't quite manage to hide the tremor in her voice. "For murdering my roommate. That's what you think I did, isn't it? You think I killed Belle."

He was glad that at least she'd stopped denying she was who she was. "Did you?" he asked softly.

Her head jerked, as if her whole being was expressing the denial she could only whisper. *"No."*

"But you know who did, don't you?" He fired that right back at her, giving her no chance to recover her composure.

This time her denial was much more emphatic—and as far as Doug was concerned, a lot less believable. Her mouth snapped shut—the spring trap, again—and she turned her head deliberately to one side, reminding him of nothing so much as an obstinate child.

"I could still arrest you," he said mildly. "For withholding information in a murder case."

"Yeah, so why don't you?" It was sheer bravado. He could see that she was dangerously pale, and he had an idea that there was a good reason why she was leaning against the wall like that.

It was no time to feel sympathy, and an even worse time for the urge he suddenly had to put his arms around her and invite her to lean against him instead of the damn wall. Taking care to keep both emotions out of his voice, he said, "Is that what you want me to do?"

He could have sworn he heard her swallow, even from clear across the room. She looked past him and whispered, "I don't know anything."

"So what do you want? Want me to leave?" He jerked his head in the general direction of the bullet-pocked wall. "Let whoever did that come back and finish the job?"

She didn't answer. After a moment Doug got up and crossed the room in an unhurried stroll. He stood looking down at her, hands in his pockets, in the manner of an elementary school principal zeroing in on a stubborn miscreant. "Look, Joy. The way I see it you've got two choices."

"*Mary Jo.*"

"Pardon?"

She gave her head a little toss. "My name's Mary Jo, not Joy. I wish you wouldn't keep calling me that."

"You called yourself that," he said softly. "Once upon a time. Didn't you?"

Her eyes seemed to flicker, like guttering candle flames, then went cold and dark, disappearing behind the curtain of hastily dropped lashes. "It was a long time ago."

It occurred to him suddenly, irrelevantly, that what gave her mouth that bruised, vulnerable look was the fact that the upper lip had very little indentation. And then for one wild moment he had the panicky feeling that he'd completely lost the thread of the conversation.

He cleared his throat and said in a hard voice, tossing it off as if it wasn't of any consequence to him one way or the other, "Okay, Mary Jo, then. Mary Jo, did you ever hear the expression, 'between a rock and a hard place'? Now, on the one hand, you've got jail—that's the hard place. On the other hand, there's somebody that seems to want you dead—that's the rock. Between, you got me. That's where you are right now. You follow me?"

She was silent, still steadfastly refusing to look at him.

In a kinder voice he said, "Look, it seems to me I'm about the best option you've got right now. Maybe it's about time you accepted that and trusted me a little."

If he thought he had her cowed, he'd underestimated her again. Her eyes flew open, striking at him like hurled pebbles, and she fairly spat the words, "Why should I?"

"Why should you?" She'd surprised him so much he hardly knew what to say, except, "Why *shouldn't* you?"

Again something flickered in her eyes, but this time, although shielded, their gaze remained steady. "Think about it, MacDougal. Two things happened to me today, right out of the blue. Number one, you show up. And number two, somebody tries to kill me. Am I really supposed to believe that's a *coincidence?*"

Chapter 5

There was a brief period when everything in him struggled to deny it. But that was it, of course, the thing that had been bothering him all night, starting from the minute he'd driven onto a quiet, middle-class residential street in San Diego and heard the unmistakable sounds of automatic weapons fire. *Coincidence?*

He dragged a hand over his face, rubbing at his eyes which seemed roughly the size and texture of tennis balls. It had been a long time since he'd slept.

"Truth?" he said finally, frowning in his effort to bring her face back into focus. "I don't know what to think. And most of what I am thinking I don't like very much."

He put the blame for what he did next on the fact that he was very, very tired; he didn't like using physical intimidation, especially on a woman. Especially this woman. In spite of that he felt himself shifting his weight, leaning toward Joy and bracing one hand on the wall above her head. With his other hand he captured and imprisoned her face, fingers on one cheekbone, thumb on the other. He spoke very softly.

"Problem is, I'm a detective, so I don't like coincidences. They make me suspicious. But I'll tell you this much. Whether your name is Joy Donnelly or Mary Jo Delinsky, or Mary Mary Quite Contrary, the fact is I've been looking for you for ten years—*ten years,* dammit. I've been looking for you because I have some questions I'm pretty sure you know the answers to. And if you think for one minute I'm going to let you out of my sight until I get those answers..."

The muscles in his jaws hurt; he made a conscious effort to unclench his teeth. He could hear the harshness in his voice, though he kept it reined in and just above a whisper.

"We have to talk, Mary Jo. You understand me?" He gave her face a little waggle of encouragement and waited for her barely perceptible nod. Then he took his hand away from her face and let go of the breath he'd been holding. "But not here. I don't want to take a chance on those guys coming back. Let's go. Get your things."

"Where..." She cleared her throat with a small, cautious sound. "Where are you taking me?"

He could see the pale imprint of his fingers on her flushed cheek, and it made him feel mean and slightly queasy. The velvety feel of her skin still vibrated on his nerve endings, aftershocks of the sensory jolt that had just sent a wave of heat right through him.

He looked around distractedly. "Never mind where." He found that he was rubbing his fingertips against the heel of his hand, and made himself stop it. "Come on, get what you need and let's—"

"I'm not going."

"Pardon?"

"I said I'm not going. I can't. I won't."

Now what? Damn the woman. But there was a look in her eye he was beginning to recognize.

Doug's temper was a well-kept secret. Very few people were aware that he even had one because he seldom lost it— a good thing, too, as close family members could have testified. When he did lose it, it was an awesome thing to behold. But while he was an extremely patient man, he did have his flashpoint, and thanks to a combination of hunger, fatigue and frustration, he was dangerously near that point now.

Slowly, enunciating carefully, he said, "What do you mean, you won't go? You don't seem to understand, I'm not giving you a choice."

Her mouth had an implacable look that was contradicted by her eyes, which were liquid and shiny, like warm maple syrup. She fixed those eyes on him and said, "I'm not leaving without Moki."

It suddenly occurred to Doug that he was not in control of the situation any longer. If he ever had been. Which is not a feeling any cop likes to have, and Doug was no exception. He felt unarmed and unarmored, which he found frightening. He felt frail and human, which he found intolerable.

The truth was, he hadn't really felt in control since the first moment he'd set eyes on Joy Donnelly. He'd been so blown away by the miracle of finding her that he'd committed the cardinal—and potentially fatal—sin of letting his guard down. And he knew he couldn't—*could not*—let that happen again. Because, whether she was a murderer or not, if she had that kind of effect on him she was dangerous. A lot more dangerous than he'd anticipated.

He made himself take a step back, both physically and emotionally, and folded his arms on his chest, consciously barricading himself against her. "Moki," he said, pleased to hear that his voice sounded calm, quiet, firm. "That would be..."

"My cat."

"Ah."

She pushed herself away from the wall and toward him, and folded her arms over *her* chest in a parody of his own stance that he was pretty sure wasn't intentional. It occurred to Doug that they must look like a couple of mismatched bookends, faced off like that.

She cleared her throat and said unevenly, "I can't very well just go away and leave him. Especially since he probably saved my life."

"A cat...saved your life."

"Well, yeah. He jumped out of my arms and I was trying to catch him, and that's when the shooting started. And, um, I guess I lost my balance." She gave an ironic little shrug as she slipped past him. "Anyway, that's how come I landed in the bushes. So I guess if he hadn't jumped, I'd probably be dead right now, huh?"

Doug said something under his breath which his mother, a devout Roman Catholic, would probably have considered blasphemous. Joy threw him a look, a wry little half smile.

"Yeah, funny isn't it, the way things happen?" She suddenly clapped a hand across her mouth and exclaimed, "Omigod—I just thought of something. I bet he knew those guys were out there. I thought he was just mad because I wouldn't let him out." She had the front door half open before he realized what she was up to.

He lunged for the door and straight-armed it shut. "Where do you think you're going?"

"Let...me...out, dammit." She was tugging furiously at the doorknob. "I have to find—"

"The hell you do." He caught her by the shoulder and yanked her back from the door, ignoring a hiss of pain that reminded him belatedly, and with a guilty pang, of her scratches.

"Yeah, but...but I know where he probably is. He must be terrified. I can't just leave him here. Please let me look for him. It'll only take me a minute. Please—I can't..." And suddenly she was crying.

Doug was no stranger to women's tears. In his business he saw a lot of them, both the real and the crocodile variety, but he couldn't remember any ever affecting him the way hers did. Then there was the fact that she was so obviously dismayed by her own tears—horrified, almost—which made them all the more gut-wrenching.

The way they made him feel reminded him suddenly and vividly of a scene from his childhood—a cold, gray drizzle, and a crowd gathered around an open grave...the sound of rain drip-dripping from the edges of an umbrella, the crack of rifles fired in salute...a flag folded into a tight, triangular bundle, and his father's rugged face, contorted and wet with what Doug had understood even then wasn't rain. He remembered the way he'd felt inside, watching his father weep for his friend and partner, killed in the line of duty. He remembered the cold, upside-down feeling that was fear.

"Hey," he croaked and, before he knew what he was going to do, turned Joy Donnelly into his arms.

At first she fought him like a frightened cat, bracing against his chest with her fists, then her forearms, growling "No...no..." in helpless fury.

But he was a whole lot stronger than she was.

"Hey," he said again, and was bemused to hear that this time it sounded almost like a croon. His hand cradled the back of her head; his fingers pushed through her hair and rasped softly against her scalp. He felt her begin to relax a little, then a little more, and finally the damp warmth of her breath and tears soaked into his shirt. Something inside his chest seemed to tighten and quiver.

"It's okay," he heard himself murmur. "It's okay. We won't leave without him, I promise. How 'bout if I go look for him?"

She shook her head, a movement that caused her face to rub against the front of his shirt in a way that felt disconcertingly like nuzzling. "You'd never find him." It was a whisper, muffled and husky. "He hates strangers. Especially men."

Oh, great, Doug thought, gazing up at the ceiling. And then he thought, Oh, Lord, I wonder if he likes mynah birds. He had a sudden, vivid mental picture of the cat making Maurice's acquaintance for the first time. Which, the more he thought about it, did cheer him up some.

"Okay," he finally said, with a sigh he acknowledged as complete capitulation. "I guess we can wait awhile...see if he shows up. He'll probably come back home once he knows it's safe, right?"

Joy mumbled something he couldn't hear.

Oh, well, he thought, what the hell. He was too tired to drive to L.A. right now, anyway. He'd rest for a little while...maybe an hour or two. If the damn cat hadn't come back by that time ... well, he'd cross that bridge when he came to it.

He didn't say anything to Joy, though. He simply didn't trust himself to speak.

Mary was busy in reflections of her own. I don't understand, she thought. How can this feel so good? This man was a cop and a stranger. But his arms were so strong around her, his heartbeat so steady against her cheek, his hand so gentle in her hair. Never in all her life before had she felt like this—wrapped in warmth, steeped in security, protected, cherished and cared for.

The sensation was so wonderful it utterly demoralized her. She felt shattered, overwhelmed by a grief she didn't understand at all. How could she feel such a terrible sense of loss for something she'd never even had?

I can't do this, she thought. *I can't.*

She heard the sounds she was making, sounds she'd never made before, sobs like those of a heartbroken child. And she heard something else, too—the cop's soft, wordless murmurs of comfort. She felt his hand stroking her hair, the bare and vulnerable nape of her neck. A shockwave of pain rolled through her, like magma boiling beneath the surface of a volcano, or an avalanche of sorrow that was utterly beyond her control.

I can't ... I can't.

But then somehow her arms found their own way around the cop's midsection, her hands clutched at his shirt, gathered it in desperate fistfuls, and she was clinging to him as she would to a rock in a flood.

Sometime later, in the darkest, quietest time of the night, Mary awoke to a strange, rhythmic sound. A harsh, but oddly comforting, sound. She was so disoriented it took her a while to figure out what it was. It wasn't a sound she could ever recall having heard before.

Somewhere, very close by, a man was snoring.

How funny, she thought. The cop—MacDougal—was snoring. And *very* close by. So close his breath stirred her hair, so close she felt the rumble of it beneath her cheek. Oh, Lord, when had she come to be snuggled on his lap, wrapped in his arms with her head pillowed on his chest, in the middle of her living room sofa? When—and how—could she have fallen asleep in the arms of a *cop?*

It was all so strange. And the strangest part of it was, she felt no desire whatsoever to move out of those arms. She felt limp, exhausted, utterly spent . . . and at the same time, unbelievably content. She remembered it all now, being in such awful pain, feeling such overwhelming sorrow. It had probably been cathartic, although at the time she hadn't really understood what she was grieving for. Even now, sheltered and protected in the arms of a stranger, she still couldn't figure out *why.*

I have so much. That was what she told herself, as she had always done. I am so fortunate. I'm thankful for my health, my home, my friends. I have so much. Why should I be sad?

Because I have lost so much. The truth came into her mind like a cold and mournful little wind, scattering her denials like so many dry leaves. She'd lost . . . oh, God, so much. Her family. Her sisters. And Belle, of course. Her dreams. And trust. And so many other things she hadn't let herself think about for such a long time. Thinking about them now should have brought more pain, more grief, but somehow it didn't. Maybe she was just too drained, too numb, but for some reason instead of feeling sad, she felt . . . empty. Not a bad kind of empty, but an emptiness that waits, like a cup or a bowl, to be filled. She felt . . . for the first time in a very long time, she felt hopeful.

She thought it was ironic, in a way. This cop—MacDougal. She'd dreaded his coming so much, been terrified of all that it would mean, but now that he was here, she found that she wasn't afraid anymore.

The rhythm of his snoring stumbled, then resumed. Mary drew an unsteady breath, then held it in wonder while something warm and tremulous came to life inside her. Incredibly, it was happiness—an urge to smile, to giggle, to laugh. Held inside, the laughter became a cool shower of sparkles, like the bubbles in a glass of champagne. With a long sigh she turned the smile against MacDougal's gently heaving chest, and with the music of his snoring in her ears, went back to sleep.

The first thing Doug realized when he woke up was that parts of him were still asleep, parts he hadn't even known were capable of that sort of betrayal. Both feet and an elbow, okay—but portions of his chest and backside?

He shifted, and a warm weight distributed all along his front stirred and rearranged itself in a way that made him acutely aware of another kind of discomfort entirely.

"Joy," he croaked, "wake up."

She made a querulous sound and burrowed her face into the hollow of his throat. He sighed, and the breeze of his exhalation made a lock of hair that was standing up in a childish rooster tail flutter and tickle his lips. He smoothed down the errant strands with his hand, then absentmindedly pressed his lips against them. The scent of strawberries filled his nostrils, evocative of sunshine and spring.

Then for a while he didn't move at all, just sat enjoying the unique and unexpected pleasure of waking up with a beautiful woman in his arms, feeling no compulsion to analyze it or explain why it should feel so good to him. What he felt mostly was a profound sense of wonder, but not because the woman in his arms was Joy Donnelly, the object of his ten-year-long search—or, some might have said, obsession. No, it was wonder—because it seemed so natural to him to be holding her like that. As if it were something he'd been doing for years and years, and would go on doing for many years more.

A sound intruded on his gentle doze, most likely the same one that had awakened him the first time. It was an unearthly sound. The effect it had on him was something like fingernails raking down his naked spine.

"Joy... uh, Mary?" He coughed, nudged her head with his chin and said firmly, "Hey, come on, wake up. I think your cat's home."

Catlike herself, she stirred, her body firming, stretching, arching against him. Then suddenly she paused . . . and sat bolt upright on his lap, which increased certain of his discomforts immeasurably.

"Moki? Really?" Her voice was sleep-slurred and husky. "Oh, God, he came back. I was afraid—"

"Uh," said Doug with gritted teeth. But she'd already hopped off his lap and gone to open the front door, leaving him free to rise, groaning, and hobble to the bathroom on legs that were still prickly with returning circulation.

He felt better after he'd relieved himself and doused his face with cold water. At that point there wasn't much he wouldn't have given for a shave and a nice hot shower, and he did consider it, with a longing look at the bathtub and its transparent shower curtain patterned with gaily cavorting tropical fish. He figured there was probably even a razor somewhere he could borrow. But he was beginning to feel a real sense of urgency about getting Joy out of that vulnerable little house and into a safer place, so he just borrowed some deodorant and a sprinkle of baby powder instead.

When he came out of the bathroom he could hear Joy in the kitchen, apparently talking baby talk to someone or something. The first thing he saw when he walked into the room was that incredible smile of hers, which was like looking into the sunrise, so it was a moment or two before he really noticed the creature that was winding itself with serpentine grace around her feet.

When he did, he blurted tactlessly, "My God—what is that?"

Far from seeming insulted, Joy turned up the volume on her smile a few megawatts and scooped the animal into her arms. "This is Moki. He's a purebred Siamese—aren't you, baby? Yes, you are. My neighbor down the street raises them. She gave him to me because she says he has some kind of flaw—too many toes, or something. Isn't he beautiful?"

All Doug could think of at that moment was that, if her name wasn't Joy, it sure should have been.

"Beautiful," he murmured, not meaning the cat, which had fixed him with a pale, opaline stare, while the last six inches or so of his mink-brown tail twitched and curled as if possessed of a life all its own. Personally, Doug thought the beast looked more like a goblin than any cat he'd ever seen before. Its neck was too long, its ears too large, and its small, triangular face much too small to accommodate those eerie, translucent eyes. They reminded him of something....

He cleared his throat warily. "Uh...did you by any chance happen to see Walt Disney's *Lady and the Tramp* when you were a kid? There were these two evil Siamese cats—"

Joy's laughter was an uninhibited bark of delight, which ended with a happy little gulp. "I know—he does look kind of sinister, doesn't he? But he doesn't even like fish, and he hardly ever hunts birds. He's really sweet, I swear to God. Once he gets to know you."

Doug said, "Right," but with a note of lingering doubt as he observed the tips of razor-sharp claws peeking out of deceptively relaxed-looking chocolate-brown paws. He sighed inwardly and firmly suppressed mental images of cartoon mayhem. It was clear she thought the world of the damn beast, so it looked like he and Maurice were just going to have to make the best of things.

He cleared his throat. "Uh...you know, we really should get going."

She nodded, but showed no sign of being through with nuzzling and sweet-talking the beast. Watching her, it occurred to Doug that she seemed different this morning—friendlier, for one thing, and a lot more relaxed around him. Nothing like a good crying jag for breaking the ice, he thought. Or maybe it had something to do with the fact that she'd just spent most of the night in his arms. Either way, she seemed to have gotten rid of most of the chip on her shoulder, not to mention her bad attitude toward cops, which in a way was going to make his position that much more difficult. It was hard enough having to keep reminding himself that she was "the target," the material witness in a homicide investigation, when she was so damned beautiful. Being physically attracted to her was one thing; if he started to like her on top of it, things were going to get a lot more complicated.

He pulled himself together, put on his best take-charge look and said sternly, "Come on, let's go. You got a carrier for that th—uh, Moki?"

She smiled at him from between the cat's triangle ears, obviously not terribly impressed by his authority. "Yeah, somewhere, but he really hates it. He'll just howl the whole time. That can really get on your nerves. It's probably better if I just hold him."

"Right," said Doug, and sighed, which was something he seemed to be doing a lot lately. His stomach was giving him warning rumbles, too. "Uh, look, that's fine, but the thing is, I'm pretty hungry, and you probably are, too. What about when we stop for breakfast? We can't just leave the cat in the car."

As desperate as he was for a cup of coffee, there was no way he was going to leave those claws alone with his seat covers. His Mercedes might be old and ugly and stagger a bit on the hills, but it did have leather upholstery.

"No problem," said Joy blithely. "We can just drive through McDonald's."

"Perfect," Doug breathed. He could already feel his cholesterol rising.

Mary broke off a small piece of an Egg McMuffin and offered it to Moki, who was perched on the back of her seat, near her shoulder. MacDougal glanced over at her and said irritably, "You sure that stuff's good for cats?"

She could think of a lot of combative answers to that, but for some reason she felt too mellow to bother. There was a strange kind of warmth inside her this morning, like the friendly glow of a nice little old potbellied stove on a cold winter's day, and all she said was "It'll have to do until I can buy some cat food."

MacDougal grunted, then began to swear and mutter under his breath as they started up a hill and his car coughed and sputtered and the speedometer needle dropped once more below the speed limit.

"Great car," said Mary dryly. She'd made that remark before, and with sincerity, when she'd first learned that the old dirty white Mercedes was MacDougal's. She thought it was kind of endearingly wacky, an unexpected sort of car for a cop to have. But then, she was finding that quite a few things about MacDougal were unexpected.

"What's her name?" she'd asked him then, to which he'd replied in a surly tone, "It's a *car,* not a pet." But she thought that if it was hers, she'd have named it. That's just the kind of car it was.

Now, already regretting her facetious remark, she looked over at MacDougal and asked with genuine concern, "What's wrong with it?"

He flipped on the turn signal and edged into the slow lane as a Cadillac swerved around them, horn blaring. "Clogged fuel filter," he muttered, scowling into the rearview mirror. "That's what I get for buying cheap diesel."

"Cheap diesel? I thought there was no such thing."

MacDougal snorted. "'Cheap' as in lousy."

She waited a moment, then said, "Why do you?"

He shook his head and slowly exhaled. "Ah... well. It's a long story."

"So? We've got a long way to go." She noticed that he was fidgeting with the steering wheel, shifting uncomfortably in his seat. Once again the notion that a cop might feel embarrassment both delighted and confused her. In fact, there were quite a few things about MacDougal that she was beginning to find confusing. She pulled her leg up and turned halfway around in her seat so she could look at him and said, "Tell me."

"I've got this friend..." He made a throwaway gesture with his hand. "Well, not a friend, exactly. More like an acquaintance. Actually—" he blurted the rest in a rush "he's an ex-con. I busted him for armed robbery. But that was a long time ago, and now he's got this gas station-garage over on Los Feliz... and, you know, I just like to try and help him out. When I can. No big deal. I just wish he'd get some decent diesel, that's all."

He indicated that the subject was closed by abruptly turning on the car's stereo. The pipe organ music from

Phantom of the Opera blared forth, sending Moki into hiding in the back seat.

Who is this guy? Mary thought, watching him in fascinated silence. He sure wasn't like any cop she'd ever known. He was unexpected...confusing...even *nice*. Not that he didn't seem capable of being tough as nails if he had to be—she'd spent half the night with his gun pressing into her hip, and she had no doubt whatsoever that he knew how to use it—but she knew firsthand that he was also capable of great gentleness. And kindness. For instance, she could tell he didn't much care for cats, and yet he'd let her wait for Moki to come home. He hadn't had to do that. He could have forced her to go with him right then—he was a cop, he had the authority. But he hadn't. Instead, he'd waited until morning, and held her while she cried.

Remembering the night just past, that strange fit of weeping, the terrible sadness and sense of loss, brought an unanticipated reprise of those emotions. She found that she had a terrible lump in her throat. And it didn't help that the stereo began playing Andrew Lloyd Weber's "Memory" just then. Of all the songs in the world... She caught a quick, panicky breath and shifted around to face front, but it didn't help; the haunting and beautiful music from *Cats* seemed to carry the ache into her chest, into every part of her.

"What did you do that for?" MacDougal asked when she stabbed at the off button, silencing the song. "Don't like music?"

She cleared her throat and looked out the window so he couldn't see her face. "Not that kind."

"You used to sing that kind of music, didn't you?" She could hear the change in his voice—the change to on-duty cop. "At the club where you and Belle worked—what was it called? Caesar's Garden?"

"Joy did." She spoke very softly, holding herself rigid. "I don't. Not anymore."

"You don't sing?" She could feel his head turn, feel his inquisitive cop's eyes on her. "Why not? I heard you were good."

She shut her eyes, trying desperately to hold the memory at bay, but it came, anyway. The caress of soft purple lights; the spotlight holding her, like a lover's embrace; the feel of the microphone, smooth and warm in her hand; and the music welling up inside her... the ecstasy, the *joy.*

MacDougal's voice was soft, an insidious invasion of her emotions. "Want to talk about it?"

She shook her head. *I can't. It hurts too much. Too many memories...*

"You're going to have to, you know," he said gently. "Sooner or later."

She didn't reply. He didn't turn the stereo back on, and after a while Moki came creeping across the back of the seat and over her shoulder like a curl of brown smoke. He didn't settle down in her lap for a snooze, as he usually did, but lay sphinxlike across her legs and watched MacDougal with a steady, unblinking gaze.

"It's a brand-new *car!*" crowed the voice of a famous game-show host, as Doug, Joy and Moki paused on the landing outside Doug's front door.

Joy said, "You leave your TV on?"

Doug stuck his key in the lock, then turned his back to the door and took a deep breath. "Do me a favor. Make sure you keep a good tight grip on that cat, okay?"

Joy looked puzzled, but nodded. The cat's triangular head was sticking up on that long neck of his like a periscope, ears alert and eyes like pale blue headlamps.

"Okay," Doug muttered grimly, "here goes." He pushed open the door.

"It's a raid!"

Doug heard a surprised gasp from behind him as he stepped into the living room. Joy followed him, all but tiptoeing.

"Damn cops!"

"Joy, uh, Mary," said Doug dryly, "meet Maurice."

There was a moment or two of thunderstruck silence. Then she crowed, "Omigod—this is just so *great*—it's a mynah bird!" and advanced upon Maurice's cage, croon-

ing, "Aren't you a pretty bird...?" She turned on Doug
suddenly. "You mean, that was all *him?* It didn't even
sound like a bird talking."

"Mynahs don't just imitate words," Doug informed her.
"They imitate voices—even sounds." He dropped Joy's
suitcase on the floor and his keys on the coffee table and
went to check his phone messages, adding absently, "It's
enough to drive you crazy sometimes."

"Well, I think he's wonderful." She bent over so she was
on the bird's eye level and began to talk baby talk to him the
way she did to the cat. Maurice cocked his head and studied her with one bright, beady eye.

The light on the message machine was blinking furiously. Doug punched the rewind button and listened to a
long string of gibberish.

"Oh, baby..." A man's voice filled the room, deep-
throated and passionate. *"Yes...yes...yes..."*

Joy gasped and straightened up as if she'd been jabbed,
then burst into great peals of laughter. Doug closed his eyes
and groaned, *"Jeez,* Maurice." He went to snatch up the
cage cover. "Believe me, he did not learn that from me."

"Where did he learn it from?" Joy inquired in a fascinated voice, husky with suppressed mirth.

"Lord only knows. Look, you wretched crow," he muttered darkly as he dropped the cover over the cage, "one
more outburst like that and you're cat food, you hear me?"

"You have the right to remain silent" issued mournfully
from beneath the shroud.

"He used to belong to a drug dealer," Doug explained to
Joy, who was watching him with a solemn expression, but
with glistening eyes and a mouth that quivered suspi-
ciously. "The guy's currently doing twenty-five to life at
Soledad. I suppose I should have warned you about his vocabulary. You haven't heard anything yet, believe me."

"I can't wait," she said demurely.

Then, for some reason, there was a strangely electric little silence while he looked at her and she looked back at
him. His eyes dropped to her mouth, and he suddenly felt
like a starving man beholding a thick, juicy steak. Then they

both moved at once, as if someone unseen had pressed the start button. He scrubbed a hand over his stubbly jaws just as she looked down at the cat in her arms as if she'd momentarily forgotten he was there.

They spoke simultaneously.

"I guess I should—"

"You probably want to—"

She yielded, and Doug gestured with uncharacteristic awkwardness toward the hallway. "Uh…guest room's down there, on the right. Bathroom's just across the hall. You can put the cat in there for now, I guess." He frowned, trying to think what he could be forgetting.

She made a tiny, throat-clearing sound. "I have his litter box. It's in the car."

"Right. I'll get it." He turned to pick up her suitcase, and when he looked at her again he saw that she hadn't moved, that she was still just standing there looking at him as if there was something else she expected him to say or do. "What?" he said, his frown deepening.

"So…I'm staying here?" Her eyes had suddenly gone wary, and her voice had a brittle, defensive edge. "With you?"

"You got a better idea?"

She didn't answer, just went on looking at him in a way that made him feel as if he were drowning.

He set the suitcase down and put his hands on her arms. The cat gave a low, warning growl, which he bravely ignored. "Look, this is the safest place I can think of. Nobody knows you're here but me, and the only way in here is up those stairs." He found that he was rubbing her arms through the fabric of her windbreaker; it occurred to him that, if it hadn't been for the cat, he'd have pulled her into his arms, and he didn't know if he was glad about that, or sorry.

"Joy," he said, surprised by the huskiness in his voice, "you're just going to have to trust me."

She started to say something, cleared her throat and croaked, "Why?"

Right—why should she, when he was beginning to think he couldn't even trust himself? He shrugged and managed a half smile. "You gotta trust somebody sometime."

Her voice was hard, angry. "No, I mean, why are you doing this? Isn't this illegal? Why don't you just quit this bull, arrest me, or take me in for questioning, or whatever it is you're supposed to do?"

He hated the way she was looking at him, last night's wariness and suspicion back again in her eyes, that bruised look around her mouth. It gave him a hot, angry feeling in the pit of his stomach that he didn't want to analyze, or try to understand.

He gazed at her for a moment, then said flatly, "I don't know. There are some things I have to figure out first. It would make everything a whole lot easier, you know, if you'd just come clean with me. I don't suppose you're ready to do that?"

She stared back at him with a look he recognized. He smiled sardonically and picked up her suitcase once more. "That's what I thought. So for now, you and your cat get to stay here where it's nice and safe, and I can keep an eye on you. Got it?"

He carried the suitcase into his spare bedroom, which was more catchall than guest, showed Joy the bathroom, waited until she and the cat had gone in and shut the door, then went back to the living room and punched the playback button on his message machine.

The first three were from Jim Shannon, in escalating degrees of impatience, from last night, probably. The fourth was from his lieutenant, left first thing this morning. He winced at the surly note in her voice; Lieutenant Mabry was a bad lady to cross. He'd filled her in before taking off for San Diego, but hadn't reported progress since then, and he was already long overdue to check in. He wasn't too worried about it, though. She'd cool off when he told her he'd just found the key to cracking one of the most notorious cases in the department's active file. Jeez, the Rhinestone Collar Murder. The press would have a field day. And he'd see to it that all the publicity went to Mabry. She'd forgive him in a hurry.

Right now, though, what it meant was that he was going to have to go down to the station and convince her to cut him some slack in this situation. He just needed a little more time. If he could just get Joy to trust him . . .

He allowed himself the luxury of a long, hot shower and his first shave in three days. When he got a good look at himself in the mirror, he thought he could understand why Joy kept giving him that "why should I trust you?" look. He wouldn't trust somebody who looked like him, either. He looked like a skid row bum.

In the bedroom next door, Mary stood gazing down at her bullet-riddled suitcase. She opened it slowly and pulled out a pair of jeans, which she held up to the light. "Yeah, right . . . trust somebody," she whispered, sticking a finger through the frayed hole just below one hip pocket.

You're going to have to trust somebody sometime.

She folded the jeans slowly, folded them over and over and then hugged the bundle to her chest, drawing comfort from their familiarity as she looked around her, surveying the room that had so unexpectedly become her refuge. A strange sort of refuge, she thought, though it probably beat the hell out of a jail cell.

The room was totally masculine, with furnishings that ran to weight benches and rowing machines, decorated with high school football trophies, marksmanship awards, old gym shoes and worn out sweat socks. This was obviously the place where MacDougal put everything he didn't want the whole world to see, the place he tossed things when he tidied up, the things he closed the door on when company showed up unexpectedly. It gave her a strange feeling, being in the midst of so much that was personal and private, almost like having him right there with her.

She closed her eyes and pressed her face into the warm, rough, familiar-smelling denim, suddenly aching with the need to cry and be comforted, as she had the night before. Her life was changing, irrevocably and much too rapidly. There was too much of the past here in L.A., too many memories, and she couldn't see the future at all. She felt scared and off balance, as if somebody had just pulled the rug out from under her feet.

You have to trust somebody.

And suddenly she knew that it wasn't just any comfort, it was *him* she wanted. MacDougal's arms around her, his big, strong body to hold on to, a buffer between her and the terrors of the unknown.

The idea terrified her. All at once she wanted nothing so much as to go home, to go back to the way her life had been before the cop from L.A. had walked into Saint Vincent's and blasted it all to smithereens. All right, so it had only been half a life—at least she'd felt safe, and she'd known whom to trust.

Moki stuck his head out from under the dust ruffle near her feet, then jumped up on the bed with a querulous and interrogative yowl and bumped her leg with his nose.

"I know," she whispered as she sat on the edge of the bed and gathered the cat into her arms. "I know...." She held him and her bullet-riddled jeans and rocked herself, back and forth, back and forth.

Oh, how she missed them—she missed them all, Preacher and Daisy and JoJo. She wondered where they were now, whether she was ever going to see them again, and whether they'd think of her at all.

"What'd you find out?" Daisy Pepper snapped at Preacher as he slid onto the bench across from her.

"Yeah," said JoJo. "Is Mary comin' back?"

"I don't know." Preacher spread his hands wide in an exaggerated shrug. "Nobody knows. She hasn't shown up, and she hasn't called. I found out something, though. That cop? He's from L.A."

Daisy hit the tabletop with her open palm. "I knew it! I told ya, didn't I? You think he took her?"

Preacher shrugged again. "That I don't know. All they'd tell me up there in the office is that the gentleman showed them a badge and asked for her address, they gave it to him and he left. That's it. And today she didn't show up for work.''

"We oughtta check on her," said JoJo, looking worried. "Make sure she's okay."

"Wish we knew her address," Daisy muttered, beating a tattoo on the table with her fingertips. "Think the office'd give it to us? If we explained—"

Preacher shook his head. "I asked. They don't seem to trust our motives the way Mary did, for some reason. However..." His eyes were gleaming. "I just happened to notice that her, ah, employee record card was lying there on the desk, and I, ah, was able to create a small diversion...." He reached inside his jacket and drew out a three-by-five card with perforated edges, which he slid across the table with a small flourish. "Haven't lost my touch," he purred, rubbing the tips of his fingers across his lapel.

Daisy hissed, "Hot damn, you got it!" and whisked the card out of sight beneath the table.

"I would suggest," said Preacher in an undertone, "that we get out of here before somebody notices that card is missing." He gave a surreptitious glance around him and rose.

"Where we going?" JoJo asked, following suit.

Daisy pulled her cap down over her eyes and began to shrug into her assortment of sweaters and coats. "To check on Mary, that's where. Ain't that what friends are for?"

Chapter 6

Lieutenant Mabry was on the phone when Doug walked into the squad room, but if he thought he was going to be able to slip past her and get to his desk without her spotting him, he ought to have known better. There wasn't much that got past the lieutenant. She gestured to him through the glass and was cradling the receiver as he stuck his head through her office door.

"Come in, Doug," she said pleasantly, "and close the door." She waited until he'd done so, then planted her elbows on her blotter and began to turn a pencil end over end, which Doug knew from experience was not a good sign. He gamely cleared his throat, but before he could launch into his prepared speech, she said in that same even tone, "I need a phone call, Doug. That's all. Is that too much to ask? We've got a backlog of cases a mile high here, as you well know. Where the hell have you been?"

"You know where—"

"You told me you had a lead on the Landon case. I gave you leave to go to San Diego to check it out." There was a pause. The pencil hit the blotter with a soft plop. "So let's hear it. What did you come up with?"

Doug figured it was okay to let his breath out. "An eye-witness—I think."

The lieutenant leaned forward, suddenly bright-eyed and eager. "You *think?* And where, might I ask, is this witness now? Did you bring him with you, or is it to be a surprise?"

Damn, how he hated it when she got sarcastic. It sure wasn't going to make this any easier. He leaned one elbow on the top of a filing cabinet and rubbed at the back of his neck. "Actually, it's a she. And ... no, I didn't bring her in for questioning."

"Why not?"

"I didn't see any point to it. She's not ready to talk."

"Sergeant, we do have ways of encouraging people to help us in our investigations."

"Look, I just need some time. She's trying to decide whether or not to trust me. Meanwhile—"

"Meanwhile..." The lieutenant's voice had gone quiet again— too quiet. "Meanwhile, we have a couple of drive-bys, a parking lot stabbing, and a Jane Doe that turned up in a house fire of suspicious origin, and that's just last night's tally. Do I need to remind you, Detective Sergeant MacDougal, that we need you here, not out somewhere obsessing over a case that's ten years cold?"

"I'm not..." Doug threw up his hand in a gesture of denial. "I'm not obsessing. It was my case, that's all. It's still my case."

He glanced over his shoulder at the wall of glass that separated him from the busy squad room, then went over and gave the venetian blind cord a yank. He came back and put his hands on the lieutenant's desk and leaned on them.

"Ann," he said, lowering his voice to a rusty growl, "I have to ask you something—don't take this wrong, okay?" He hesitated, took a breath and dived in. "Who besides you knew about that San Diego lead?"

Lieutenant Ann Mabry was in her mid-forties, of a somewhat exotic mix, ethnically speaking, and as immaculately turned out as a Rodeo Drive saleswoman. She had a flawless oval face and cafe-au-lait skin, and wore her hair

sleeked back from her face and bound into a large knot on
the back of her head in a manner that in no way made her
look frumpy. She looked elegant, intelligent and capable, all
of which she was. Doug respected her a great deal, for all of
those reasons, and also because she was a damned good cop.
At his question her features had remained perfectly still,
except for the slightest twitch of her perfect blackbird's wing
eyebrows. But deep in her eyes a light flared.

She said only, "I didn't keep it a secret, Doug. That case
is big news."

"So... ?"

"Probably everybody in the precinct." There was a pause
while Doug swore under his breath. "You want to tell me
why you'd ask me such a question?"

They traded long, hard looks. Then Doug said in a
monotone, "I tracked the witness to the place where she
works, a skid row shelter named Saint Vincent's. Before I
had a chance to take her into custody, she made me for a
police officer and, uh, was able to effect a getaway. I per-
suaded the shelter management to give me her home address and drove out there immediately. I arrived just in time
to observe my witness going down off her front doorstep in
a hail of automatic weapon fire. The suspect or suspects left
in a hurry upon my arrival, and I did not give chase, thinking it more important to determine the condition of the
witness. She was shaken up, but uninjured, and I was sub-
sequently able to convince her to put herself in my protective custody. That's where she is now." He let his breath out
and straightened, leaving the lieutenant to draw her own
conclusions.

It didn't take long; that was one of the things Doug liked
about her. For a moment of two she didn't say a word, just
picked up her pencil and once more began to turn it end over
end. Then she dropped it and murmured, "You don't think
it could be a coincidence—a run-of-the-mill drive-by?"

He shook his head. "She's safe as can be for ten years,
and then one day I show up and *whammo?* I don't think so.
Plus, she doesn't trust cops. And she's not the type, know
what I mean?" He put his weight on his hands and leaned

across the desk again, his voice low and urgent. "Ann, you weren't here then, but this is just the way it was before, back then when I was working on the case with Jim Shannon—"

"That's right," Mabry interrupted, "I'd forgotten he was your partner. I hear he was quite a guy. What's it looking like for him, do you know? Think he'll be our new boss?"

Doug's smile came and went. "Don't know—but I'm sure betting on him. Nobody deserves it more. Anyway, back when we were working on this Rhinestone Collar case together, things like this kept happening to us. We had evidence lost, tests botched, files turn up missing. We got to wondering if the damn case was jinxed. Once we had a tip—a female caller told us she knew who the killer was, that she'd seen it go down. She wanted to meet us, so we set up a rendezvous. Shannon was sick that day, so I went alone. She never showed. Day or so later she calls again, absolutely terrified, said she'd been waiting at the meeting place when somebody fired three shots at her. I didn't know what to think, whether she was some sort of excitement junkie, or what. Anyway, we agreed to another meeting, and again—no show. Nothing. Never heard from her again after that. At the time Jim and I were pretty sure it was a nut case, but now..."

"You think it might have been her—your San Diego witness?"

Doug straightened up, swearing and rubbing at his neck. "I don't know what to think."

Lieutenant Mabry said softly, "You want me to contact IA?"

"God, I don't know." He turned away from her, fighting it. *It* being every cop's worst nightmare, that somebody he works with, depends on, trusts literally with his life, might be dirty. "Can you hold off for a little while?"

"What have you got in mind, Sergeant?"

He shut his mouth and just looked at her. After a few pregnant seconds Mabry abruptly leaned back in her chair and brought her hand down flat on her desk in exasperation.

"Oh, for heaven's sake, Doug, use your head. Ten years ago I was a graduate student in criminal law at the University of Washington. You're looking at somebody who had to be around here back then. That ought to narrow it down some."

He'd known that, of course, but hearing her say it eased the tension in him a little. He let go a little gust of rueful laughter by way of an apology and said, "Yeah, well, I'd like to see if I can narrow it down some more. I thought I'd try a few things . . . set a few traps. See what happens."

The lieutenant's eyes held a hunter's gleam. "Okay, Doug, you've got your time. But let's be careful, now, you hear? If anything happens to this lady, you know I'm going to have your handsome head on a platter. Meanwhile—"

"Thank you, ma'am," said Doug with a grin and a small salute. He started out of the office, then hesitated and turned back. "Meanwhile, she's at my place. Thought you should know—just in case anything happens."

Her gaze was steady, her features immobile. "Is this one of your little traps, Sergeant?"

"What? No! Like you said, it'd have to be somebody—"

Lieutenant Mabry made a pistol out of her thumb and forefinger, pointed it at him and murmured, "Gotcha."

"This is the right place," Preacher announced, squinting first at the card in his hand, then at the neat white stuccoed duplex. "I believe that must be it, right over there."

"Her car's here," said Daisy. "Looks like she's home."

They started together up the walk. As they got closer to the duplex's front steps, JoJo began making a moaning noise and hanging back. Daisy said, "Come on, what's the matter with you?" and tried to take him by the arm.

"Ooh, I don't like this," moaned JoJo, shaking her off like a Saint Bernard evading a persistent kitten. "I don't like this. Let's go. . . ."

Daisy and Preacher halted at the bottom of the steps. "Holy mother," said Daisy.

"This does not look good," agreed Preacher.

"Try the door," said Daisy. Preacher gave her a look, but mounted the steps and knocked gingerly on the splintered panels of the front door. "Holler," instructed Daisy. "Maybe she's hidin', and don't know it's us." Preacher did, to no avail. He and Daisy looked at each other. "JoJo could probably kick it in," said Daisy. They both looked at JoJo, who was walking around in rapid circles at the foot of the steps.

"I'm afraid that would be apt to bring us unwanted assistance from the police," Preacher sighed. "I suggest we try the back door first."

They scurried around to the side of the duplex, leaving JoJo pacing and wringing his hands in front of some pyracantha bushes.

"Locked," muttered Preacher a few moments later. He felt around in his pockets and pulled out a small pocket-knife, unfolded a slender blade and stuck it into the lock. "Ah," he breathed with satisfaction as he turned the door-knob, "haven't lost my touch...."

"Come on," Daisy hissed at him, slapping his hand, "put that thing away. We gotta see if Mary's in there. She might be hurt—maybe dead."

A little while later, after they'd looked pretty much everywhere there was to look, including under the beds, they met in the living room. "At least we know she's not dead," said Preacher.

"We don't either know that," said Daisy, scowling. "We just know she ain't *here.* Where do you s'pose she's at?"

"Perhaps we should contact the police, after all," Preacher said with reluctance. "It does seem as though—"

"We already had a cop," snapped Daisy, "and look what happened."

"It does seem like an odd coincidence," Preacher said, scratching his beard, "but I find it hard to believe any cop was responsible for *that.*" They both looked in silence at the arch of bullet holes that decorated the living room wall.

After a moment Daisy shook herself and said briskly, "Okay, then, he musta took her. It was her he came looking for, and she ain't here, and there ain't any blood, so he musta come here, found her and took her to L.A. with him. That's the way I see it.''

"I'm inclined to agree," said Preacher with a sigh. "It does seem like the logical conclusion."

"So, what are we going to do about it?"

"I don't see that there's anything we can do." Preacher opened the front door and held it for Daisy, then followed her outside. "Our Mary's gone, and that's that."

JoJo was sitting on the grass beside the steps with his head in his hands, snuffling and rubbing his fingers back and forth over a shiny pink worm of a scar that could just be seen through his close-cropped black hair. Daisy Pepper went to him and began to stroke his head and neck.

"Come on, JoJo, it's okay. She's not in there. Nobody's hurt. Get up, now. Let's go home. Everything's okay...."

The big man lumbered to his feet, still sniffling a little. Something jingled in his hand. Daisy said, "What's that you got there, JoJo? Give it here—let me see."

"I—I found 'em," JoJo said as he handed over the set of car keys. "I never stole 'em. They was just lyin' there in the grass." He pointed to the tall, scraggly grass where the lawn met the bottom step.

"These are Ford keys," Daisy said, squinting hard at them. She looked at Preacher. "They gotta be Mary's."

"One way to find out." He snatched the keys from her hand and strode briskly across the lawn to where a maroon Bronco was parked on twin tracks of grass-pocked concrete. Daisy scurried after him. After a moment JoJo followed, knuckling his eyes like a child.

"Not locked," said Preacher. He opened the door, then handed the keys back to Daisy. "You try."

Daisy elbowed him aside and slid under the steering wheel. An instant later the Bronco's engine cranked and roared to life.

"You drive," yelled Preacher as he slammed her door. "JoJo, you get in the back. Come on, hurry up, before somebody catches on."

JoJo could move with surprising agility when it was in his best interests to do so. He ran around to the passenger's side and squeezed into the back seat. Preacher climbed up after him and slammed the door just as the Bronco began to roll backward down the driveway.

"Where we goin'?" JoJo asked, hitching himself forward so he could see over the front seat.

"To find our Mary, that's where," said Daisy grimly. She was hitched forward, too, trying to see over the steering wheel.

Beside her, Preacher relaxed back with a long sigh. "It may be a wild-goose chase, I'm afraid. Los Angeles is a very big place. Where do we even begin?"

"A cop took her," Daisy reminded him. "That's a place to start."

Preacher snorted. "That narrows it down to twenty or thirty precincts, who knows how many thousand cops."

"She used to live in Hollywood," said JoJo.

Both Daisy and Preacher turned to stare at him, to the extreme peril of everyone in the immediate vicinity. "How do you know that?" Preacher demanded when Daisy had the Bronco more or less under control again.

JoJo shrugged. "She told me."

Daisy and Preacher looked at each other. "Then that's where we start."

Doug's partner, Jeff Burnside, had been a little sulky about getting stuck with all the paperwork on the murder-suicide, but he got over it when Doug briefed him in private about the Landon case. Jeez, the kid was so young he'd never even heard of the Rhinestone Collar Murder.

On the one hand, that sort of made Doug feel old, but on the other, it did make it a reasonably safe bet he wasn't the person responsible for the attack on Joy Donnelly. Even so, Doug found himself being a little bit selective about what he actually told his partner. Mostly history, and the fact that he had a witness in protective custody. He didn't say anything about what he and Mabry suspected; it was too soon, and he still hoped like hell he was wrong.

Burnside had been assigned one of the drive-bys, which had taken place in a mostly Hispanic neighborhood, so for the sake of community relations he'd been temporarily partnered up with Carl Rodriguez. Doug wondered if he had the lieutenant to thank for that arrangement. What it did was leave him pretty much free to pursue any other "opens" he happened to see fit.

By the time he'd taken care of everything he couldn't find a way to postpone and checked out of the squad room, it was nearly noon. When he was driving out of the lot he started feeling uneasy and jittery, the way you do when you think you've left the water running at home, or the iron plugged in. Ah, hell, he told himself, it's natural enough to be edgy about leaving a stranger alone in my house, right? And the minute he thought that, it began to seem like just about the stupidest thing he'd ever done in his life.

What had he been thinking of? The woman had been a fugitive for ten years, she was still officially a suspect in a homicide investigation, at the very least she was a key witness who'd had at least one attempt made on her life. And he'd pretty much just dropped her off and left her there at his place, all alone.

He told himself he'd covered everything. He was pretty sure he'd impressed on Joy the importance of staying out of sight, not answering the door or the phone. He was pretty sure he believed her when she'd promised him she wouldn't try to run away again. The fear in her eyes had been real enough; she might not trust him enough to tell him what she knew, but at least she was smart enough to know he wasn't the one trying to shut her up permanently. But his uneasiness only got worse. He'd been in too much of a hurry. He'd been worried about checking in with Mabry. He hadn't had much sleep. He might have overlooked something.

But he knew he hadn't. And he knew why he was worried. The bottom line was, he was a cop. And no matter how much he wanted to, he knew he couldn't really trust Joy Donnelly. Or Mary Jo Delinsky. Whatever in the friggin' hell her name was!

He probably should have stopped right then and asked himself why that fact should make him so angry and tie his stomach up in knots. But he didn't.

He had to stop at the supermarket for cat food and litter; he had no choice about that. And then, of course, the express checkout line was a mile long, and the lady ahead of him found out too late—she said—that she wasn't supposed to write a check in that lane, and did so, anyway. He'd always wondered what, exactly, was meant by the term "gnashing his teeth." By the time he got out of that store he was pretty sure he knew.

Now he was in the middle of lunch hour, and probably the most hectic and hair-triggered traffic of the entire day. Companies and businesses might stagger going-to-work and quitting times, but the entire human race, it seemed, was beset with the same urge when the clock struck high noon. Everybody wanted food; most of them had to go somewhere else to get it and, after that, run any errands that couldn't wait until after work. And they all had exactly one hour to do it.

It was only a short distance from the market on Melrose to his house, which was on one of the unbelievably narrow, winding hillside streets north of Franklin, but to Doug it seemed a lot like a broken field run through a mine field in the midst of an artillery barrage. When he pulled up onto the short apron of concrete between the street and his garage, he was shaking from a surge of adrenaline.

He took the short way up, through the garage and the laundry room, up the inside stairs and into the kitchen. The house was ominously quiet. Even Maurice was still sulking under his shroud and would only mutter a surly, "Stupid bird," when Doug lifted up one corner.

There was no light blinking on his message machine, and no sound at all from the rest of the house. "Ah, Joy..." he breathed, hoping and praying she was only napping.

The bathroom door was open. The towels he'd left for her were damp and cold, the air was still humid and smelled of strawberries.

He knocked on the guest room door, listened intently, then cautiously eased it open and stuck his head inside. The bullet-scarred suitcase lay open on the bed. In the middle of it, the cat Moki crouched like a sphinx, his pale, opaline eyes fixed upon the door to the hall with almost hypnotic intensity.

Doug shut the door carefully, fighting for calm. It helped a little to swear, so he did, in a constant bitter stream, all the while opening every door and sticking his head into every nook and cranny in his entire house. But there wasn't any doubt at all that she was gone.

Think, he commanded himself. You're a detective, dammit—act like one.

Okay, she hadn't *left* left—she'd never leave without that cat. So in spite of all his warnings she'd gone out somewhere, the stupid little fool. But *where?* And why? Could she have gone for the cat food herself? But it was too far to walk to the nearest supermarket, and she didn't have any—

Transportation. That was it. Wherever she'd gone, she had to have transportation, and to get transportation, she'd have to have used the phone.

Back in the living room, he snatched up the phone, stuck the receiver between his ear and shoulder and punched redial while he pawed through the litter on his coffee table for a pen. The number twittered in his ear.

"Yellow Cab," a male voice grumbled.

For the first time in quite a while, Doug felt like smiling.

He found her sitting on a bus stop bench on Sunset, just sitting there in the hot October sun with her hands pushed deep into the pockets of her blue windbreaker. A mild Santa Ana riffled through her hair, reminding Doug suddenly, and with an acute little jolt, of the way it had tickled his lips in the night . . . the way it felt, the way it smelled.

She didn't even glance at him when he sat on the bench beside her. He felt only the slightest movement, the almost undetectable rise and fall of her chest and shoulders, before she said in a soft, dry voice, "I keep forgetting I'm dealing with a cop."

He'd had all sorts of stuff ready to throw at her—mad-as-hell stuff, worried-sick stuff, stern, cop-type lectures. He didn't know what made him decide to keep it all to himself, or where he got the wisdom and insight to say instead, in a quiet, mildly curious tone, "What are you doing here, Joy?"

She didn't answer right away, and again he thanked God for giving him the good sense to keep his mouth shut. When she did speak, she sounded remote and sad. "It's not like I remember it."

"No," he said, "I suppose it isn't."

She nodded, finally, at the square, faintly art deco building on the other side of the street. "When did they paint it *purple?* It's so... ugly." She jerked one hand out of her windbreaker pocket and brushed it angrily across the back of the bench, where black spray paint had all but obliterated an insurance company's advertising. "It's all ugly—all this graffiti and stuff. I hate it. Why doesn't somebody clean it up?" She looked away, but not before he saw the painful little ripple of movement in her throat.

When she spoke again after a moment, it was in a sad, faraway voice. "There was a time, you know?... when I thought this had to be just about the most beautiful place in the whole world. I loved it all, even the sleazy stuff on Hollywood Boulevard, if you can believe that. I just thought it had so much... excitement. So much *energy.* And the palm trees—oh, man, I had this thing for palm trees. I used to go down there, south of Melrose—what's the name of that street? Anyway, the one with all the palm trees down the middle of it. I'd take my camera... one time I actually had this *gardener* take my picture with those stupid trees. I used to look at all those huge, gorgeous houses—you know, the ones from the 1920s—and try to imagine what it would be like to live in a place like that. I thought they must be just about the most incredibly rich, incredibly beautiful, houses in the world."

"I imagine they are." Doug cleared his throat. "They're still there, you know. Still just as rich, just as beautiful. The blight hasn't made it much past Melrose, yet."

She snorted softly and shook her head. "Doesn't matter. I'm pretty sure the people who live in those houses aren't any happier or wiser than anybody else. Of course, I hadn't figured that out yet, back then. It was my goal, you know—

to live in a house like that someday. And that—'' She nodded toward the purple monstrosity across the street. "That
was going to be my ticket. Caesar's Garden..." She was silent for a moment, head tilted, studying the building with a
critical eye. "When in the world did they turn it into a
comedy club?"

"Uh...maybe two, three years ago. But they closed down
Caesar's long before that. That kind of club kind of went
out with the eighties, I guess, except maybe for places like
Vegas. The big thing's comedy now. From what I hear, I
guess they really pack 'em in."

"Yeah..."

Once again, Doug didn't know what inspired him. He
nudged her with his elbow. "Want to go in?"

She shrugged matter-of-factly. "Can't—they're closed. I
checked."

He got to his feet and held out his hand. "Come on, let's
try again." When she just looked at him, he smiled and said
wryly, "Hey—there are some advantages to being with a
cop."

What is it about this guy? Mary wondered as she felt her
hand being swallowed up in his. Her heart was racing like a
runaway train, her stomach full of butterflies. She'd never
had stage fright like this before in her life. And yet...why
was it that the minute he touched her, in spite of everything, she felt...all right? As if nothing but wonderful
things could happen to her now.

The Don't Walk sign was blinking. "Come on, come on,"
MacDougal said, giving her an impatient tug, "let's *go.*"

What the hell. She heard the surprising sound of her own
laughter as she ran with him across the street—the breathless giggle of a venturesome child. The child she'd once
been.

A pretty young woman came to the door of the comedy
club in answer to Doug's no-nonsense pounding, looking
bright and cheery and all set to disappoint an eager beaver
without discouraging a potential customer. When Doug
took out his badge and held it up to the glass, she abruptly
disappeared.

A few minutes later a man—obviously the manager—appeared instead. He was thin and balding, and had the look of an accountant whose columns weren't adding up. He opened the door warily, as if he might want to shut it again in a hurry. "Yes? What's the problem?"

"Oh, no problem," MacDougal assured him. "No problem at all. Sorry to bother you. Just hoping you might be able to help us out." He cleared his throat loudly. "I'm Detective Sergeant MacDougal, with, uh, Missing Persons. We've got an amnesia victim here, says this building looks familiar to her. What I'd like to do is let her come in and look around for a few minutes, if that's all right with you. Could we do that, sir? We'll try not to disturb you in any way. We're hoping she might remember something."

Remember? That was the last thing Mary wanted to do. For so long she'd tried not to remember, had fought her memories is if they were enemies to be vanquished, or at least held at bay. Now suddenly she felt as if she'd been caught up in a flood and was being swept helplessly toward some unseen disaster. She couldn't stop it, couldn't avoid it. It was going to happen, whether she wanted it to or not.

"Sure," the manager said with a shrug, "why not?" He moved aside and waited while they stepped into the foyer, then locked the doors behind them. "Come on in. Take all the time you need."

He lead them into the main dining room, then wandered off toward the back of the club with a vague wave of his hand. "I'll be in my office if you want me. Let Rhonda know when you're ready to leave." His voice and his footsteps faded away, pulling silence after them.

Mary jammed her hands into the pockets of her windbreaker. "This feels weird," she whispered. "It's so different."

MacDougal didn't say anything, just kept pace a few steps behind her as she began to weave her way slowly through the maze of tables.

The room looked smaller than she remembered it. And of course it had the slightly tawdry look all nightclubs have in daylight.

"There used to be a fountain here," she said, trailing her fingers across a tabletop. "And a skylight..."

"Guess they wanted more room for the customers." MacDougal's voice seemed too loud in that empty room.

"This used to be a really happening place," Mary said, turning in a slow circle. "It was really nice in here then, believe it or not. Plus, it was *hot*. I mean, it was *the* place to be, if you wanted to see and be seen, you know? All the stars, important people used to come in here. And Belle—" She stopped.

"Belle?"

Mary began moving again, shoulders hunched inside her windbreaker. "Stage is still the same," she murmured. "No piano, though. Guess stand-up comics don't require much in the way of musical accompaniment."

MacDougal remained silent, even when the silence began to seem like another presence in the room, crowding them with its company. He had a way of doing that, she'd noticed, a way of not asking the questions she knew he most wanted the answers to. She thought about digging her heels in and waiting him out in some sort of childish battle of wills, like a staring contest. But the truth was, deep down inside she really did want to give him those answers, because carrying them around all by herself had gotten to be too much of a burden. She was just...so tired. And she was pretty sure he knew it.

"I'll never forget the first time I saw this place," she said softly. "I walked in looking for a job. I mean, I was right off the bus, you know? I was staying in this scuzzy hotel downtown by the bus depot, almost out of money. Anyway, I was desperate enough, even though I figured a ritzy place like this wasn't ever going to hire me, not even as a cocktail waitress, but I thought...what the heck, I've got nothing to lose by asking, right?"

She could feel MacDougal behind her, big and broad, solid and strong. Strangely, now she found his silence more encouragement than goad. He wasn't going to rush or pressure her, or try to direct her into memory paths of his choosing. He was letting her explore any sidetracks she wanted to, take all the time she needed, including time to close her eyes, to touch, taste, smell and hear...to feel again. To *remember*.

Chapter 7

Caesar's Garden seemed dark and cool to her after the sunshine brilliance outside. The sun was shining in the dining room, too, a slanting cone of light that came through a skylight above the marble fountain in the middle of the room. But it was cool, magical light, with a milky, shimmery translucence that made being in that place seem almost like being underwater. Mary could hear the silvery music of the water in the fountain, too, and feel its chaste kiss on her hot cheeks.

Beyond the cone of sunlight it was dark, except for a soft purple glow coming from a stage near the back of the room. As she moved toward it, she could hear a different music—piano music, light and playful. Then there was laughter, and a voice as sweet and pure as a crystal bell.

"Oh, I like that, Ronnie—let's put that in the transition, okay? Now—let's try it from the chorus, second time through...."

"I even remember the song—it was 'Sweet Caroline,'" Mary said. "A Neil Diamond oldie. But I swear, it seemed as though I'd never heard it before. And her voice—God, that voice. It was really different from her speaking voice, you know. Rich and gutsy, like it came from way down *here.*" She pressed her fist against her stomach.

"And that was Belle?" MacDougal asked softly.

"Yes." She said it on a whispery exhalation. "That was Belle. I remember thinking, Oh, God, if I could just sing like that! I mean, there'd be no stopping me. She really had something. If she'd wanted to, she could have gone anywhere. Madonna?—shoot, she was better than Madonna. She was the headliner here, you know, and all these big-name stars that used to come here—they really loved her. Everybody loved . . ."

The last word got caught in her throat. She cleared it hastily and moved on again, mounting the two wide steps to the stage, which was bare except for a high metal stool with a chordless mike lying on top of it. She picked up the mike almost without thinking and hitched herself onto the stool, hooking a foot around one of the legs. She felt the microphone grow warm in her hand.

"But you got the job," prompted MacDougal.

She glanced at him guiltily. He'd followed her up onto the stage and was standing a few feet away, hands in his pockets, watching her with shadowed, unreadable eyes. His suit jacket was hitched up, so she could see the smooth leathery sheen of a gun holster on his hip. It gave her a jolt to see it there; it had been a while since she'd thought of him as a cop. It was getting harder and harder to remember that about him.

"Yeah," she said dryly, "I got the job. The manager comes running up, see, and he's ready to give me the heave-ho, and I'm arguing and begging him to give me just a chance, just one chance. Belle heard the commotion, I guess, because she stopped singing and came over to see what was going on. I don't know what she saw in me, I really don't." She laughed, a rocky chuckle that hurt her throat, and self-consciously jammed a hand through her hair. "I must have been a pitiful sight.

"But anyway, Belle says, 'Oh, come on, Charlie, give the kid a break.' I mean it—I'm dead serious, that's what she said. Like it came straight out of one of those old Hollywood musicals, you know? I swear, I thought I must have fainted from hunger, or something, and was having this incredible dream. I thought Belle was Carole Lombard, Greer Garson and Carol Channing all rolled into one.''

She looked down at the microphone, which she'd begun to roll back and forth along her thigh. After a moment she shrugged. "So, that's it. I got the job. Belle took me home with her and fed me and gave me a place to stay. It was supposed to be just temporary, you know, while I was getting on my feet. But... somehow, we got to be really good friends, and uh..."

She had to stop again, struggling with it, trying, with deep breaths and short, dry laughter, to keep the pain at bay. Not counting last night, she'd never cried for Belle; she'd never had a chance. Someday she thought she'd have to, but not now. Please, God, she thought. *Not now.*

"I just never moved out," she went on, when she knew her voice was steady again, speaking rapidly, because she wasn't sure how long her self-control would last. "We were—she was kind of like my big sister. She was always looking out for me, giving me advice on how to get along in the big bad city, how to stay out of trouble. Of course, I didn't always want to stay out of trouble, right? I mean, that's what I came to the 'big bad city' for. If I'd wanted to stay out of trouble, I could have stayed in—" She caught herself, just barely in time. "I'd have stayed home."

She shook her head, letting her shoulders slump and the microphone dangle between her knees. "I don't know why she put up with me."

MacDougal came closer, casually strolling. "But you sang here, too, didn't you? You weren't just a cocktail waitress."

Mary nodded. There was a terrible lump in her throat, and the mike burned like cold iron in her hands. "Yeah." She cleared her throat. "That was Belle's doing, too. Whenever she could manage it, she'd let me go on for her. You know, just a song or two, sometimes when she wasn't feeling well, or had a sore throat, or something. No big deal."

"No big deal?" MacDougal said gently. He was directly in front of her now. She looked up bravely to meet his eyes and found them gleaming with a little spark of curiosity... and something else deeper down, like the soft, steady glow of candle flames. "Wasn't that what you wanted? To be a singer?"

She looked away again and hitched one shoulder, a movement that was more defensive than dismissive. "Sure. That's why I came here. I wanted to be a singer, dancer, movie star—everything. Oh, I had big, big dreams."

His voice was still gentle, not quite teasing. "And... were you that good?"

Remembered feelings surged inside her—power, pride, confidence and anger. "If I didn't think I was, I wouldn't have come, now, would I?"

"Easy." He touched her chin with a knuckle, nudging it downward. The light in his eyes softened. "Hey, I believe you. The way you look right now, sitting there with that microphone in your hand... you look right at home. Natural."

He was still touching her, brushing his knuckles lightly along the edge of her jaw. She felt a desperate need to swallow, but her throat seemed paralyzed. It had become too warm in that room, too dark, too... close. She gave her head a quick, painful shake. "It was a long time ago. A lot's changed. Everything... has changed. I've changed."

His fingers slowly uncurled, fanning along the side of her neck. She had to fight the urge to close her eyes.

He shook his head and murmured, "I can see you, the way you must have looked back then... with that soft light, then the spotlight... your hair..."

Her hand flew unbidden to the back of her neck, and found his there already. "I don't look anything like I did then. My hair—"

She felt his fingers weaving through the short hair on the nape of her neck, ruffling it, then smoothing it down. "Your hair's different, I know. A lot shorter."

"How...? You didn't—" Unreasoning panic seized her. Her eyes clung to his.

His smile slipped, became wry. "No, no, I never saw you—heard you sing." The warmth of his hand pooled at the base of her skull, gently massaging. "I've seen your publicity photos. You had—" he laughed, his voice turning husky "—an awful lot of hair."

"Oh, man—masses of hair." She found that she was laughing, too, in unaccountable confusion, suddenly incapable of looking at him. "Movie star hair. Oh, well..." She scrubbed at her head with her fingers, making it awkward for him to keep his hand where it was. He let it drop away from her, allowing her to comb her fingers through her hair, leaving it in deliberate and total disarray.

The laughter died. "I told you—a lot's changed. I've changed. That person..."

"Joy Donnelly?"

She nodded, all at once too overwhelmed to speak. After a moment she whispered, "That's not me anymore, don't you understand? I left that all behind me. Years ago."

"But... don't you ever miss it? I mean, the music... the life?"

She couldn't answer, except to shrug and look away from him in feeble denial.

But he pursued her, his words soft and relentless. "How could you not miss it? The music, at least. You don't just give something like that up. It must still be there, inside you somewhere. Mary or Joy, it's still got to be a part of who you are, right?"

She'd closed her eyes, but his words assaulted her, anyway, pounding like hailstones upon the frail shelter she'd erected over her emotions. Furious with him, she pivoted on the stool, twisting away from him, out of reach of his pelting words. But one last one found her, anyway, whispered softly, like a single drop of rain.

"Right?"

Oh, God, she thought. And then there was no more thought, only feeling, great, howling storms of feeling. She felt helpless, buffeted, scared and alone. She heard the music—*felt* it—first as something faint and faraway, like a child crying in the storm. It grew closer and louder until it seemed a part of the storm, too.

She sat rigid and still on the stool, the microphone trembling in her hand, while the tumult of her own emotions threatened to deafen her, and the pressure grew and grew inside. She felt her chest straining to draw breath into a space that had no room for it, no room for anything, except for pain, and...memory.

The opening notes of the Andrew Lloyd Webber song, fragile, almost crystalline, impossibly high, then the dizzying drop down, down, to the very bottom of her register. She could *feel* it vibrating in her chest, sultry and rich, like a bow stroking across the strings of a cello. Oh, how she ached to let it out, to open her throat and her mouth as she had that wonderful night and just let it go, to feel the power of it once again, and the *joy*.

The pressure was terrible. She thought it would tear her apart. Her throat ached with the strain; she felt as if she couldn't breathe, as if there was a band around her neck, choking her.

A band... bloodred, studded with diamonds.

The music and the tumult inside her faded away suddenly, leaving her cold and empty. She became aware of the mike in her hand, clammy and sweat-slippery, and the press of the metal stool against her bottom. She drew a deep breath and after a moment said in a flat, dead voice, "Let's get out of here."

Outside, the Santa Ana had picked up a little, swirling around corners and chasing debris down the gutters. After the chill inside the club—and inside her—it felt good to Mary, at least the heat of it did, even though she knew it was turning her hair to straw and her skin to sandpaper. The hot, dry winds from out of the Mojave Desert could do strange things to people. Maybe, she thought, that's why I feel like this...so precarious and edgy.

She glanced sideways at MacDougal, wondering if the winds were bothering him, too. He certainly looked as if something was bothering him. He was squinting, lips pressed tightly together and jaw hard as rock, while the wind lifted the tails of his jacket and whipped his pant legs and generally played havoc with his hair. He looked grim, she thought, and out-of-sorts. He'd looked like that ever since they'd left the comedy club. That sense of comradeship she'd felt earlier, when he'd taken her hand and they'd run across Sunset together, those strange moments of communion in the club…they might never have happened at all. He was all cop now, and in a hurry to get somewhere.

Mary had long legs, but she had to really stretch to keep up with him, and by the time they reached his car she was hot and out of breath.

"Santa Anas get to you?" she asked only a little tartly as she waited, hip-shot and puffing, for him to unlock her door.

"No, why?" He barely glanced at her.

"Just wondering." The car was like an oven. She tossed her windbreaker into the back seat and waited for him to open his side and create a cross breeze. "I thought you seemed a little…edgy, that's all."

Now he did look at her. "I have a lot of work to do," he said pointedly, "and I'm late getting started. So if you don't mind…" He waved her into her seat and she complied, if somewhat gingerly, with a soft hiss as she touched the metal seat-belt buckle.

"What is it you do?" she asked him when they were on Sunset again, heading east with the air conditioner blasting a hot wind in their faces. "Exactly…"

Doug glanced over at her in surprise, the question jolting him out of the quagmire his thoughts were in. Those moments with her in the club…they'd changed him somehow, in some way he couldn't figure out. He'd felt so close to something…something he'd been searching for for a long, long time. He didn't know exactly what it was, but whatever it was was gone now, and his sense of disappointment and loss had left him brooding and cranky.

But now she was waiting, those big brown eyes of hers fixed on him without a trace of irony or guile. Was it possible he hadn't told her?

Then it occurred to him, with a sense of shock, that he'd only known her a few hours—less than a day—and that he hadn't had time to tell her much of anything. Plus, in the time they'd been together he'd been focused on getting her to tell *him* something, right? And anyway, he told himself angrily, why should he tell her about himself? She was just a witness he was protecting, a temporary part of his life. It wasn't as if they were starting off a relationship, or something.

"I thought you knew," he said gruffly. "I'm a detective. Homicide. I, uh, investigate homicides."

"Oh—right," she said, and was silent for a moment. Then, without inflection, she asked, "Was it your case?"

He didn't pretend not to know what she meant. "Yeah, it was my case—along with a lot of other people, of course. There was a whole team assigned to that one."

"Why?"

The hard edge in her voice made him curious. He didn't ask about it, though, just shrugged and said, "It was a big case—sensational. The news media got into the act, played up the Hollywood angle, so there was a lot of interest nationwide. The public wanted the killer caught. So did we." He paused and added grimly, "We still do."

She didn't reply to that, didn't say anything at all until he was sitting at a light, waiting to turn south on Vine. Then, her head swiveling as she watched a hooker making her unhurried way up the street, she said in that same, tight voice, "What if it was her? Would you go to so much trouble?"

"What?" Doug glanced over at her, but she was still gazing out the window at the hooker. He looked, too, noticing that the woman had a folded wad of money tucked away in the bosom of her dress, which he'd swear was so tight he could almost read the denominations on the bills.

"That girl—what if *she* was the one they found strangled, instead of Belle? What if the media didn't give a damn, what if there wasn't any nationwide interest?" Now she was looking straight at him, with eyes that seemed too bright. "Would you be trying so hard to find the killer?"

"Absolutely." He said it with quiet conviction, and watched that strange glow fade from her eyes. "And I'll tell you why." He faced forward as the light up ahead changed and traffic began to move again. "See, that girl, no matter what she's doing now, is somebody's daughter. We try never to forget that."

He felt her head turn once more to gaze silently out the window as he turned the corner onto Vine Street.

"Sunset and Vine," Preacher announced, craning to read the street signs. "I guess this is it."

"Hollywood," said JoJo with a happy sigh.

"Yeah," said Daisy, "now all we have to do is find the police station. Any ideas?"

"We could ask," suggested JoJo.

Preacher shook his head. "I think the less attention we call to ourselves, the better. We don't need anybody wondering why individuals like ourselves are driving a nice car like this. Perhaps if we just drive around for a while, we might stumble upon it."

"Uh-uh," said Daisy. "Bad idea. We're runnin' low on gas. I don't have any money—you got any money, Preacher?" He shook his head sorrowfully. "JoJo?" Same response. "Okay, then. First thing we gotta do is park this thing someplace. Someplace where they ain't gonna tow it off, or put a bunch of parking tickets all over it."

Preacher thought for a moment. "Shopping center parking lot, I would think. Attract less attention than we would in a residential neighborhood. Pick one with a nice big supermarket, Mrs. Pepper, or at the very least, a restaurant. I'm feeling the need of a little sustenance."

Daisy shot him a look. "If you're talkin' about food, me, too. You think they lock up their Dumpsters in this neighborhood?"

"One way to find out," said Preacher. "Here, this looks like a good one. Pull in here. JoJo and I will go scout around and see what we can find. You'd better stay here in case we need to make a—"

"Wait," said Daisy, "I got a better idea. Look over there. Ain't that a school?"

"Hollywood High School," read Preacher, swiveling as they drove by. "Well, well . . ."

Daisy stuck her arm out the window to signal and made a last second left turn. "It's past lunchtime," she said with a hungry gleam in her eyes. "Trash cans'll be overflowing with goodies. You wouldn't believe what those school kids throw away."

"Um-umm, smart move," Preacher agreed, while JoJo began to bounce on the back seat in eager anticipation. "Very smart, indeed. Okay—food first, then we look for the police station. Look sharp, now. Try not to attract any undo attention."

Daisy Pepper snorted. "You kidding? Look around you, man. This place is full of weirdos. We're gonna fit right in."

It was early evening, and the squad room was winding down after another busy day in Tinseltown. Most of the desks were empty; the phones rang sporadically. People called to one another, brief snatches of small talk and laughter, a little coarse humor as they scraped back chairs, gathered up jackets and called it quits—hopefully, but probably not, for the night.

Doug was still at his desk, trying hard to stay awake. After he'd dropped Joy off at his place, he'd come back to the station, intending to spend the afternoon catching up on paperwork. There'd been a few distractions. He'd started a routine check on the name Mary Jo Delinsky, for one thing, which so far hadn't turned up a thing, not even a parking ticket. He hadn't really expected it to, but he needed all bases covered. Then he'd checked in with the San Diego PD, to see if there'd been any progress on the "drive-by," or a make on the partial plate he'd been able to pick up at the scene. Nothing on either one. But then, he hadn't expected much on that score, either.

Along about five o'clock he'd finally accepted a call from Jim Shannon, since ducking him was beginning to raise a few eyebrows. God, he hated to have to do this, keep Jim shut out of things, but he knew it was for his ex-partner's own good. But it was hard, when he could hear the tension and frustration in his friend's voice—shoot, he knew just how he felt, like an old fire horse getting a whiff of the smoke.

But much as he'd have loved having his old partner working with him on this case again, just like old times, he knew he couldn't let Jim take the risk, not with so much at stake. The man was like a brother to Doug. He had a real good shot at the chief's job, and after that, who knows? For a guy like Jim Shannon, the sky was pretty much the limit. No way in hell Doug was going to let him screw all that up over one hostile witness.

Ah, yes. The witness. Mary Jo Delinsky—he thought she'd told him the truth about that being her name, although there was a part of him that was always going to think of her as Joy. It just seemed to suit her, somehow. By any name, she was all he could think about.

Who are you, Mary-Joy? Where did you come from, with your big dreams and your heartbreaking smile and your eyes full of hope? What did they see, those eyes, that you're so afraid to tell me?

Trust me—that's what he'd said to Jim. Trust me, partner, I swear I'll let you know the minute I find out anything. I think she'll open up to me, if I can just get her to trust me.

Trust me. Doug pressed his fingers against his burning eyelids and released a soft huff of silent, ironic laughter. It was a hard thing to have to admit to himself, because he was used to being trusted, but after this afternoon, he was beginning to wonder if she ever would. Damn—she was just so...so bottled up. So full of pain. It was driving him crazy, not being able to reach her, not being able to get at what was eating her alive.

The thing was, he kept wanting to...to reach *for* her, touch her, hold her in his arms and make it all go away. And that was driving him crazy, too. He was afraid he was getting too close to this one. Too close to *her*.

Ah, hell, he was tired, that's all. He'd been operating for a couple days, now, with nothing but a few hours' nap on a sofa with a long-legged woman in his lap. He'd just as well give it up, go on home, turn in early, call it a night. And hope the phone didn't ring.

He drove home through a soft purple dusk. The Santa Ana had died its usual fitful death, the air had a cool sweetness to it, and already streaks of mauve clouds were reaching like fingers over the mountains to the north. It was getting into the dinner hour, and except for frantic housewives rushing to and from the supermarket, traffic was light. There was a kind of peacefulness about the streets—that pause, sometimes infinitesimal, between daytime business and nighttime business, like the quiet of the jungle just before the predators come out to prowl.

Doug damn near fell asleep at the traffic light while he was waiting to cross Franklin. God, he was tired. In spite of that, he made himself climb the outside steps; he hadn't been getting enough exercise, lately, or eating right, either, and he was beginning to feel it in his legs and around his middle. But, oh, Lordy, those steps had never seemed longer. He noticed that they'd gotten a pretty good layer of bougainvillea blossoms built up, and made a mental note to get them swept off before the fall rains started. They could be slippery, and downright dangerous, when wet.

When he opened his front door, Maurice greeted him with a reference to his mother that sounded almost affectionate. Once again the place was empty and silent, but this time there was a light on in the kitchen, a box of cornflakes on the counter and a cereal bowl and spoon in the sink. And permeating the whole house, a subtle warmth, an indefinable aura made up of all sorts of scents—coffee, cat food, orange juice, soap... and something mystifyingly foreign, but unmistakably female.

He dropped his mail on the coffee table, checked his phone messages—all of which were from Jim—then headed straight for his bedroom, tugging on his tie as he went. The guest room door was closed. He hesitated beside it, then knocked softly and listened for a response. When he didn't hear anything, he opened the door several inches and stage-whispered, "Joy? Everything okay?"

A silvery wraith streaked across the bed, struck the floor with a muffled *thud,* and vanished under the dust ruffle. There was an incoherent murmur, then only the rhythmic whisper of breathing.

Doug pushed the door open farther, letting the light from the hallway fall across the sleeping woman's face. And then for some reason he just stood there and looked at her, and went on looking, as if she were a puzzle he couldn't crack. But at the same time, all the while he was gazing at her, his brain was refusing to work on the puzzle. It seemed to have stopped working entirely. He couldn't think of anything except how incredibly lovely she was, and how terribly vulnerable.

He couldn't think, but he could sure feel, more than he ever wanted to. He felt anger—a fine, white anger made up of equal parts frustration and some kind of primitive instinct for protection and possession. There was an ache he recognized as loneliness, a certain longing that came upon him sometimes, such as holidays and his friends' anniversary barbecues and the arrival of a new niece or nephew. And there were other aches less familiar to him and far less identifiable, deep-down-inside aches that had nothing to do with desire—although, God knows, he felt that, too. It hadn't been that long since he'd held that long, supple body in his arms and felt the warm, firm weight of her thighs pressing excruciatingly against the most sensitive and responsive part of him. That was a night neither he nor his body were likely to forget for a long time. But this was something else, this new ache. Something gentler and much more subtle than the primitive urge to procreate—and infinitely more complex.

And he was much too tired to figure it out now. He closed the guest room door and went into his own room, pulling off his tie and shrugging out of his jacket on the way. He remembered sitting on the bed to take off his shoes....

He awoke to find himself sitting full upright on the edge of the bed with his bare feet on the carpet and his hands pressed down on the mattress, ready to launch himself into... what? Flight or action? His conscious mind didn't know, and instinct didn't care; adrenaline would take care of either scenario. And he was awash with it, clammy and quaking, with his heart going ninety miles an hour.

What the hell? he thought. His shirt was unbuttoned, and both it and the T-shirt underneath it were soaked with sweat. He stripped them off and tossed them vaguely toward the foot of the bed, then lurched to his feet and groped his way to the bathroom. He had his shaking hand on the faucet and was about to turn the water on when he heard the sounds. Small, heart-rending sounds.

"Jeez—what the hell..." He spun out of the bathroom, swearing under his breath. He was almost to the hallway when he heard the sound that turned his body cold and raised the hair on his arms and the back of his neck... an eerie, undulating howl straight out of a horror movie. Swearing aloud and in earnest, he crossed the hallway in one bound and threw open the guest room door.

Chapter 8

From the doorway, Doug could see the Siamese cat Moki crouched on the bed, his dilated eyes reflecting the light from the hall with a demon glow. The cat uttered another of those ghastly yowls and then vanished, and now, above the thunder of his own heartbeat, Doug could make out those other sounds again, smaller sounds... but infinitely more terrible to hear. Desperate, whimpering sounds, like a child pleading for mercy.

"No... no... no... no..."

He could see her clearly. She was lying on her side, curled into a tight little ball with one arm covering her head, as if, he thought, she was shielding herself from blows—or from a sight too ghastly to bear. Oddly, she wasn't fighting it, striking out or thrashing around the way he thought people usually did during nightmares; later he wondered if it might have been that utter defenselessness that got to him the most.

Right then, though, he didn't think at all. He didn't consider whether it was a wise thing to do, going to a vulnerable woman's bedroom in the middle of the night, or for that matter, whether it was even all right to wake someone in the throes of a violent nightmare. He didn't wonder whether the nightmare had something to do with the secret he'd been trying so hard to get out of her, nor did it occur to him to use the moment of her vulnerability to accomplish his purpose. He simply reacted. He went to her and touched her, and felt her shrink away from him, instantly, instinctively, like a sea anemone he'd once found in a tide pool.

Her cries came even more desperately, harsh and shrill. "No! No!" God—he couldn't bear the sound!

Filled with a sense of terrible urgency, he threw back the covers, sat on the bed beside her and began stroking her back, her shoulder, her hair, talking to her, calling her name. He tried to get her to relax her body, to uncurl enough so he could pull her into his arms, but she was stiff and unresponsive as a hedgehog, all knees and elbows and cold bare feet. Then all at once she was fighting *him,* as if he was even a greater threat than her nightmare, as if she was more afraid of him than of whatever unspeakable horrors populated her dreams.

"Mary," he cried hoarsely, "for God's sake, it's me, Doug. *Wake up.* Jeez, honey, wake up—it's all right, it's over now. *Joy...*"

He heard a small, sharp gasp, and realized that her eyes were wide open and staring at him. Then suddenly she was clinging to him as if she were drowning, her arms wrapping around his neck and her face burrowing frantically into the hollow below his chin, while shudders claimed her body in wave after uncontrollable wave.

Doug heard himself murmuring, "Easy...easy, honey. It's okay, it's okay...." He felt dazed and shell-shocked.

She didn't cry. Never uttered a sound, in fact, beyond that first cognizant gasp. Little by little, though, the tremors diminished and her body began to relax, to grow warm and pliant.

He became aware of her warmth at about the same time he realized she was wearing absolutely nothing but panties and a soft cotton T-shirt, but he still wasn't allowing himself to think, much less analyze the position he was in and the consequences of staying there. If he had, he wasn't sure

it would have made any difference. She needed him. It was
as simple as that. She needed his arms and his body, his
warmth, his strength, his comfort. And every functioning
part of him commanded that he give her what she needed.

With a strong feeling of déjà vu he lifted and resettled her,
making her position and his more comfortable, and felt her
snuggle and mold herself around him. He stroked the long,
supple lines of her back and felt the soft press of her breasts
against his chest, felt their heat melt like warm oil through
the thin fabric of her shirt and into his skin. He felt her
hands ease their death grip on his neck, and their touch become a sensory exploration instead, seeking out the varied
textures of his hair and skin.

Even then he didn't stop. He closed his eyes and let his
chin, then his cheek, come to rest on the top of her head. He
felt his own arms tightening, drawing her still closer, while
in the hollow of his neck her lips moved, tasting, searching.
He turned his head slightly and felt the silky tickle of her
hair on his lips, then the velvety warmth of a temple, the
damp coolness of a cheek. She tipped her face upward,
blindly, unerringly... and that was when Doug found that
the need wasn't only hers.

Her lips were so soft, and like her cheek, bore the slight
salt-tang of tears. When they lightly brushed his, a little
shiver took him, like the riffling of a breeze across the mir-
rored surface of a pond. For a moment his heart stopped
beating; he forgot to breathe. Oh, God, he thought, this
feels so good. And instantly he felt tears spring into his eyes
at the sheer inadequacy of the thought.

He'd have sworn it wasn't what he wanted, and certainly
not what he meant to do; kissing Joy simply wasn't right,
and doing so promised complications he didn't even want to
think about. And he knew that in all his life he'd never
wanted anything so much.

He opened his mouth, only a little at first, because he was
still fighting his own scruples and desperately hanging on to
a measure of self-control. And there was still a tentative-
ness about it, too, a kind of quivering, breathless suspense,
a sense of miraculous discovery. His awareness seemed

heightened. He was acutely conscious of everything—the warm, winy flow of her breath across his lips, the soft sounds she made, tiny, inarticulate whimpers of wonder.

Then all at once there was simply the two of them, and he didn't know anything at all, not even where he left off and she began.

Once before he'd felt like that—when he was eight years old, coasting down Suicide Hill with his best friend Roger in their Radio Flyers. One minute, he remembered, he'd been in complete control, full of himself, whooping and hollering with the wind in his face and the rumble of the wheels in his ears—and the next minute he was hanging on out of pure gut instinct, his mind a blank. Only when the wagon finally dumped him on Dead Dog Curve had reason returned, along with the exhilarating realization that he was still alive.

But this time there wasn't any Dead Dog Curve to put an end to the ride. He was on his own, with nothing but his own willpower standing between himself and disaster.

He had to stop this. He *had* to. What he was doing was unconscionable. But she felt so good, and she fit him so well, and he knew it was going to hurt like hell to separate himself from her. He could feel it already, like a dull throbbing in his belly. He wanted to postpone it, just a little longer. Please, he thought, just a little longer....

Her mouth was incredible—so soft, so sweet, so responsive. And she seemed so *right* in his arms, her head cradled in his hand as if one had been custom-made for the other. Meanwhile, his other hand had found its way under her T-shirt and was lightly brushing her back, riding slowly up and down along the gentle undulations of her spine, savoring the velvety texture of her skin. So smooth...broken randomly by the roughness of healing scratches.

Scratches. It was that small thing, reminding him so tangibly of past events and present circumstances, that brought him finally back to reason and responsibility. But it wasn't easy. He managed to turn his mouth aside from hers long enough to draw a gasping breath, and to groan, from deep in his chest, from the bottom of his soul, *"Joy..."*

As soon as he said that he felt a stillness in her body, and then the warm sigh of an exhalation along his cheek. He began to stroke her hair in a way that was meant to soothe him more than her, and this time when he spoke, he remembered to say, "Mary..."

Then he gave it up and tucked her face into the hollow under his jaw, and for a while just held her like that, smoothing her T-shirt down where it belonged while he waited for his runaway vital signs to coast back to some semblance of normalcy.

When he was pretty sure he had control of himself again, he nudged her head with his chin, patted her back and said gruffly, "Hey, you okay?"

"Yeah, sure," said Mary. "Fine."

But she didn't feel at all fine. She knew she should move, get off MacDougal's lap. She knew he wanted her to. She could tell by the way his body felt now—like rock, as if he'd hardened himself against her. But what she wanted more than anything in the world was just to go back to the way they'd been a few minutes ago, when his arms had surrounded her and his whole body had seemed to open up and welcome her like a harbor a long-lost ship. If she moved away from him now, she thought, she would only be cast adrift again, to be once more cold and lost and alone.

"This is getting to be kind of a habit," she said, testing her voice, laughing a little to cover the shake in it.

"You were having a nightmare," MacDougal said. She could hear the gravel in his chest, feel the rumble of it under her cheek. "I was, uh...I didn't mean—look, I'm sorry. I don't want you to think—"

"Think what, MacDougal?" She sniffed and pulled her face from the warm place near the base of his neck, and with one palm pressed flat against his chest, managed to ease herself more or less to a sitting position. "That you were—how did you put it—trying to ravish my body?"

"Something like that."

She'd been trying to laugh it off, lighten things up, as much for her own sake as for his, but he didn't sound at all amused. His voice was thick with emotion, almost surely that embarrassment she'd found so fascinating before. In spite of it, though, he didn't avoid her eyes. Instead, he held them with a gaze that was determinedly steady, like a little kid, she thought, a good, honest kid who'd just hit a baseball through a window and was all set to face the music.

But there was something else in that look, too, something she couldn't put a name to. She thought he seemed almost puzzled, as if he were searching for something but didn't know quite what it was. Whatever it was, the look made Mary feel confused herself, and her heart began to beat with a slow, heavy tread.

She said dryly, "That'd be hard to do with your pants on, MacDougal." Yes, he was wearing pants. But he wasn't wearing a shirt. Her fingers had made that discovery already, and had begun to curl on his chest, it seemed of their own volition.

He made a sound deep in his throat and captured her hand, halting the tentative forays her fingertips were making into the springy thicket of his chest hair. Then, in that same low growl, he said, "With or without my pants—that's not something you ever need to worry about. Believe me, in spite of—"

"Hey—I'm not worried." Oh, but she was, sick with it. Because she could hear in his voice that the cop was back, and she was afraid to the bottom of her soul that those moments in his arms were never going to happen again, that he was never going to kiss her again. That she was never going to feel that wonderful again.

"Oh, yeah? Why not?" He sounded surprised, a little curious, and maybe even a bit wary. "It seems to me you should be, I mean—under the circumstances..."

She shook her head and forced a teasing note into her voice, while inside she was trembling and hollow with longing. "You know, MacDougal, for a smart cop, you really are dense." She'd startled him. He jerked back slightly, and she touched his lips with a light, playful finger. Her throat ached; she wanted to swallow, but couldn't, so her words came out thick and just a little slurred. "Maybe you didn't notice, but I was kissing you as much as you were kissing me."

He frowned. "Yeah, but you were upset. I don't think you knew what you were doing. Anyway, I shouldn't have let it happen. I'm sorry—it was inexcusable."

"Why?" Her lips twisted painfully. "Because you're a cop?"

For a moment or two he didn't answer. Then he said quietly, "Yeah. Because I'm a cop. And you're..."

She stood abruptly and moved away from him, not even caring that she was wearing only skimpy panties and a T-shirt. Let him look, damn it. Let him eat his heart out. Oh, *God,* how she hated cops.

"Look..." His voice came softly, almost as if he'd read her thoughts. "I know you don't think much of me right now, but I really am one of the good guys. I just want to keep it that way. Understand?"

Carefully keeping her back to him, Mary lifted her arms and scrubbed her fingers through her hair. "Sure, I understand. You're a regular Boy Scout. Well, listen—since I'm all okay now...no more bad dreams...why don't you just, um, go on back to whatever it is you were doing, okay? I'll be fine. Terrific."

"You're sure?" She heard the rustling noises he made as he stood. "You want me to—"

"Yeah, I'm sure." She'd begun to shiver. She folded her arms over her breasts and jerked her head toward the door. "Go on—beat it."

"That nightmare..." She held her breath; gooseflesh prickled across the back of her neck. "Sure you don't want to talk about it?"

She heard more faint sounds of movement. Was he coming closer? If he touched her now...if he put his arms around her...

"No." She turned, arms covering her hard-pebbled nipples, to find him standing by the door with one hand on the knob. "It's gone now. I don't even remember what it was about. Swear to God. I'm fine."

"You're sure?"

"Yeah, I'm sure."

"Well, if you need anything..."

"I will—I'll holler." *Go—please, just...go.*

"All right, then. Good night..."

"G'night. Oh—MacDougal?" He leaned around the half-closed door, eyebrows questioning. She cleared her throat. "Thanks. For, um..."

"Sure. Anytime." The door closed softly.

For a long time Mary went on standing just as he'd left her, folded arms pulled tight against her ribs as if she didn't quite trust them to contain her wildly pulsing heart. She heard MacDougal's footsteps go down the hall toward the kitchen, heard bumps and thumps, the sound of water running, then the footsteps returning, and the click of a closing door. Only then did she let herself go, draw a long, shuddering breath and grope her way to her own door, feeling wobbly-legged, as if it was her first time out of bed after a bad case of flu.

She went down the hallway to the bathroom, washed her face, got a drink of water, then crept back to her room and into bed, cringing at the clammy feel of the sheets, still damp with her sweat. She lay there shivering, thinking of warmth—of strong arms around her, a wonderfully solid body pillowing her cheek, gentle hands stroking her, a mouth like...like nothing she'd ever known.

Oh, God, she thought, why did you do this to me? She felt as if she'd been given a piece of heaven, only to have it snatched away again.

Oh, how I hate cops.

I'm one of the good guys.

"One of the good guys..." Those words began to play over and over in her mind like a snatch of song, perhaps a lullaby.

As quiet settled in once more, Moki came creeping up across the rumpled covers to find his usual nest on her pillow, and shortly was adding his own rhythmic accompaniment. And before she knew it her body's own heat had driven the chill from the sheets, and she lay relaxed, hovering, incredibly, on the edges of sleep. Normally she wouldn't

have expected to sleep at all, after such a nightmare—
wouldn't even have dared to try. But tonight, for some reason, she felt none of the lingering effects of the dream, neither the icy-cold horror nor the throbbing sickness in the pit
of her stomach. There was even a puzzling sense of relief,
almost of contentment....

I'm one of the good guys.

And suddenly she believed it. Suddenly she knew, beyond any doubt, that Detective J. T. MacDougal *was* one of
the good guys. She could trust this one. Everything was going to be all right. He was a good guy, and somehow, that
made everything all right.

Even the way she was starting to feel about him.

Doug woke with a sense of having overslept. He had a
pretty good awareness of time, which ordinarily, along with
a primitive wake-up response to daylight, made it unnecessary for him to rely on alarms. But this morning his inner
clock seemed to be off; he thought maybe it had something
to do with the fact that the weather had turned dark and
cloudy during the night.

The house was quiet, so at least it looked as if Joy was
sleeping in. He felt relieved about that; he wasn't sure he'd
have been able to face her this morning. As it was, he
showered, shaved and dressed with a kind of edgy awareness of her presence in the house that he found extremely
annoying. It was a complication he hadn't counted on.

While the coffee was brewing he turned on the TV, remembering to keep the sound low, and caught a morning
weather report that said that a winter storm front from the
Gulf of Alaska was working its way down the coast and was
currently due to arrive in L.A. just in time to threaten can-
cellation of the second game of the League Championship
Series, scheduled to be played that evening in Dodger Stadium. The morning sports news that followed reported that
the Dodgers had won the first game in a thriller, 3-2, which
came as a real shock to Doug. God—was it possible that
he'd completely forgotten about it? Something was definitely wrong with him.

For one thing, he reflected as he sipped his coffee, he hadn't gotten much sleep after the interruption last night, for reasons that put him ruefully in mind of certain episodes in his adolescence involving his unresolved passion for a blond cheerleader named Monica Stiller. He was sure those same reasons were what was making him so achy and stiff this morning. He found the state he was in annoying in the extreme; it had been a long, long time since he'd felt a sexual need strong enough to cause him physical discomfort, much less any lingering side effects.

One of the down sides of being a cop was that he got to see everything that was lousy and wrong with the world. Every day he got reminded how dangerous it had become these days for a single person just to seek a little human companionship. On the up side, it also gave him the knowledge and the contacts that made it possible for him to find safe and reliable female company when he needed it. He had a long-standing arrangement with a woman named Carmen over in Silverlake, no emotional strings attached, just a comfortable little business association that suited them both perfectly. Over the years they'd even become friends, in a casual sort of way. In fact, lately he'd found himself going to her more just out of loneliness than from any compelling physical need. Maybe, he thought, that's all it is. Time to give Carmen a call.

Except he knew damn well it wasn't Carmen he wanted. Or any other woman, for that matter. Just...one particular woman.

Her picture was there on the coffee table, buried under yesterday's junk mail. Joy Donnelly's eight-by-ten glossy head shot, with the cascade of hair and the million-dollar smile. He pulled it out and looked at it, and was instantly engulfed in total recall, an avalanche of sensory memories—the strawberry scent of her hair, the slippery dampness of it in his palm, the salty taste of the moisture on her cheek, the silky-smooth texture of her skin. And her mouth...the taste, the warmth, the full, firm feel of her lips, the soft, whimpering sounds she made, the first tentative, fluttery response of her tongue...

His stomach churned audibly, prompting Maurice's hopeful carol from under his cage cover, "It's a brand new *car!*"

Doug dropped the photo as if it had suddenly burst into flames. "Shut up, Maurice," he muttered as he went to rinse out his cup and put it in the dishwasher. The damn bird was going to wake up Joy, which was the last thing he needed right now. Or possibly just what he did need—he was damned if he knew which.

That was the worst thing about the way he felt—realizing that his discomforts weren't only physical. Maybe he *was* lonely. He hadn't thought much about it, up to now. He'd made the decision never to marry a long time ago, and he still believed it was the right one. He'd watched the torment his mother'd had to put up with, married her whole life to a cop. He remembered cops' funerals, and the anguish on the faces of their widows, and he remembered sitting with Carol Shannon in the hospital through that long, long night after Jim had gotten shot. And he'd made up his mind right then and there that he was never going to put somebody he cared about through that kind of hell.

Plus, of course, it was a statistical fact that cops' marriages didn't last, Doug's parents and the Shannons being the exceptions that proved it. He thought it probably had something to do with the way cops had to bury their emotions when they were on the job. It could get to be a habit that was hard for a man to put aside when he walked through the door of his own home. In any event, as far as Doug was concerned, cops made lousy husbands, and he'd decided as long as he was the one, he wasn't going to be the other.

Of course, he'd also had to accept the fact that that pretty much nixed any kind of committed relationship, since in his experience women tended to give up pretty quickly on a man who wasn't ever going to allow himself to love them.

But he had accepted it, damn it. So maybe he got a little bit lonely now and then—so what? On the whole, he liked his life the way it was. He liked being a cop. He had great friends, a great house, a great car, when it was running right—hell, he thought as he pulled the cover off Maurice's cage and got his usual "good morning" in the form of a jubilant invitation to go and commit a physically impossible act with himself—he even had a great pet.

Life was great. He was a happy man. Or he had been.

What he didn't understand was how he could have been brought to such a state of confusion and discontent by a *witness*, of all people. Worse—technically, he supposed, she was even still a suspect in a homicide investigation, one he was involved in. He was responsible for keeping her alive. At the very least he needed information out of her, and by God, he was determined to get it.

Bad enough to think he might be falling for the woman, but to even consider following up on his carnal urges—God help him, it went against every moral scruple he'd ever had.

No doubt about it. What he had to do was stop pussyfooting around with Joy—or Mary, rather—and get her to tell him what she knew. The quicker he got to the bottom of this thing, the quicker she could go back to San Diego and her buddies at Saint Vincent's, and he could go back to being a happy man again. She had the answers, he was sure of it.

He snatched up his jacket and car keys, then paused and looked grimly toward the silent hallway and the closed guest room door. So near, he thought. And yet, so far...

Tonight, he promised himself, clenching his teeth so hard a muscle in his jaw twitched in protest. He'd been patient long enough.

Mary heard the front door close and felt the tensions in her body relax, then melt away. She didn't know whether to be glad or sorry that MacDougal had gone off without a word to her, and that she was alone again—except for Moki, of course, and that silly Maurice. He really was the most amazing creature, that mynah bird. He was funny, in spite of such an awful vocabulary. He made her laugh.

On the heels of that thought came another: she felt like laughing now, at this very moment. It was true—in spite of the fact that she didn't much care for mornings, especially those that were dismal and dark, like this one, she could feel laughter only a careless breath away, lurking somewhere inside her like a child crouched in hiding, stifling giggles of delicious suspense. How was it possible, she wondered, when the world outside was so cloudy and gray, to feel as if the sun was shining? She felt warm and good, as if the sun had come out after a cold spell, and she wanted to bask in it. She felt *light,* as if a burden she'd been carrying around for a long, long time had suddenly been lifted from her shoulders.

The lightness prompted her to get out of bed with considerably more than her usual enthusiasm, to the disgust of Moki, who shot out one sinuous paw in protest before curling himself back into the shape of a large tawny doughnut and going instantly back to sleep.

"Lazybones," she murmured fondly, indulging in a few bone-cracking stretches herself. Then she stood looking around her, at the room that held so much of MacDougal, with a curiosity that was suddenly as sharp and demanding as physical hunger.

Yesterday she'd felt like both a prisoner and an intruder in this room. She'd felt strange about touching anything, or even looking too closely at the private pieces of a man she'd had no wish to get better acquainted with. She'd resented him and the decisions he'd forced upon her, feared the changes in her life those decisions would inevitably bring. She hadn't wanted to know him—certainly she'd never wanted to *like* him, much less ever dreamed she'd find herself kissing him, and wishing with every part of her being that she might do it again sometime soon.

But she had. Oh, she had, and now she seemed to have an insatiable desire to know all there was to know about the man who had held her and chased away her night terrors, then kissed her until her bones turned to butter. Who was this man, this J. T. MacDougal? How was it that a cop could make her feel so wonderful? How could he have such gentle hands?

He had exercise equipment—a weight bench, a rowing machine, a stationary bicycle. Did he worry about gaining weight, keeping in shape? He'd played football in high school, in a place called Ferndale, Michigan, and been awarded trophies, for Defensive Player of the Year and Most Valuable Player. Had he been one of those popular jocks, the ones who went out with the Homecoming Queen? God, she really hoped not—she'd always thought those guys were such *meatheads*.

He dressed like a jock, around the house, anyway—lots of old sweats and holey baseball jerseys and athletic socks. But... his taste in music ran to classical, judging from the pile of tapes she found in the bottom drawer of a dresser, which didn't sound much like a meathead.

The stuff on the walls was mostly framed certificates, diplomas and things—he'd graduated from the police academy right here in L.A., was a great shot with a pistol and had been awarded a couple of service citations. Hmm... impressive, she thought, but wasn't really surprised. He did have that *way* about him....

The few photographs seemed to be group shots—a black-and-white of a football team, several color photos of Little League teams, along with plaques expressing appreciation for "Coach Doug MacDougal." That made Mary smile. All right—it made something extremely warm and squishy happen deep down inside her, she wasn't going to deny it. She wondered if it was possible to fall in love with someone, just going through his stuff.

She wondered if he'd ever been married. He was definitely a bachelor now, and if he had been married, she hadn't seen any signs that there were children involved—no indication that this room had ever been used for weekend visits, for instance. No family photographs. Of course, she reminded herself, pictures of his family would probably be in his room, and... she wasn't *that* nosy. But she did wonder whether he had a mom and a dad back in Ferndale, brothers and sisters, nieces and nephews. What kind of a child he'd been...

Then she noticed another group picture, also black and white, this one of a troop of—incredulously, she leaned closer to get a better look, and gave forth a little spurt of delighted laughter. "Well, I'll be darned," she gulped, "he really *is* a Boy Scout."

That was when she knew what the lightness inside her was all about. Sometime between last night and this morning, without even knowing it, she'd made a decision. She was going to tell MacDougal everything. She could trust this man. She *knew* it. He'd take care of everything—take care of her, protect her. Everything was finally going to be all right. That knowledge, that *certainty*, was sunshine and champagne to her. She felt warm and giddy, light and young and free. For the first time in so very long, the terrible burden of knowledge she'd carried like an albatross was gone. For the first time in a very long time, she felt like singing.

Doug had barely settled into his chair when the phone rang. A familiar voice barked, "My office, Sergeant." That was followed by a click and a dead line. He sighed and pushed himself away from his desk; it looked as if the scrambled-egg burrito and coffee he'd picked up on his way to work were going to have to wait.

"I've been doing some reading," Lieutenant Mabry said without preamble before he'd even closed her office door. She picked up the file in front of her and shoved it in his direction.

Doug nodded. "The Landon case." He didn't have to pick it up to know which one it was.

Mabry nodded. "Reads like a horror story. What in the *hell* happened to that case?"

He let out a gust of pure exasperation and snapped, "Don't you think I wish to God I knew?"

"Look, Doug," Mabry said quietly, "you and Jim Shannon are the best there is—I know you didn't botch that case. But frankly, I'm having a hard time believing deliberate sabotage, either."

"You think I *like* it?" Doug glanced over his shoulder and hastily lowered his voice to a growl. "Dammit, Lieutenant, I work with these guys—some of 'em I've known for years. I want to think I can trust every single one of them—I have to think that, or how am I going to go out there with them

and put my life on the line, huh? You tell me that. Ah..."
He dragged a hand through his hair, then rubbed angrily at
the back of his neck. "Hell, I don't know if it's sabotage. I
can't for the life of me figure out why, what the connection
could be. Maybe... I don't know, that club was a hangout
for a lot of big-money people—lot of wise guys, too.
Maybe... somebody was on somebody's payroll who
shouldn't have been. Belle worked there, maybe she saw
something. Maybe she tried to cash in on what she saw. I
don't know. All I know is, I've got an eyewitness who seems
to get shot at every damn time she makes an appointment to
talk to me, and I want to know what the hell's going on!"

Chapter 9

"Take it easy, Detective," Lieutenant Mabry said calmly. "I want to know what's going on, too. And trust me, I will."

Doug turned away, furious with himself for losing control and fighting to regain it. This case, the situation, everything—it was getting to him, in a way nothing had ever gotten to him before. And he couldn't let it. He couldn't.

"What about this eyewitness of yours?" Once more the lieutenant's voice was nothing but businesslike. "Any progress there?"

"Not yet." He frowned...cleared his throat. "I'm working on it."

"I think you'd better bring her in."

The quiet statement punched through the thin veneer of his self-control like a high-caliber bullet. He whirled, to find the lieutenant's hand upraised like a traffic cop's.

"Doug, I've cut you quite a bit of slack already, you know I have. But we have a situation here. I can't—"

"You can't bring her in." He had his hands on her desk, curled into fists, urgency like a knot in his belly. "What if you can't protect her? Huh? What then? What happens to the case?"

Mabry's eyebrows lifted. "Whoa, Sergeant. Are you sure it's the case you're worried about?"

"What do you mean, am I sure it's the case? What else do you think it is?"

She just looked at him. A moment or two of that was all his conscience could take, so he pushed away from her desk with a hiss of exasperation and turned his back to her again, rubbing fruitlessly at the tension in the back of his neck.

"Look, if you're asking me if I care about the witness, you bet I do. Of course I do. I'm responsible for her safety, dammit. I don't want her hurt."

"I mean," Mabry said softly, "I think you more than care. This is personal with you, isn't it?"

Doug snorted. "Personal? Come on." But he didn't dare let her see his face; he wasn't that good an actor.

And Mabry was too good at reading people. *"Personal,"* she repeated with her special brand of implacable calm. "I think you're emotionally involved. And you've been around long enough I don't have to tell you how dangerous that is. That's why I want you to bring her in. Doug, we'll take every precaution. If she cooperates, I'll see she gets the full program. Witness protection—"

"No." He ground the word through clenched teeth. "Dammit, I know she's close to trusting me. I just need a little more—"

"Are you sleeping with her?"

"What?" He pivoted, the word coming out in a rush of breath, as if she'd punched him in the gut.

Mabry had her hands clasped in front of her like an old-fashioned school teacher. "You heard me. You said she's at your place. Are you sleeping with her?"

Doug, on the other hand, felt like a ten-year-old, sweaty and fraudulent. "Lieutenant," he said softly, "you are way over the line."

Her gaze didn't waver. "I don't think so. Are you?"

"No," he growled, "I'm not sleeping with her. Not that it's—ah, jeez." He stopped and began to swear quietly, in a completely different tone of voice.

Lieutenant Mabry caught the change and looked for the reason, then sat up straight and said, "Oh, wow." Her tone had taken on a new note, too, something uniquely feminine. Jim Shannon had that effect on people—especially women.

Doug watched his ex-partner weave his way through the squad room, graceful in spite of a left knee that was mostly stainless steel, answering greetings with a grin and a wave and shaking hands like a damned politician. No doubt about it, he thought, the man did have charisma. In spite of the nerves that were still jumping and fluttering in his belly, he was grinning himself as he opened the door of Mabry's office.

"Ah, hell," he said with a grimace, "there goes the neighborhood."

Shannon laughed and gripped his hand. "Good to see you, too, partner." The handshake held a while, the way it does between longtime friends.

"So," Doug said, "what're you doing way up here, slumming? Not enough excitement for you downtown these days?"

"Couldn't stay away." Shannon moved past Doug to extend a hand to the lieutenant, who was just stepping out from behind her desk, smoothing down the front of her skirt as she came. "Lieutenant Mabry—hope this isn't an imposition."

"Assistant Chief Shannon. Of course not, sir—it's an honor."

"Oh, hey—just Jim."

Doug rolled his eyes. "God, yes—we're going to have to be calling him 'Chief' soon enough as it is."

Shannon laughed and modestly waved that aside. "Hey, I wanted to hear firsthand what you've got on this Landon case. Doug tells me he's located the missing roommate. You know," he said to Mabry in a conspirator's murmur, jerking his head toward Doug, "the two of us pretty near busted our butts trying to find that girl. I thought sure she was fish food—didn't you, partner?" Expanding his focus to include both Doug and the lieutenant, he went on, "Anyway, I just thought I'd drop over and see how it's going."

Doug and Mabry exchanged a look. The lieutenant cleared her throat. "She's, uh . . . not in custody—"

Shannon waved a hand. "It's all right, Lieutenant, Doug told me what happened in San Diego. He tells me he's got her in a safe house somewhere. Won't tell me where, though." He grinned ruefully. "Seems to think he's keeping my ass out of the fire."

Mabry said quickly, "Sergeant MacDougal—"

At the same moment Doug coughed and said, "Look, Jim—"

Shannon held up a hand, cutting them both off. "No, I understand. It's your ball game, and I know you're going to handle it the way you think best. Just wanted you to know, though—I can't help but take a personal interest in this one. I hope you'll let me know if there are any developments. Anything at all."

"Of course," Mabry murmured. "Absolutely."

"Count on it," said Doug.

"Just one thing. The Donnelly woman—how's it looking? You really think she's an eyewitness? She can ID our killer?"

Mabry glanced at Doug. He cleared his throat. "I'm not sure," he said. "I think so."

Shannon exhaled slowly and audibly, shaking his head. "Oh, boy. Wow. Well . . ." He looked from Doug to the lieutenant and back again. "I won't take up any more of your time. I hope you'll let me know as soon as anything breaks."

"You bet, partner," Doug murmured. "You can count on it."

Shannon nodded toward Mabry. "Lieutenant."

She acknowledged that with a nod of her own. Doug opened the door and held it for his ex-partner, then followed him out of the office.

"I gotta tell you," Shannon said with an exhalation as he walked with Doug to his desk, "I'm having a hard time with this. I don't like being out in the cold."

"It's for your own good." Doug picked up his cardboard cup of fast-food coffee, took a swig of it and made a face. Stone cold. Figured.

Shannon was eyeing the burrito with something like revulsion. "Come on, you're not going to eat that, are you? You hate fast food."

Doug shrugged. "Gotta eat something. Didn't have time for breakfast this morning. Overslept."

"Tell you what. Since I can't get you to let me in on the Rhinestone Collar case, at least let me buy you a decent breakfast."

"Is this a bribe?"

"You bet."

Doug grinned. "Okay, partner—you're on."

"Preacher! Preacher—look there," Daisy said in a raspy stage whisper. "It's him. That's the guy."

Preacher stirred irritably beneath his open newspaper; he and Daisy and JoJo had been watching the police department parking lot for hours, now. It was turning colder by the minute and he was beginning to stiffen up. He was also beginning to work up a powerful thirst. He made querulous noises, then muttered, "What?"

"Look there—coming out the front. The big guy. That's the cop took our Mary. Told you we'd find him."

Preacher considered for a moment, squinting. "I believe you're right, Mrs. Pepper. Who do you suppose the other fellow is? The one with the limp."

"Who cares?" Daisy was already on her feet. "Where's JoJo at? We gotta get the car."

Preacher groaned and managed in careful stages to achieve a standing position. Panting and swaying slightly, he said, "Might I . . . ask why we . . . require the car?"

"We gotta follow him. Hurry up—ah . . . *shoot.*"

"Never mind," Preacher said comfortingly as they watched the two men get into a shiny brown BMW and drive away down the street toward Hollywood Boulevard. "At least we know we have the right place. I'm not certain tailing a police officer is the best course of action in any case. I believe—" He cleared his throat loudly and thoroughly and gave his coat a few cursory swipes with the back of his hand. "I believe it's time I made a few discreet inquiries."

"Yeah," said Daisy, "and then what? What are we gonna do if she's in jail?"

"Then," said Preacher with a shrug, "we see what we can do to get her out."

Daisy considered that gloomily. "We better hope she ain't, then. Okay, so what if she's not in jail?"

Preacher straightened himself up to his full height, smoothed down his hair with both hands and gave his lapels a tug. "In that case, we will have to proceed to Plan B." Daisy looked blank. "We tail the cop," he explained with dignity. "I suggest you and JoJo go and retrieve the car, just in case."

Doug spent the morning trying to ID the Jane Doe in the arson case. According to the autopsy report, she'd had enough drugs in her system to kill a horse, which kind of put a whole new slant on things. Had it been a homicide, or just another accidental overdose, with the arson as a cover-up? He made the usual check with Missing Persons and the runaway file, but inspiration eluded him. His instincts were dormant on this one; his mind kept wandering.

Around one o'clock he told the lieutenant he was checking out.

"Going to lunch?" she inquired, eyebrows arching.

He gave her a half smile with no humor in it. "Going to go talk to a witness."

Mabry didn't smile at all. "Doug—I meant what I said. I want her in here tomorrow. *Tomorrow*, understand?"

He left without answering.

Outside, the day had turned as dark as his mood; rain seemed imminent. It was one of the few days in Southern California that actually felt like fall. There was a chill in the air, a certain smell that reminded Doug suddenly and with a nostalgic twinge of his boyhood back in Michigan, of playing touch football at twilight through a swirl of leaves on a tree-lined street, and then waking up to the very first fall of snow.

He turned off Franklin and began the steep uphill climb to his house, his car coughing and choking in its usual irritating way. "Gotta get this damn thing fixed," he muttered to himself as he shifted into low gear. It didn't help much. His speed kept dropping until he was chugging along at all of twenty miles an hour. And to make matters worse, now he had a car on his tail.

"Sorry, buddy," he said to the headlights in his rearview mirror. "This is as fast as I go, and there's no place on this damn street where I can let you by."

At least they didn't seem to be in a great hurry, whoever they were. He didn't think it was one of his neighbors, at least not one he recognized. A Bronco, it looked like. Dark red, or maroon. When he pulled off into his own driveway it roared on past, and the people inside, just silhouettes in the premature dusk, didn't wave or even look his way.

"What do I do, what do I do?" Daisy was saying in a hoarse whisper, as if there was a danger she'd be overheard. JoJo was bouncing nervously up and down on the back seat.

"Keep going," said Preacher. "There must be a place to turn around up here somewhere. It's a two-way street."

"How can it be a two-way street?" demanded Daisy, scowling over the top of the steering wheel. "There's only room for one car. If we meet somebody, we're dead."

"Up there," said Preacher suddenly. "Pull into that driveway."

"What if somebody comes?"

"Nobody's going to come. They're out of town."

"How do you know?"

"There's a whole bunch of newspapers, that's how. Hurry up—pull in, pull in."

"Okay, okay," said Daisy. The Bronco bucked over a shallow curb and lurched to a halt. Its three occupants sat for a few moments in dead silence.

After a while JoJo mumbled, "He has a nice house."

Daisy took off her baseball cap and scratched her head. "So, what do we do now?"

"Be quiet," said Preacher. "I'm thinking."

Doug climbed the steps to his front door in the heavy quiet that sometimes falls just before rain. There wasn't a sound from inside the house, either. Not even when he stuck his key in the lock.

What the hell? he thought. What could be wrong with Maurice? Had the cat got his tongue—and the rest of him along with it?

He opened the door slowly and silently, all his nerves vibrating with suspense, and a premonition that wasn't quite alarm. What he saw instantly reassured him as to the condition of Maurice, if not his tongue. It also mystified him completely. The mynah bird was in his cage, safe and whole. He had his head cocked and one eye riveted with glittering intensity on *something*. Something in the kitchen.

Doug never knew what instinct kept him silent. He closed the door without a sound, and had taken a single stealthy step when he heard something that froze him in his tracks. It was an ordinary enough little sound—the thorough and careful clearing of a throat. What followed that, however, was anything but ordinary. It sent a shiver up his spine. It prickled his skin with goose bumps.

Doug didn't think he'd ever heard anything quite so lovely. It moved him unexpectedly, caught him like a sucker punch with shock wave of emotion that made his eyes sting and his throat ache, like organ music wafting from a small country church on a warm summer Sunday, or choirs of small children singing "Silent Night." The closest he could come to giving the emotion a name was *homesickness*. But if that's what it was, it was for a time and place he'd never known, and wasn't sure had ever really existed.

> "I once was lost, but now I'm found,
> Was blind, but now I see."

The last poignant note died away to a whisper, leaving

Doug shaken, uncertain what he should say or do next. He felt as if he ought to tiptoe out and come in again, as if he'd intruded on something so intensely private it would embarrass him to ever have her know he'd listened. So he just stood there beside the door in an agony of indecision.

And then she giggled. He heard it clearly, as fat and smug as any giggle could be, full of pride and delight and self-satisfaction. It was infectious, too; laughter rippled through his insides and broke out in a smile.

She launched at once into a new song and Doug moved forward again, still tiptoeing, still feeling like an intruder but no longer sorry for it. He felt like a little kid about to catch Saint Nicholas red-handed.

This time it was "Song Sung Blue," a Neil Diamond standard. She began it soft and slow, with a whispery sweetness in her voice, like a very young girl, but picking up tempo, volume and richness as she went along. By the time Doug got to the kitchen door she was belting it out with the full-throated confidence of a stage performer with a whole orchestra behind her. Her back was toward him but he could tell she was holding something in her hand, pretending it was a microphone. She was wearing a man's shirt—one of his, he suspected—and apparently not much else. Her feet and legs were bare, and the tails of the shirt brushed the backs of her thighs as she swayed and danced to the rhythms of her own making.

When she finished the song she threw her arms out and her head back and held the pose as if she were listening to the rising swell of applause. Doug wished he could have provided it for her, but the best he could manage was a soft and heartfelt, "Wow."

Oh my. She uttered a single sibilant swear word—obviously out of pure shock—and whirled around, eyes wild and bright, chest heaving, cheeks flushed. He'd never in his life seen anything so beautiful. So passionate . . . so sexy. His belly churned with a surge of pure, primal lust.

Then he saw what she was holding in her hand, and the lust got tangled up with so many other emotions he felt as if he'd been turned wrong-side out, upside down, tied in knots. Tenderness and pride, wonder and fear...other things he didn't dare name.

"Joy," he said, his voice soft and quivering with laughter, "what in the world have you got there?"

She looked at the thing in her hand, her erstwhile "mike," and burst into a bright cackle of laughter, a starburst of delight that was colored only slightly with embarrassment. She crowed, "It's a SaladShooter. I can't believe you've actually got a SaladShooter!"

"Actually, my mother gave it to me," he said. "Christmas, I think—no, it was my birthday." He wanted to go to her, take the thing out of her hand, and...but he couldn't seem to move from his spot in the doorway.

"Birthday? Oh—when?"

"May."

"Ah—a Taurus," she said, as if it explained something.

A Taurus, Mary thought. Yes, of course. *He makes me feel safe.* Taureans were rock-solid dependable, fiercely loyal. Slow to anger, slow to love, but when they did...

"Um...do you actually *use* it?" Her voice was hushed and bumpy with laughter; everything inside her felt loose and shaken, like pebbles in a tumbler.

He lifted one shoulder. "Yeah, I did for a while. I was..." He coughed in that discomfited way she found so appealing. "I was trying to lose some weight. I thought maybe becoming a vegetarian would help, but..."

But I like you this way, Mary thought. I like the way you feel when I put my arms around you—so big and broad and solid.

But she couldn't say *that.* So instead she said, *"Vegetarian?"* on ripples of wondering laughter.

He shrugged again. "Yeah, well, it didn't last. Apparently I'm a confirmed carnivore." He nodded toward her, his eyes gleaming. "What were *you* doing with it?"

"Me?" she gulped. "I was...I was looking for something to eat. Yeah. I was just going to fix some lunch. Are you hungry? Would you like me to fix you something?"

She knew she wasn't answering the question he'd really asked. She was somehow hoping if she kept talking fast and long enough she could keep him from pursuing it. She didn't quite know why, but she couldn't talk about what had just happened—not to him. Not yet. It was too much, too private. All the emotions . . . so close to the surface now, yet connected to the innermost part of her being, the part she'd never shared with anyone before, except, in a way, through her singing. Oh, she thought, but to share that part of herself would be such an act of intimacy, much more than simply taking off her clothes, or even sharing her body in the act of lovemaking. It would be like . . . like stripping away all the layers of her person, and sharing her naked soul.

"I didn't expect you back so soon. I hope it's all right. I mean, I don't want you to think . . ." She kept talking because he wasn't doing anything to stop her, damn him. Oh, how she hated it when he did that—just stood there looking at her with those eyes that seemed to see everything inside her head, so that she felt compelled to babble on and on, throwing up words like a smoke screen. "I wasn't snooping, in case you were wondering. I was, um, looking for a frying pan, actually, because I was going to maybe make some scrambled eggs, or . . . something." She waved the SaladShooter vaguely, then put it down on the countertop.

That was when she noticed the sleeve of the shirt she was wearing. She gave a little gasp and snatched her hand back, rolled the sleeve a couple more times, shoved it above her elbow and folded both arms across her waist.

"I, uh . . ." she said, then stopped and cleared her throat, not knowing where on earth to look. For goodness sake, she was wearing his shirt, and nothing but panties underneath. She'd only meant to borrow it. She hadn't expected him until much later. What must he think of her?

"I'm sorry . . . I hope you don't think . . . my only clean jeans had a hole in them. I put the others in your washing machine. I found this in a pile in the guest room. It had a couple buttons missing, so I thought—"

"Looks good on you," MacDougal said, absolutely deadpan.

She felt a panicky little catch in her breathing as he moved out of the doorway, finally, and came straight toward her.

The shirt suddenly felt transparent to her; her nipples cringed against the smooth, soft fabric. But it was the refrigerator he was heading for, and she had to sidestep out of his way, suddenly clumsy and off balance.

He didn't even look at her. She noticed that his eyes no longer had that penetrating gleam, and that his expression seemed guarded. But not his cop-look, she thought. It was more as if he was protecting private places of his own.

"Why don't I fix us both something?" he said evenly as he opened the door of his refrigerator. From its depths, after a few scuffling noises, came the muffled question, "Okay... chicken or shrimp?"

"Oh—gee, anything." She shrugged in a bemused, thoroughly fascinated way; her nerves were still jangling because of his unexpected appearance, plus she'd never had a man fix a meal for her before. The idea was curiously exciting. She caught her lower lip in her teeth and murmured, "Uh... chicken's fine." Besides, she knew very well that shrimp was hideously expensive.

"Chicken it is." He took a package of boneless breasts out of the freezer and put them in the microwave. While they were defrosting he turned on the oven, got a brown-and-serve sourdough baguette from the freezer and slapped it on a cookie sheet, and then began assembling an assortment of condiments and spices, utensils and bowls.

"I'm impressed," Mary murmured. She was reading the label on a jar of French mustard. "You really do *cook.*"

MacDougal glanced up from what he was doing, which was chopping the tops off a bunch of green onions. "What did you expect? I'm single."

"So am I, but I mostly just defrost." She unscrewed the lid of the mustard jar, took a tiny bit on her finger and popped it into her mouth. After a moment she shrugged judiciously and said, "Hmm..." then replaced the lid, put the jar back on the counter and dusted her hands. "I don't know, I just think most single people probably don't go to this much trouble."

He shrugged without looking up. "I guess it depends."

"On what?"

"On whether you think of being single as a permanent condition or not." The microwave beeped; he swooped upon it with the efficiency of long practice.

Mary waited until he'd removed the chicken breasts from their disposable package and arranged them on his cutting board before she ventured, "And you do?"

Now he did look at her, a brief flash from those dark eyes, like a searchlight in the night. "Yeah," he said, "I do."

"How come? You seem like a—" she coughed and finished carefully "—a presentable-enough guy."

"Thanks—I think." He smiled wryly and picked up a mallet. Then he shrugged and said, "I'm a cop."

"So what? Cops get married, have families."

"Yeah, I know." He began pounding the chicken breasts, methodically, efficiently, first one side, then the other. "My dad was a cop."

She watched his hands, frowning. "But if—oh, I see. Your parents—it didn't work out, is that it? Because of his job? Or... oh, God, you said *was*. He didn't—"

"Nah—he was wounded a couple of times, but managed to live to enjoy his retirement." He was still smiling, but even in profile, Mary could see that there wasn't any amusement in it. Just something dark and ironic. "These days he fishes and makes furniture. He and my mom will have been married... let's see, forty-three years, I guess it is. Next month."

"But then I don't understand why—"

"I saw what my mother went through." He put down the mallet and gathered up the flattened pieces of chicken, then looked at Mary and said very quietly, "Every day of my life, when I was growing up, I saw how much she suffered, worrying about my dad. He got shot once. So did my partner—took a bullet that should have been mine, as a matter of fact. I remember what it was like, sitting with Jim's wife in the emergency room, watching what she went through." He shook his head and turned away. "I never wanted to be anything else but a cop like my dad, but I also knew I never wanted to put anybody I cared about through that kind of hell."

That was punctuated by the sizzle of meat dropping into a hot buttered frying pan.

Mary didn't say anything. While the chicken was browning she watched MacDougal throw together a salad of butter lettuce, water chestnuts, mandarin orange sections and slivered almonds, and top it off with poppy-seed dressing. After that he added green onions, parsley, freshly ground pepper and mustard to the butter in the frying pan to make a sauce that smelled like pure heaven. And all the while she watched, she wondered whether she'd be able to eat a bite of it. There was a lump in her stomach that felt like lead, and she couldn't for the life of her explain *why.*

Why should she care whether MacDougal ever married or not? It had nothing whatever to do with her. Why should the loneliness she'd glimpsed in his eyes make her *ache* so? Until a couple of days ago she'd considered her own single state pretty much a permanent one, and she'd accepted that. Or, she thought she had. Why *now* was she suddenly so acutely aware of her own aloneness? Dammit, of course she wanted a home, someone to love...babies. She *did.* Oh, God...yes, she did. And now, when for the first time in ten years it seemed the chance to have those things might be given back to her, why didn't she feel hopeful...*happy?*

A little while ago, in this same kitchen, she had felt happy. Now she felt...bleak.

At least, Doug thought, the exercise of cooking, doing something creative with his hands, was helping him regain a measure of control over his rampaging libido. With that accomplished, and as long as he didn't let himself look at Joy too long or too often, he figured he should be able to restore his priorities to their proper order. That was important. He could not forget his reason for being here—which was hard when there was an unbelievably gorgeous, long-legged woman dancing in his kitchen, wearing nothing but one of his shirts with a couple of buttons missing.

Whew. The problem was, she was just so damned *cute.* Scrubbed, tousled and barefooted, there was a hoydenish

quality about her that made him feel young and irresponsible. It made him want to laugh. It made him want to spend
the day doing carefree things with her—like tossing a ball on
the beach in the rain, picking flowers from someone else's
garden, making love in all sorts of playful and sensual
ways... cuddling, tickling, romping together like kit-
tens....

He had until tomorrow to get some answers out of her, or
he was going to lose her. He didn't know why he was so sure
about that, but he was. He had to get Joy to talk *now*—tonight. That realization made him feel grim and edgy, the
way he used to feel on a stakeout, just before all hell broke
loose.

While they were eating he told her more about his family, especially his mom and dad back home in Ferndale,
Michigan, hoping that might loosen her up some, get her to
feeling relaxed, trusting him more. But for some reason he
couldn't for the life of him figure out, it seemed to be having the opposite effect. Okay, so she listened and made interested noises, but her face was fragile and transparent as
blown glass, her eyes had that lost waif look again, and
carefully avoided meeting his.

He was so frustrated by his own lack of success, finally,
that he shifted gears rather more suddenly than he'd intended to. He put down his fork, picked up his coffee cup,
hunched forward and said a little too brusquely, "Okay,
Mary Jo, your turn. Where're you from? You have a family back home somewhere?"

It was clumsy, and she responded to it that way. Her head
jerked up and her eyes went wide and startled. A look of
such exquisite pain flickered across her face that he instantly wished he'd kept his mouth shut.

She said, "My... my family?" Her mouth looked swol-
len and bruised. He saw her throat move convulsively, as if
her last bite of food had gotten stuck there.

He hardened his resolve, and the effort it cost him rasped
in his voice. "Yeah—family. You know, mother, father,
sisters, brothers—stuff like that."

She gave her head a small, quick shake. Her eyes slid away, in that way she had that told him she was lying. "No—no family. I'm, uh . . ." She shrugged. "There's just me."

"Okay," he persisted grimly, "so where are you from? You weren't born in Hollywood." He'd heard something in her voice, not much, and not often, but sometimes. Just a hint, he thought, of the South.

Again she shrugged, refusing to look at him. "Just a small town. No place you'd know. The kind of place nearly everybody leaves, sooner or later." And then there was silence, complete and impenetrable.

Doug sat very still, staring at the wall she'd thrown up between them, until he felt his temper begin to roil and swell. Then he got up, carefully picked up his plate and hers, and carried them to the sink. When he came back to the table he placed one hand on its surface and the other on the back of Joy's chair, leaned close to her and said very softly, "Mary Jo, I don't normally come home for lunch, did you know that?"

She flashed him one brief, alarmed look and shook her head.

"I didn't come home today because I felt hungry. Do you know why I came home?" She didn't move, didn't look at him, didn't answer. "I came home because I have to get some answers from you. And I have to get them *now*." He turned her chair with a loud scraping sound and growled, "Do you understand?"

Her eyes were clinging to his now, so full of anguish and appeal he almost wished she'd look away again. He felt like a sadist, and that made him angry. He felt a childish desire to break something, bite through nails, swear. The last of those he could do, at least, and did, putting Maurice to shame. And it did help, a little.

He straightened, finally, with a long exhalation, rubbing at the back of his neck. The most frustrating thing was, he had a feeling she really wanted to tell him. It was almost as if she didn't know *how*. She was just so . . . bottled up, he thought—the way she'd been yesterday down at the club, up there on that stage, wanting so badly to let the music out....

And today she was singing. Joyfully, unrestrainedly singing. He had a feeling that if he gave her enough time she'd find a way to let go of the secrets she'd been keeping locked up inside her for so long, just as she had the music. Trouble was, he couldn't give her that time. He had to find a way to break through her barricades somehow. He had to find something—

He turned back suddenly, bending over her as he had before. Only this time his voice was gentle, almost intimate.

"Joy...I'm sorry. I wish I didn't have to do this. I hate like hell to have to do this." He touched her arm...her shoulder...her hair, then murmured, "Come with me, okay? I want to show you something."

Chapter 10

He took her hand. But Mary knew it was nothing like the other times, when his hand had seemed to swallow up hers, wrap it around with warmth, security, safety. She felt as if she were standing too close to a forest fire. Her skin burned; she felt buffeted, half suffocated.

"C'mon." He tugged her to her feet, encouraging her with a casual jerk of his head.

As soon as she was upright she pulled her hand from his grasp, but then gave him a nod of reluctant acquiescence even as she hesitated still, rubbing both hands mechanically on the long tails of her borrowed shirt.

Why am I doing this? she wondered. She'd already made up her mind to tell him. Why, then, was it so *hard?*

She had that stage fright again; her belly felt hollow, her legs like rubber. On those precarious legs she followed him through the living room, then down the hallway that led to the bedrooms. To *his* bedroom.

The first thing she noticed was that his bed wasn't made—at least, not very well. A dark maroon comforter had been carelessly thrown over a jumble of sheets and pillows. She caught a glimpse of a masculine print—wild geese, or perhaps ducks.

She noticed those things and so many others while she stood just inside the bedroom door, shivering in the borrowed shirt, with her crossed arms clutched tightly against her middle. She noticed them in spite—or perhaps because—of the fact that she was teetering on the brink of an emotional precipice. She'd been peering over the edge of that precipice for ten years now, in utter terror of the shadowy unknown that lay at the bottom. Well, here she was, finally, about to jump—or be pushed—over the edge, and her mind was filling up with details, inconsequential, everyday things, *anything* to distract her from what was coming.

Wild geese, rumpled comforters . . . the room was wholly masculine and typically untidy. There were clothes, of course—clean underwear and socks that had been folded but not put away, shirts and slacks that had been taken off and carelessly dropped across the back of a chair, on the foot of the bed, the floor. And there *were* pictures—family photographs—on the walls and dresser top, and on the white-painted mantelpiece above an old-fashioned wooden fireplace that unexpectedly graced the far end of the room.

The fireplace elicited an exclamation of surprise and appreciation from her, which she stifled instantly. MacDougal looked up from the box he was rummaging through just long enough to give her a distracted frown, which left her feeling as though she'd committed some grave indiscretion, like giggling at a wake.

Jittery and ill at ease, she ventured farther into the room, pausing now and then to examine a particular photograph more closely. She recognized MacDougal's parents easily, and several family groupings that could only have been brothers and sisters, nieces and nephews. He had a large family, she realized. Which made it even harder to fathom his being the way he was. The way he'd apparently made up his mind to be. Alone . . .

"Joy."

MacDougal's voice had a rasp in it that acted like sandpaper on her exposed nerves. She started and turned so abruptly she dropped the framed photograph she'd just picked up.

"Oh, God," she gasped, dropping to her knees, "I'm sorry. I didn't mean to—"

"It's okay. Forget it." He seemed edgy, almost impatient.

He came around the bed and bent down to take her elbow and lift her to her feet, but she shook him off and picked up the photo and frame, babbling breathlessly, "I think it's okay. It's not really broken, it's just come apart. See?" She looked at it herself and saw that it was a color snapshot of four men in ski gear, standing in front of a snow-covered mountain cabin. One of the men was MacDougal; two she didn't know. The third—

"Leave it," said MacDougal. "I'll fix it—don't worry about it. Here..." He removed the snapshot and the pieces of its frame from her fingers. She heard him mutter, "My God, your hands are like ice." And then he said urgently: *"Joy?"*

"What?" She stared at him for the space of a few painful heartbeats without any comprehension at all.

"I said, it's okay. Come on, it's only a photograph."

She blinked him into focus, surprised to find that he was on her level, balanced on the ball of one foot, and that he was holding both of her hands, his thumbs rubbing back and forth across her knuckles, chafing warmth into them.

"Come on—leave it," he said suddenly, gruffly. "I want you to look at something." Once more he raised her to her feet, then roughly turned her, holding her by her upper arms. "There—look, dammit." The rasp in his voice made it more like a growl. "Take a good...long...look."

More photographs. A half dozen or so, she saw, maybe more, all in vivid color. He'd spread them out across the bed, on the comforter, giving them a background of deep maroon. Like dried blood...

Reality teetered, shivered, dissolved. It was her dream, her waking dream. These were the frozen frames from the

movie. They were all there—the body, the flowing hair that
had lapped across the toe of her shoe...the smeared lipstick...the one white breast, so shockingly exposed...the
slash of crimson across the pale throat, glittering with diamonds....

Mary's whole world seemed to tilt, and she felt herself
sliding helplessly, inexorably, toward that precipice. She put
out a hand, groping desperately for something to hold on to.
But there was nothing. Nothing to stop her from going over
the edge.

"You *were* there that night, weren't you?" There was no
gentleness in MacDougal's voice now. It was hard and
strained, as though he'd forced his words through tight-
clenched teeth. "You saw her...Belle...just like that. Didn't
you? *Isn't* that what you saw?" He gave her a quick, hard
shake, full of barely restrained violence. His fingers were
like steel bands around her arms. *"Tell me, dammit."*

She nodded rapidly, desperately. One stricken little sob
escaped before she could stop it; the others she kept back the
only way she could—by holding her breath.

Doug thought it was possibly the worst thing he'd ever
done. He knew for damn sure it was the hardest. To be
holding her like that, so cruelly, ruthlessly, when all he really wanted to do was simply...hold her. Every instinct,
every desire in him, demanded that he pull her back against
him, wrap her in his arms and shield her eyes from the horrors spread out on the bed before her. It took all his strength
to fight the demand; his whole body quivered with the
strain.

Dear God, he thought suddenly, with the shock of someone confronting divine revelation. I *love* this woman. What
in the world am I going to do?

"Joy—Mary..." He said it gently now, pleading with her
with everything he had. Because he felt suddenly that so
much more was riding on this than just a ten-year-old murder case. Without stopping to think about it or to analyze
why he felt that way, it seemed to him to have become a
matter of life and death—*his* life, Joy's life. And maybe,
just maybe...his future, too.

"Something happened that night." He eased his hold on her arms, rubbing the places where he knew his fingers must have bruised her. "Something terrible. Something ugly. I think you know what happened. I think you've kept that inside you all these years. What I want to know is *why*. I want you to tell me why, Joy. I want—I need you to tell me what happened."

"I want to." Her voice was faint and airless. He bent his head low in order to hear it better and felt the cool brush of her hair on his cheek ... like a child's sweet, impulsive kiss. "I just don't know if—"

She stopped there, as if she'd bitten off the rest. He closed his eyes and let out a breath.

"You *can,*" he said fervently, finishing what he thought she'd wanted to say. But she shook her head and mumbled something he couldn't quite hear. Something about ... his not believing her.

Fear clutched at his insides, the cold, sick feeling that accompanies unthinkable thoughts. *What is she hiding? God—did she do it after all?* She was strong enough, tall enough...at least five-eight. Belle had been tiny, all of five-two....

No. The answer slammed home with the finality of absolute certainty. Joy could never kill anyone. She was protecting someone. That had to be the answer. And he had to know who it was.

Still holding her by the arms, he turned her to face him. But she kept her face averted and stubbornly refused to look at him. So he moved his hands upward, feeling the soft-crisp fabric of his cast-off shirt slip and slide over her shoulders. When he got to the collar he pushed away the cloth and slipped his hands inside next to her skin, next to the warm, slender column of her neck. His thumbs lay along the undersides of her jaw ... he could feel the flutter of her pulse against his palms.

"You were singing that night," he said softly. "Weren't you? At the club—at Caesar's. You went on for Belle."

She nodded. "Second show." Her voice was uneven, like a motor trying to start on a cold morning. She cleared her throat, and it got better. "Belle said she . . . she had something she wanted to do. She was going to meet someone."

"Someone?" Doug prompted. "She didn't say who? Or what it was about? Was it business? Or do you mean like a date?"

"I don't think—not business. She was . . . she seemed . . . excited. Happy." Her voice broke, became a whisper. "She had that look, you know? She'd had it for several days. I remember thinking, *Uh-oh, Belle's in love!* But she never would tell me who it was, and I never saw her with anybody, you know, around the club. Whoever it was, she was keeping it a secret, even from me. She didn't want anyone to know...." Her throat muscles contracted under the heels of his hands.

"Tell me what happened after the show," he urged her gently, bending closer, creating an intimacy between them. "The manager said you left almost as soon as you finished singing. Did you go home?"

She nodded. Once more he felt her swallow, and his own throat ached in sympathy. "I wanted to tell Belle." Her lashes quivered and finally lifted, unveiling eyes that burned with a fierce and joyous anguish. "The most wonderful thing had happened. There was this producer in the audience—he'd come to see Belle, and instead...anyway, he gave me his card and told me to come and audition for him. I couldn't believe it. It was like, my most perfect dream, and it was coming true. I wanted to tell someone. I wanted to tell Belle. It was late—after midnight—and I thought she might be home...."

It was a moment or two before he realized she'd stopped speaking; somehow he'd become lost in her eyes. They were clinging to his, it seemed, with a kind of desperate faith, as if he held the rope to which she clung, dangling over the side of a cliff. It was that small, painful convulsion in her throat that alerted him to her silence. In response his hands moved slightly, unconsciously kneading, trying, in the only way he knew, to ease her pain.

"You went home...." He spoke so softly, and yet it seemed too loud. Suspense was a pulse in his head, like the ticking of a clock. "And then?"

"I had my key out, like I always do, but then...the door wasn't locked. I was so glad, I thought—Belle's home! I couldn't wait to tell her. I opened the door, and..." She grabbed desperately for a breath. "I heard this...sound. I don't remember exactly...where I was when I...she *fell*. She just sort of...fell. As if somebody had...dropped her. Right at my feet. Her hair was...on my shoe. Her lipstick was all smeared, and her...dress was twisted around so it didn't...cover her. Her eyes were looking up at me. And there was...there was this...thing around her neck. It was...cutting into her neck. At first I thought it was blood, but it wasn't. It had—" she paused, then finished it in a horror-stricken whisper "—diamonds on it."

"Rhinestones," Doug murmured. She nodded, her eyes slowly closing, displacing quivering beads of moisture. His mind raced on, past the horror, past her pain, and ran head-on into the incredible truth. And it was as he'd suspected all along—as he'd hoped. "My God—he was there. The killer was still there. Wasn't he? You saw who killed her?"

She was shaking her head—that rapid little shudder, the way she did when she knew denial was futile. "*No*. I didn't. I ran. I...didn't even think. I didn't see—"

"He saw you," Doug said slowly. Gradually the door was opening, letting in the light. "That's what this is about, isn't it? You saw him, and he saw you. *Isn't that right, Joy?*"

He gave her head a shake, jarring loose one sharp, tormented gasp, and his muscles cramped and quivered with the effort it took for him not to haul her straight into his arms and cradle her head against his shoulder, gabbling vows and promises. But it wasn't over yet, dammit. She hadn't finished. She hadn't answered the most important question, and until she did, he couldn't let her go. He *couldn't*.

"Joy?" He left one hand cradling the side of her neck and with the other raised her chin so that she had no choice but to look at him. God—her head, her neck, felt so fragile, so vulnerable; her eyes were so full of pain and fear, and yet in a strange way, trusting.

He was suddenly reminded of a time during his street patrol days, when he'd stopped a speeding car and ended up delivering a baby in its back seat. How vividly he remembered the look in that woman's eyes, the way they'd clung to him—just the way Joy's were clinging to his, right now. And he thought, with a grim, inner smile, that in a way, what he was doing here wasn't all that much different. He remembered feeling strong and scared to death, back then, both at the same time. He remembered how he'd fought to keep his voice calm....

"Joy, I know you saw this guy—it *was* a guy, right?" She sniffed, then nodded. *Yes,* he thought. *Yes—now we're getting somewhere.* "Did you know him?"

She shook her head. "No. Not then..."

"Not then?" Doug pounced on that, while a little current of excitement went zapping through his nerves... the primitive thrill of the hunter. "But later? You saw this man later and recognized him, is that it?" *Tell me, Joy. For God's sake, get it over with. Just... tell me.*

Her lips parted; words hovered achingly on the tip of her tongue. He could almost see them there, quivering... the suspense like an audible hum in the air between them. But no sound came out of her mouth.

Doug's muscles tensed; he drew breath to exhort her. And that was when he saw the shutter fall across her face. She said in a flat, final voice, "No. I didn't recognize him. I've no idea who he was."

She was lying—he knew she was. He gave her head a small, restrained shake, and heard the tiny sound she made as she caught her breath, and then nipped her lower lip between her teeth. He didn't know which he wanted to do more, throttle her or kiss her. It was impossible to look at her mouth, remember the way it had tasted in the night, the salt-sweet taste of it, moist with her tears, and *not* want to kiss her. But there was too much frustration in him right now, too much violence, and he knew that if he kissed her now he might not... Ah... damn. Later, he promised himself. *When this is all over...*

"Ah...jeez," he groaned. "Joy..." There had to be a way to get it out of her—there *had* to. If only he could figure out what it was.

It shocked him, suddenly, to realize that what he felt more than anything was *disappointment*. It hurt more than he'd thought possible that she didn't trust him enough to tell him what she knew. He wanted her to trust him completely, believe in him unreservedly, have absolute faith in his ability to keep her from harm. Which was unfair of him, he knew. She'd known him...what...two days? Plus, he was a cop, and she obviously didn't have a very good opinion of cops. Hell, if she wasn't so damned scared, she probably wouldn't be tolerating his company at all.

And yet, last night...

Last night she'd wanted him to stay.

Sure, he reminded himself, but last night she was scared to death. It was just comfort she'd wanted. A warm body to hold on to.

Comfort...a warm body. For the first time the idea crossed Doug's mind that he could use that vulnerability and need to get the answers he wanted. And he shivered, as though something cold and slimy had crawled across his skin. He couldn't—wouldn't do that. It was a dangerous idea, a reprehensible thought.

And besides—the knowledge was forming in his mind and in his soul with the solidity of concrete—it wasn't just answers he wanted from Joy now. He wasn't sure when or how it had happened, but he knew he wanted more. A whole lot more.

"So." He took a deep breath and added, almost to himself, "I guess it's back to square one."

She was still gazing at him, her eyes wary, full of apology and appeal. He realized that she was holding on to his wrists, and that her thumbs were moving back and forth along the rigid tendons. For a moment his mind blanked, as if there'd been a brief power glitch, erasing all his recently programmed logic and resolve. He closed his eyes and willed himself ruthlessly back on-line. Damn, he thought. When this is over...

He sighed and said softly, "Joy, I know you're scared. Don't you realize, if you tell me what you know, who you saw that night, it'll all be over? We can protect you. There won't be anything more to fear. *Come on*..."

She spoke in a whisper, as if her vocal cords had rusted. "I wish I could tell you."

"You *can*."

She shook her head. He felt her trembling. He thought, If I kiss her... if I hold her...

The phone rang. Even all the way from the living room it seemed unbearably strident and loud.

Joy's body jerked; his went rigid. She let go of his wrists and he moved his hands to her shoulders, then they both waited, tensely listening to Maurice's profanity and counting rings, until the answering machine clicked on.

Joy cleared her throat. "Shouldn't you answer it?"

He shook his head. "If it's important, they'll call my—"

His beeper went off. Swearing, he snatched it from his belt and punched it into silence. "It's the station," he muttered. "I have to..." He started out of the room, then on second thought ducked back in and scooped the forensics photos into a pile and dropped them into the box he'd taken them from. "Don't go 'way— I'll be right back."

In the living room, he barked "Shut up, Maurice" as he picked up the phone and punched his most often used pre-programmed button.

"MacDougal," he said into the receiver. "What've you got?" He took out his notebook as he listened, asked a couple of questions and jotted down some brief directions. "Got it. I'm on my way."

When he went back into the bedroom, it didn't look as if Joy had moved a muscle. She was standing right where he'd left her, still holding her arms across her middle as if she had a stomachache, looking lost and scared.

"I have to go," he said tersely. "Sorry..." He was already in the closet, scraping hangers. First storm of the season, and he never could find his damned raincoat. There.

He hauled it off its hanger, turning to look at Joy as he shrugged it on over his suit jacket. "You'll be okay here. Just remember—don't answer the door, no matter what. Got that? Probably wouldn't be a bad idea to leave the lights off in the front rooms, and stay away from the windows, just in case. Okay?"

She nodded.

"Okay. I don't know how long I'll be. . . ." He had to leave, but oh, how he hated to. All of a sudden he felt like a nervous parent, leaving his kids without a sitter for the first time. His stomach was tied in knots of dread he told himself were *not* premonition. "I'll be back as soon as I can," he told her, and went out into the October dusk.

A moderate rain had begun to fall.

"Look, he's leavin'," said JoJo.

"Shoot—watch out," hissed Daisy, backing hastily into the shadows behind the trunk of a large eucalyptus tree and dragging JoJo with her.

Preacher, who was already in hiding, peered out over her head and murmured, "Well, well. Looks like here's our chance to see if our Mary's hidden away in there. As soon as he's out of here—then we go."

"Right," croaked Daisy.

They watched the garage door tilt open, and a little while later an old white Mercedes backed out of the driveway and took off down the hill in a cloud of diesel smoke.

"Okay, *now*." The three eased cautiously out of hiding, looked up and down the narrow, deserted street, then scuttled across like wind-driven leaves.

"I sure do hate rain," Daisy grumbled, sniffing as she turned up the collar on her topmost coat and pulled down the brim of her baseball cap.

"Be glad it isn't worse," Preacher remarked. "I wouldn't like to climb these steps in snow, for example."

"Yeah," said Daisy, "better watch your step. They're kinda slippery." She didn't object when Preacher took her arm; after all, he wasn't getting any younger.

"That's all right," said Preacher cheerfully, glancing over his shoulder at JoJo, who was plodding stolidly behind them. "If we do slip, JoJo will catch us—won't you, my friend?"

"Yeah," said JoJo, smiling his jack-o'-lantern smile. "I'll catch ya."

They reached the top, breathing hard. "Ring the doorbell," Daisy instructed.

"Wait." Preacher put out a hand. "I hear someone." He leaned closer to the door panels. "Dear me. He seems to be yelling something about . . . cops."

"Probably the TV," said Daisy. "Lotta people leave the TV on when they're away, to make people think there's somebody home."

Preacher suddenly reared back as if he'd been poked with a sharp stick. "My word—I don't believe they allow language like that on television."

"Cable," said JoJo, nodding wisely.

"Ah," said Preacher, looking profoundly uncomfortable. "Yes . . . harrumph. Perhaps an X-rated channel."

"Never mind the damn TV," hissed Daisy, punching him in the arm. "Ring the doorbell. How we gonna—"

"Somebody's comin'," said JoJo.

"Shoot!" Preacher and Daisy spun around simultaneously, backs flattened against the door panels.

All they could do was stare in frozen dismay at the man in the dark coat who was making his way steadily up the long flight of steps. He appeared to be finding it tough-going, as if he had a bad leg, or something.

Anyway, he was concentrating hard on the job, watching his feet, so he was maybe a third of the way to the top before he even looked up. When he did, a look of absolute shock came over his face. He turned, awkwardly and without a word, and started back down the steps, moving much more rapidly than he had been on the way up. When he reached the bottom he turned right and headed up the hill at a good fast clip.

Preacher and Daisy waited until the man had disappeared from view in the darkness and rain, then simultaneously exhaled. "Whooee," said Daisy, "who d'you suppose *that* was?"

"Some friend of the cop's," said Preacher, mopping his brow with a handkerchief of undetermined age and condition. "I do believe it's the same one we saw him with this morning. Dropped by for a visit, no doubt."

"Uh-uh," Daisy declared. "So why didn't he come on up, say howdy, like regular folks? I don't like this." She was already on her way down the steps. "He's probably goin' to find a phone right this minute. Come on—I don't know about you guys, but I ain't waitin' around for the cops to get here."

"What about Mary?" JoJo asked, looking forlornly back at the door. "Maybe she's in there. Maybe we oughtta holler, like you done down at her house."

Daisy paused and looked back at Preacher. Preacher shrugged. "Why not? It'll only take a second, and then we'll know." He opened his mouth.

"It's the cops!"

Preacher and JoJo looked at each other, then scrambled over each other, making for the steps. Daisy was already halfway down and picking up speed; she could move pretty well for somebody her age.

"What now?" she panted, when they were all three safely back in the Bronco, streaming water and breathing hard.

"We wait," wheezed Preacher grimly, one hand on his chest, approximately over his wildly pumping heart. "And watch."

It was a long time after the sounds of scuffling footsteps had faded into the general rush of the rain before Mary was able to stop shivering. She felt cold...so cold. Her neck and shoulders were cramped with tension. Her fingers were stiff from clutching that damn shirt of MacDougal's, as if holding it close to her body could somehow infuse more warmth into it. But what she really wanted—what she longed for—was *his* body, *his* warmth. If only he were here, she thought, if only he would hold her, wrap his arms around her, she would never be cold, nothing bad could ever happen to her again.

What should I do? What should I do? She'd done exactly what MacDougal had told her to do—left the lights off, kept quiet, stayed away from the windows, even though everything in her had wanted to *look*. She still wished she'd tried to see who it was that had come creeping up Mac-Dougal's steps, then scurried off again in such a hurry. She really didn't think it could have been *him*. He'd come alone—somehow she knew that. This had sounded like more than one person—kids, probably—but if she'd looked, than at least she'd have known for sure. But she'd been too afraid, literally frozen with fear. She was so sick and tired of being afraid.

If you tell me what you know, it'll all be over. You'll have nothing left to fear.

Oh, God, she thought, if only that were true. A wave of terrible desolation swept over her; she looked around the room, up at the ceiling, everywhere, like a trapped animal searching for a way out. But there wasn't one. No matter which way she turned, she could only lose.

Here in MacDougal's bedroom, surrounded by his clothes, his keepsakes, pictures of his family, she'd never felt so isolated, so utterly friendless, so *alone*. She had no one in the world to turn to except a cop who only wanted from her the one thing in the world she couldn't bring herself to give him. In a way, she supposed it had a kind of bitter irony.

The mantelpiece was there, an arm's reach away. She did reach out a hand, finally, wistfully touching first one photograph, then another. A portrait of MacDougal's parents... another of a man who bore a striking resemblance to MacDougal, with a pretty woman and three smiling children.

There were others, too, that she knew weren't family. A wedding group, with MacDougal as best man. MacDougal holding a baby in a christening gown, flanked by the proud parents, with the photo signed, "To 'Godpapa' Doug, with love and thanks from Jim, Carol and David."

She stood there staring at the last one for a long time. Then she turned slowly, a little stooped, like a very old person or someone in great pain, and groped her way to the bed. When she sat on the edge of it, something sharp poked her in the thigh. She pulled it out from under her and discovered that it was the snapshot and the broken frame. MacDougal and his three buddies. She clutched it in her hand, rocking slightly, back and forth, back and forth. A tear rolled down the side of her nose and dripped off the end, landing with a minute splash on the glossy surface of the photograph.

I can't tell him, she thought. Not now. Not ever.

MacDougal would simply never believe her. And he would hate her forever for telling him such a terrible lie.

Chapter 11

It was another blonde...very young, but much too old. And at one time, probably pretty. *Someone's daughter.*

Doug thought of those words and of the woman he'd spoken them to as he stared down at the sprawled and crumpled body, like a sodden doll abandoned in the rain.

"Workin' girl," said Burnside, who was balanced on the balls of his feet beside the body. "Looks like she had an expensive habit to support, too." He glanced up at Doug, the raindrops on his glasses turning to crimson in the flashing lights of a black-and-white.

"Yeah?" Doug growled. "Well, she's somebody's daughter—and don't you forget it." He bit off the last word, turned up the collar of his raincoat and went to greet the arriving detectives from North Hollywood Division.

The blonde—and the case—technically belonged to North Hollywood, since she'd been dumped on the north side of Mulholland, but since odds were she'd met the john, dealer or pimp who'd beaten her to death down on Hollywood Boulevard, they flipped for it. Doug lost.

Normally he'd have hung in, anyway, since it looked as if it was probably going to be a co-op case, but tonight he had unfinished business on his mind. Burnside, who was probably a little wary after his partner's surly remark and looking to score some points, offered to stick around and take notes. So as soon as the ME showed up, Doug checked out and headed home.

Someone's daughter... All the way back to his place the phrase kept playing over and over in his mind, but the face that went with it wasn't the dead blonde's. It was Joy Donnelly's. She was somebody's daughter, too.

Who are you, Joy Donnelly—or Mary Jo Delinsky? Whose little girl are you?

Funny—a few days ago the burning question had been, *Where* are you, Joy Donnelly? Now it was *who*. But the things he wanted to know about her now had nothing whatsoever to do with his being a cop. Sure, he wanted to know where she'd been born, what kind of home she'd grown up in, whether she had parents, brothers, sisters... but only because he wanted to see in his mind's eye the kind of child she'd been, hear the embarrassing, intimate little stories families tell on each other to perfect strangers with such loving glee. He wanted to know if she'd ever worn pigtails, stained her chin with a cherry Popsicle, climbed a tree in her Sunday best dress. He wanted to know if she ate Oreos inside out, and whether she liked going to the zoo, sharing a shower, reading the funnies sitting cross-legged in bed on Sunday morning.

A far cry from "Just the facts, ma'am."

Since it was pouring buckets when he got home he took the inside stairs, from the garage through the laundry room, then the short flight up to the kitchen. On the way through the laundry room he noticed Joy's jeans spread out on top of the washer to dry, which brought vividly to mind the utterly delightful vision she'd made dancing in the middle of his kitchen, wearing his cast-off shirt.

What in the world was he going to do about the woman? How could he have allowed himself to fall in *love* with her?

He'd gone through life so carefully, taking no chances, making sure he never got to know anyone well enough to fall in love. And now look. It seemed that, while he'd been watching his step and tiptoeing around all the relationship possibilities in his path, his heart had been ranging recklessly ahead on a quest all its own.

He wondered why Joy hadn't put her jeans in the dryer, but when he checked he found the reason—there was already a load of his things in there, hopelessly wrinkled now, of course. He dumped them all into a plastic hamper, put the jeans in the machine and turned it on. Upstairs he could hear Maurice going into his usual "Cheese it, the cops!" hysteria. Good old Maurice, he thought wryly. A regular security alarm—better than a watchdog.

He left his raincoat dripping in the laundry room and went upstairs. The house was dark, and except for Maurice, very still. For once there was no light blinking on his message machine, so he went straight on through the living room without stopping, conscious of a quickening in his heartbeat, a tightness in his belly. Anticipation, he knew that's what it was. He was looking forward to seeing Joy again, as if his absence had been a matter of days instead of hours.

What was he going to do about this?

The guest room door was closed. Doug's disappointment was as acute as it was undeniable. And silly. Why had he thought she'd wait up for him? And why because she hadn't did his house seem so empty and cold all of a sudden? He'd lived alone all his adult life, for cryin' out loud! He was used to coming home to a foul-mouthed bird and a blinking light on his answering machine, chasing the emptiness with TV and the cold with a good, hot shower. What the hell was happening to him, anyway?

His bedroom was as dark as the rest of the house. He didn't turn on the light, and he paused on his way to the bathroom just long enough to take off his jacket and toss it in the general direction of a chair that was already pretty much buried under a pile of his clothes. His tie followed, and then his shirt. He really was going to have to take some time to get caught up with his domestic chores, he told himself. The last few days had been a little... unpredictable.

He turned on the light in the bathroom and leaned across the sink to study himself critically in the mirror, rubbing his jaws with a raspy sound. When he stopped that, another sound just as commonplace made his skin go cold and his scalp prickle and the fine hairs lift on the back of his neck. A rustling sound, coming from his bedroom. An instant later he was flattened against the wall next to the open door, his heart in his throat and his gun in his hand.

While he waited there, quivering with tension like a cocked bow, the sound came again—rustlings, and then . . . the softest of sighs.

Doug closed his eyes: adrenaline began to ebb from his body, leaving him frail and jangled. Swearing raggedly, he holstered his gun, then took off both holster and belt and laid them carefully over a towel rack. Leaving the bathroom light on, he walked slowly to his bed. And then for a while he just stood with his arms folded on his chest, gazing down at the woman sleeping there.

Why, he wondered, as a cool drop of rainwater slipped from his hair onto the bridge of his nose. Why, Joy Donnelly, or Mary Jo Delinsky, of all the women in the world, did it have to be you?

It was impossible, unethical, damned awkward, unbelievably complicated, and made no sense at all!

I love her. His heart gave him the answer with the quiet implacability of the child at the animal shelter who, after hearing all his elders' experienced and well-informed advice on suitability and bloodlines, gathers in the squirming stray with the big, sad eyes and says simply, "I want *this* one, Dad."

He loved her. It was as simple—and as complex—as that. He didn't know when it had happened. Maybe he'd always loved her. Maybe he'd fallen in love with her picture all those years ago, which, when he thought about it, was a revoltingly adolescent thing to do.

But he knew one thing—it wasn't a fantasy, an eight-by-ten glossy he was in love with now. It was a flesh-and-blood, all-too-human woman, with a quick temper and an even quicker laugh, and a stubborn streak a mile and a half wide.

He sat gingerly on the edge of the bed, on the narrow strip she'd left him, overwhelmed, suddenly, by the enormity of what was happening to him. He reached out with a careful finger to touch away a strand of hair that seemed to be tickling the outer corner of her eye, but then, with a sharp intake of breath, halted and drew it back again, arrested by the moisture he saw pooled there beneath her lashes. The thought of Joy lying in his bed weeping hurt him in ways he'd never known before. Amazing, the way she seemed to have become almost a part of him, and in such a short time. Amazing how *familiar* she already seemed.

In fact, when he thought about it, he really was amazed at how much he knew about her, considering how little time he'd spent with her, and the fact that she seemed bent on telling him as little as possible about herself. He knew, for example, that she actually *liked* fast food. Also ugly animals. And that she had the kind of imagination that imbues machines—like his car—with human personalities. He knew that most of the time she didn't wear makeup or a bra, that she shampooed her hair with something that smelled like strawberries. That she knew old hymns, and loved to dance, and that both millionaires and homeless people adored her. That once upon a time she had dreamed big dreams ...

He knew that ten years ago this rare and beautiful woman had witnessed an unspeakable act and with it the death of all her dreams, and the most amazing thing of all was that neither the horror nor the tragedy had left a blight on her soul. She was as quick to laugh, to love, to give, as anyone could be.

No wonder, Doug thought, his chest growing tight with an unaccustomed tenderness. No wonder I've fallen in love with her. How could I help it?

He was suddenly taken by a white hot burst of pure rage—a most uncoplike rage, a completely, imperfectly *human* rage—against the unknown someone who had caused his beloved such pain. In a very real way, he realized, the killer had taken two lives that night. And more than he'd ever wanted anything in his life, Doug wanted to give Joy's life back to her.

Trouble was, he didn't see how he could do it without her help, and she seemed bound and determined not to give it to him.

Ah ... well. He leaned over once more and this time did touch her, oh, so carefully fingering that one impish lock of hair back behind her ear. She stirred a little in her sleep, and he saw that she had the snapshot and frame—the one she'd dropped and broken—in her hand.

Shaking his head, aching with tenderness, he slid it from her fingers and placed it on the nightstand. Then he brushed her cheek with the backs of his fingers and whispered her name very softly, because he wasn't all that sure he wanted to wake her.

The truth was, he didn't know quite what else to do with her. She wasn't actually *in* his bed; she'd simply curled up on top of the comforter and pulled it over her from the other side. He didn't want to disturb her, but if he left her where she was, then *he* couldn't go to bed. She had all his covers. He didn't relish the idea of sleeping in the guest room, either, not with a man-hating feline on the loose in there.

Perhaps, though, he could take the comforter from *that* bed, bring it in here ...

He was about to risk doing that, feline and all, when Joy suddenly opened her eyes wide, raked a hand through her already tousled hair, threw back the comforter and sat bolt upright. She did all those things with the trembly jerkiness of a rudely awakened child, then frowned, and in a husky murmur said, "Wha'time izzit?"

"Late," said Doug gently, not bothering to hide his smile, or to stop his fingertips from exploring the heat-flushed curve of her cheek.

"Omigod," she mumbled, looking stricken. "I musta fallen asleep."

"Yep," said Doug, "you did."

"I'm sorry."

He shrugged. "'S'okay. I was about to turn in myself."

For a long while, then, she didn't say anything, while her eyes seemed to search every inch of his face—*seemed*, because they were only dark smudges in the dim light and he couldn't read their expression. In a way, he was glad. Finally she looked away distractedly, jamming her hand through her hair in a gesture he was beginning to recognize as a sure sign of self-consciousness.

"So," she said, with a small and careful throat-clearing, "how did it, uh . . . go? Is everything all right?"

"Yeah," said Doug. Then amended with a quick shrug, "Well—in a manner of speaking. *You* know."

"Oh. Right. Sorry." She touched his hair, suddenly and impulsively, catching her breath as she said, "You're wet."

"Yeah." He smiled, but it felt awkward. "It's really coming down out there."

"You must be cold," she whispered, staring at his naked chest as if she could see that his heart was beating a mile a minute inside it. Her mouth seemed blurred . . . impossibly lush.

"No . . . not that cold." *Hot.* On fire. Burning up inside. He suddenly felt parched, as if he were dying of thirst and her mouth was a sweet-water oasis.

And then, once again, there was silence, a silence as tense and fraught with inevitability as a launchpad the last few seconds before blast-off.

He felt Joy's hand on his chest, a touch as cool and healing as a blessing. *His* hand lay on the gentle join of her neck and shoulder, but it seemed a tremendous weight, too heavy for him to move. From somewhere, though, came the strength to bring his other hand to bear on her roving fingers, to corral them, hold them prisoner right over his rampaging heart, and to croak her name in feeble protest.

But perhaps it wasn't strength, after all, but only the gravest folly. Because it felt so *good* to him to have her touch him like that. So incredibly, unbelievably good. The pleasure of it pierced him like a bullet, shattering his resolve all to smithereens. Instead of confining her hand, he found himself caressing it, making love to it the way he wanted to make love to all of her, stroking the delicate fan of tendons with his fingertips, then dipping into the sensitive valleys between her fingers . . . using his thumb to probe the warm, moist hollow of her palm in slow, sensual circles.

There was a moment when he heard her swallow, felt her tremble . . . just the tiniest spark, the barest flickering of reason. But it was too late—the rocket was leaving the launching pad, and the shockwave generated by its lift-off snuffed out what was left of his convictions. He wasn't even aware of closing the distance between them at last . . . like a thirst-crazed wanderer plunging face-first into a life-giving spring, he was aware only of the sweet, blessed taste of her mouth.

His lips were rain-cooled and smooth, the kiss so light, so very gentle. Before, when he'd kissed her, Mary had thought her biggest fear was that he might never kiss her again. Now she knew she'd been wrong. This was a miracle—this man, the way he made her feel. She'd thought such a thing could never happen to her. To lose such a miracle—to have it and then lose it—*that* would be agony too terrible to bear. But oh, how tenuous, how fragile, how achingly lovely it was . . . like a bubble balanced on the tip of a finger, shimmering with all the colors of the rainbow. A breath, a blink . . . and it would be gone.

Afraid of risking more, afraid of bursting the bubble, she caught just a tiny sip of air, holding herself motionless except for the trembling she couldn't control. Her throat *ached* so; she felt as if her chest might burst. Her eyelids came down on warm pools of tears; thus displaced, they ran in cooling trails down her cheeks to mingle their salt with the sweetness of the kiss.

She knew he must taste her tears. Oh, God, what would he think?

But he made only a small, interrogative sound, less a question, really, than an acceptance. *Hmm . . . so that's the way it is with this woman.*

His acceptance seemed to her like a gift; she felt encouraged by it, emboldened. She moved her lips, tasting his. Neither guided nor impeded by the fact that he was holding it, her hand crept over his chest, fingers weaving upward through the thicket of his chest hair. When it reached the smooth, warm ridge of his shoulder, he pressed it briefly against him, then left it to explore farther where it would.

And yes, oh, yes...it would. Released and validated, her hand was free at last to touch and explore as it had wanted to do for so long. What exquisite pleasure it was, just to *touch* him. Every nerve ending was super-sensitized; her fingers seemed to burn. Up, up they rode along the taut cords of his neck, not hurrying, pausing to measure his pulse, thrilling to the power and urgency in it, tracing the hard line of his jaw, rasping over the day's growth of beard and coming finally to the place where their lips met. Her fingers trembled; she uttered a tiny wordless whimper of purest joy.

It was as if he'd been waiting for such a signal. He made a sound of his own, born of similar needs but wholly masculine in timbre, and slipped his hand around the back of her neck. The kiss grew warm, liquid. It poured into her like honey, like melted sunshine, filling up that brand-new emptiness inside her.

So this is it, she thought. This is what it feels like. This is what Belle felt like. And she shuddered, because it was so much more precious than she'd ever dreamed, and she was so desperately afraid that, like Belle, she was going to lose it.

"Joy..." Her name was a groan that seemed torn from the deepest part of him; breathed into her open mouth it went straight to the deepest part of her.

She'd been so caught up in her own sensations, her own emotions, she hadn't felt the heat and tension in him, the quivering restraint in his hands. Poor MacDougal, she thought, aching for him now, for the struggle she knew she must be putting him through. In a way she even wished she had the strength of character to stop it, but she knew she didn't. She was too selfish, too hungry, and she wanted this too much.

"I'm sorry," she whispered against his lips. "I'm sorry...."

"What for?" He pulled her face from his as if it cost him a tremendous effort and held it cradled between his two hands, brushing away the residue of her tears with his thumbs.

She could only look at him. *What for? For wanting you. For loving you. But most of all ...*

"Joy? What is it? If you don't—"

With a sharp sound of frustration and longing she reached for him, took his face in her hands and pulled it toward her and kissed him. I don't care, she thought—though it was more like a prayer. *I want this. Even if it's all I ever have of love. Please, God ... I want this.*

In an instant the melting warmth became molten, a cauldron, a volcano. He made a sound low in his throat, a guttural cry that was response at the most fundamental level, primitive male, raw and unreasoning. And though it was a sound she'd never heard before, something in the depths of Mary's being thrilled to it, like a she-wolf rising to her mate's call echoing across a cold, moonlit plain. She opened to him with a fierce, primal joy, plunged into the cauldron with total trust and complete abandon. Her body arched toward him, taut and trembling. Her breasts, her nipples, every nerve felt charged, electrified ... waiting for his touch.

And then his hands—those big, strong hands she loved— were pushing impatiently under the long tails of her shirt, fitting themselves first to her waist, but only briefly, as if to establish coordinates before venturing upward again. On they skimmed, lightly, shivering her skin to roughness, to find her aching breasts at last. His palms cradled and measured them, warmly nested them, oh, so gently kneading. And—it felt so good ... so good.

She tore her mouth free, laughing with relief and the most exquisite delight she'd ever known. She kissed his jaw, his ear, the side of his neck, the cove above his collarbone, then joyously threw back her head to give his mouth access to her arched throat and the deep-plunging V of her shirt.

MacDougal wasn't content with such limits, not for long. But being MacDougal, he didn't tear the shirt open or thrust it roughly up under her chin, but instead dealt with the but-

tons one by one in heart-stopping suspense, then oh so
gently, and with an expression of profound wonder, drew
the two sides apart and pushed them up and over the tops of
her shoulders... and down her arms. Even then he didn't
take what lay open in wholehearted offering to him, but
slowly raised his eyes to her face, almost as if he were asking...

Her heart seemed to burst, flooding her with tenderness.
Laughing and dizzy, she pulled his head to her breasts and
cradled it there, kissing his hair, burying her face in it,
measuring its length on the back of his neck with stroking
fingers. With a great sigh he put his arms around her and
drew her close against him, wrapping her in the incredible
heat and power of his body. And she thought, this is all I've
ever wanted. Please... let me have this man forever.

Slowly, he laid her down, supporting her weight with his
arms while he kissed her throat, her breasts, each nipple... nursing them to softness in the liquid warmth of his
mouth, teasing them hard again with his tongue. She floated
on waves of sensation, breathing in quick, shallow breaths
as his mouth skimmed downward, lingering to kiss a healing scratch, probe the shallow cup of her navel, gauge the
nerve-flutters in her taut belly.

Those infinitesimal betrayals of the tension in her seemed
to give him pause. She sensed that there was... not a cooling of the fire inside him, exactly; it was as if the coals had
been carefully banked, so as to burn even hotter and last a
longer time. His kisses grew languid, his stroking sensual
and slow. She began to feel it deep inside her and to move
to its sultry rhythms, to the pulses that throbbed in every
part of her, like primitive drums. They filled her mind
completely; she couldn't think at all, only *feel*.

She hadn't thought it possible to feel—for any human
body to feel—such sensations. And at the same time she
wondered how on earth she had endured living so long
without them. Without *him*. This man—this MacDougal.
It was as if she had no consciousness at all, as if nothing in
the world mattered except him, except now, this moment.
Nothing that had happened in her life before this moment

was of any consequence; beyond this she had no existence at all. His body, his mouth, his hands, were her universe. He was...everything.

Dimly, she felt him ease her underpants over her hips, felt the heat of his mouth on the mound at the juncture of her thighs. She gasped, electricity curling through her from the soles of her feet to the roots of her hair...but her legs parted of their own accord.

His thumbs gently opened her; his tongue pushed between her protective folds and found the sensitive place they guarded. A shaft of pure sensation, silvery and bright as a sword, pierced her to the very core of her being, and she writhed away from him with a low, frightened cry.

Instantly he slid up over her body, holding his weight away from her while he kissed her. "It's all right," he whispered against her mouth. "Shh—it's okay. I won't if you don't want—"

She shook her head rapidly, urgently. "It's not that. It's too much. I can't—"

He kissed her again so she could feel his rueful smile. "Honey, I know. But I'm not sure how long I can hold on. I just wanted you to—"

Again she shook her head, almost panic-stricken. She understood what he meant, what he wanted to give her, but there was something more important, something she wanted more. Something she desperately needed. She didn't even fully understand it, but she felt so terribly empty... incomplete...as if the most vital part of her entire being was missing. The pain of her incompleteness was sharp and raw, as if the wound was new.

"It doesn't matter," she gasped. "I don't care—I just want *you*. Please..." She muffled the plea in his mouth. Her hands sought his belt buckle.

"*Joy*—" He broke from her like a drowning man gasping for air. His voice sounded husky and pained. "Just a minute—I have to—I just remembered something. Be right back."

And just like that, he left her.

In the bathroom, Doug yanked open the medicine cabinet and scanned the contents with an avidness born of utter futility. Then he closed it again carefully, gripped the edge of the sink and leaned on his hands, closing his eyes against the unforgiving brightness of the light.

Nothing. He had nothing. Why would he? He'd never had a woman here. Never in his life had he felt such frustration and disappointment. It hurt. It actually *hurt*—physically. And it was still nothing compared to what he was going to have to do next, which was go back in there and tell Joy—

"It's not going to happen, is it? Between us . . ."

She was there in the doorway, leaning against the frame. She'd pulled the shirt around her but hadn't buttoned it, just held it together more or less in place with her folded arms. Doug swiveled his head enough to look at her, but didn't straighten up or turn around; he felt stiff and achy in every muscle and joint and sinew.

"Not tonight." He didn't bother to clear the ton of gravel from his throat. "I don't have a thing. I'm sorry." He could see the protest forming in her eyes and silenced it with a single upraised finger before she could open her mouth. "Look, I'm a cop. Nobody knows better than I do what the risks are." He turned back to the mirror and growled, "I won't. I can't. I'm sorry."

There was a little silence, one that seemed to scream with unvoiced anguish and frustration. Then Joy cleared her throat and in a very low voice said, "You probably won't believe me, but for what it's worth, I haven't been with anybody since high school. And I've never done drugs, so . . ."

He jerked himself around, vibrating like an out-of-balance wheel. She wasn't looking at him, she was staring down at the floor, and her face, except for the blossoms of embarrassment in her cheeks, was deathly pale.

"Joy," he said, and was amazed at how much it hurt his throat to speak. He tried it again, whispering, and that was better. "Joy, I do believe you." But she still wouldn't look at him, and he wanted her to. He wanted her to *know,* to see in his face and his eyes what he couldn't allow himself to tell her until after this whole bloody mess was over. "Hey..." he demanded harshly, "look at me."

Then all at once she did, and he wasn't sure he was going to be able to survive it. Her chin came up and her eyes were glowing like old brandy, but her mouth looked soft and bruised, like overripe fruit. That combination of fight and vulnerability—it got to him every time. "Joy," he said huskily, in a voice that shook with entreaty, "of course I believe you. Dammit, don't you understand? It's you I'm trying to protect."

Her face lost all remaining color. "You don't mean you—"

He shook his head and drove a distracted hand through his hair. "For Pete's sake, Joy, a long time before there was AIDS there was another good reason for using condoms."

"Oh." It was a soft little intake of breath. The expression on her face was indecipherable and to Doug, utterly mystifying. She looked at him for a long time, and although he could almost see the wheels turning inside her head, he couldn't for the life of him interpret what she was trying to say to him with her eyes. He watched, helplessly in suspense, while she struggled with it, and then, just when he thought she wasn't going to take a shot at telling him at all, she cleared her throat and said, "But what if—"

"Cops! Hide the stuff! It's a raid!"

"Jeez—Maurice." Nerves jangling, Doug began to swear vehemently. The bird did have the worst possible timing.

Then all at once he froze. Joy had uttered a squeak of nervous laughter; he held up a hand and put his finger to his lips to silence her, then dove past her and hit the light switch. He listened, ears straining, but all he could hear was the rain.

"Raid! Raid! Hide the stuff!"

"What—"

"Hush—someone's out there." Doug had already snatched his gun and belt off the towel rack. Now he grabbed Joy's arm and shoved her bodily through the door.

"Let's go—keep down, away from the windows. Move, *move.*"

On the way through his darkened bedroom he snatched an armful of clothing from the pile on the chair, hoping and praying it was the jacket and shirt he'd just taken off, or at least something like it. Thank God, he thought, that things hadn't gone any further than they had—at least he still had his pants and shoes on.

In the hallway he felt Joy's hesitation. "Forget the damn cat," he growled. "Let's go—and for God's sake, keep *down.*" He stopped dead in the living room doorway and threw out an arm like a barricade. "*Listen.* Look there...."

Even in the darkness Maurice's cage was plainly visible, silhouetted against the lighter rectangle of the window. So was Maurice. And even in silhouette it was plain to see that he was staring intently at the front door.

Doug could see it, too, now, gleaming dully in the reflected light from the window. The doorknob was slowly turning.

Chapter 12

From the way Joy's arm had suddenly tensed in his grasp he knew she'd seen it, too, and silently blessed the instincts that kept her silent. Although the fact was, with the racket Maurice was making, it was unlikely anybody would have heard even if she'd screamed bloody murder. So while he was sending up thank-you-Gods, he added an especially heartfelt one for the providence—or preoccupation—that had made him forget to cover Maurice's cage tonight.

After that, there wasn't much time for any kind of thinking.

"Kitchen," he hissed, and gave Joy's arm a yank, aiming her in the right direction.

Since he expected in the next instant to have his front door bang open and then to die in a burst of machine-gun fire, he knew it must be pure adrenaline that carried him, with Joy in tow, through the house and out the kitchen door. And it was gratifying to discover that he could move so quickly, even pushing forty.

But while he was running headlong down the backstairs he felt a surge of something that was much more than just adrenaline rush. It was part exhilaration, part rage, and a primitive, purely instinctive call to battle. What was he doing, dammit? He was a *cop,* he wasn't supposed to run away from the bad guys!

But of course that was crazy thinking. First, there was Joy. He was responsible for keeping her alive—that was his number-one priority—and he still had a vivid memory of that arch of bullet holes across the front of her house in San Diego, and the sound of the machine-gun barrage that had almost killed her. And while he'd have given just about anything to know who was on the other side of his front door right now, he also knew that this was no time to be playing cops and robbers without any backup. No doubt about it, these guys meant business. And why not? he thought grimly. If what he suspected was true, somebody had an awful lot to lose.

Going through the laundry room, Joy pulled loose from his grasp. "Clothes," she gasped. "I don't ... have anything—"

He grabbed his raincoat and tossed it to her. "Here—put this around you." While she was doing that, he took the moment to buckle on his gun belt. Then, thinking of her jeans, he snatched them out of the dryer, rolled them up and added them to the bundle of clothing already tucked under his arm. "Come on," he rasped, taking a good grip on her elbow, "let's get out of here. You can put 'em on in the car."

The garage was damp and cold; the rain seemed closer, louder, wetter. Doug heard Joy's sharp hiss as her feet touched the bare concrete floor and remembered belatedly that she wasn't wearing shoes, either.

Ah, well, it couldn't be helped. And it wasn't all that important, considering the fact that in a very few minutes, depending on what was waiting for them outside that garage door, they would very likely be dead, anyway.

He opened the car's back door and half helped, half shoved Joy inside. "Don't shut it," he growled at her. "Wait until the last minute."

His keys were already in his hand. He slid in behind the wheel, stuck the key in the ignition and turned it, then counted the longest eight seconds of his life until the coil heater light went out. He turned the key farther and the engine fired.

"Old Faithful," he muttered to himself in gratitude, thinking about what Joy had said about naming the old car. Why not? Old and faithful she truly was, even if a little slow and creaky on the hills.

"Get down," he snapped at Joy, who had hitched herself up to look over the back of his seat. "Shut your door and *stay down.* Don't get up for anything, understand?" She nodded and dropped out of sight.

"Okay...here goes nothin'," he muttered grimly, and hit the garage-door-opener button.

"What do you suppose he's been doing up there so long?" asked Daisy, scowling through the rain-washed windshield of Mary's Bronco.

Preacher ducked down so he could see better. "He's picking the lock, that's what he's doing."

"No!" Daisy turned to look at him in disbelief. "Preacher, you know you can't see nothing from this far away, in this blinkin' rain. How you know that's what he's doin'?"

Preacher reared back, looking gravely affronted. "And who, I ask you, should know better than I? The cop's got a deadbolt lock, that's why it's taking so long. But he's picking it, no doubt about that."

"I thought you said the guy was some kinda friend."

"So it appeared, Mrs. Pepper, so it appeared.... Although I must say—oops, there he goes. He's done it, he's in."

"Look there," said JoJo suddenly, reaching over the back seat to point. "Here he comes."

Two heads jerked around to see what he was talking about. Then all three watched in silence as the garage door rose slowly to emit a feathery tail of diesel smoke.

"Uh-oh, here comes trouble," said Daisy. All three heads swiveled, like spectators at a tennis match, in time to see the figure in the dark raincoat burst from the door at the top of the stairs and start down them in a big hurry. An unwise move, as it turned out.

"Ouch," said Preacher, "that looked painful."

"Told you them steps was slippery," sniffed Daisy. "Where do you s'pose he's goin' in such a hurry?"

"To get his car, I should imagine," said Preacher. "He does seem to be wanting that cop, for whatever—"

"Look!" cried JoJo, pointing again. Back came the heads, as if they were on springs.

The white Mercedes had backed into the street and was now headed downhill away from them, picking up speed. They barely had time to catch a glimpse of the pale face looking back at them through the rear window.

Preacher and Daisy looked at each other. JoJo was bouncing excitedly on the back seat. Then all at once they shouted in a joyful chorus, *"It's Mary!"*

"Mrs. Pepper," said Preacher in some alarm, grabbing for a good handhold in the vicinity of the dash, "what do you think you're doing?" Daisy had already started up the Bronco and was putting it in gear. "We can't chase them down in this—you said yourself, we're almost out of gas!"

"Shoot," said Daisy through gritted teeth as the Bronco bucked over the roots of a eucalyptus tree, "you can't tell nothing from a gas gauge, anyhow. Sometimes you can go for miles on empty. Way I see it..." There was a pause, and two simultaneous gasps, while the Bronco's muddy rear tires fishtailed on wet pavement. Daisy down-shifted like a trucker, then continued, "...Is that he's takin' our Mary someplace, and the only way we got a chance in hell of findin' out where, is if we tail him. We got no choice. Got to give it a shot. Go as far as we can. If we run dry, well...then that's that."

"Somebody's followin' us," JoJo announced. "Comin' *fast.*"

Daisy and Preacher looked at each other; in the excitement of finding Mary, they'd both forgotten about the guy in the dark raincoat.

It didn't take long for everything to click into place.

"Mary..." Once more they said it together, now in soft tones of dread. "It's our Mary he's after," said Preacher, nodding somberly. "Not the cop."

Daisy was watching the rearview mirror. "He sure does want by," she said grimly. "But he ain't gettin' there. Not on this street, he ain't."

It got very quiet in the Bronco. Up ahead, the taillights of the Mercedes winked out around a bend in the narrow street. Behind them, headlights loomed huge and bright. A horn blared angrily.

"Speed up a little," Preacher urged. "We're almost to the bottom of the hill. If we don't see which way they turn..."

Daisy nodded, her eyes still glued to the rearview mirror. She pressed down on the gas pedal. The Bronco coughed, wheezed ... and began to slow down.

"Uh-oh," said JoJo dolefully. "Outta gas."

They were approaching Franklin; the street was leveling out. Up ahead a traffic light blinked a blurry green. The Bronco had slowed to a crawl when Daisy suddenly looked over at Preacher and grinned. Then she stomped down hard on the brake and yanked the steering wheel to the left. The rear tires slewed giddily in the syrup of mud that had washed down the hill in the rain. The Bronco came to a dead stop crossways in the street, blocking it completely.

Preacher let his breath out. "Well done, Mrs. Pepper."

Daisy nodded. They watched the white Mercedes turn left at the light and disappear into the rain.

"Hey," said Mary, "that looked just like my car!"

MacDougal jerked around to look at her, then quickly faced front again. "*Get down!* What in the hell—didn't I tell you to get down and stay down? What are you trying to do? Are you trying to get yourself killed?"

"I'm sorry." But she was only momentarily contrite. "It did, I'm telling you. I'd swear that was my car back there."

"What, a maroon Bronco? Do you have any idea how many maroon Broncos there are in this town? Every other one ever made must have been painted that color. Come on..."

"But—" It hadn't just been the car. She'd have sworn she'd recognized . . . but that was simply not possible. Of course MacDougal was right, it was a very popular, very common kind of car. Like a tan Ford sedan.

"Well, anyway," he said on a heavy exhalation, "I think we lost 'em at that light." Mary could see his eyes in the rearview mirror. They were hard and steely, like his voice. "For now." He gave her another quick, over-the-shoulder glance. "Get yourself into those jeans. I'm going to pull over here in just a minute. . . ."

The words were barely out of his mouth when he suddenly moved over into the right lane and made a quick turn onto a street lined with apartment buildings. Halfway down the block he found an open space in front of a driveway, eased into it and cut the lights, leaving the motor running. Turning half around in his seat, he snapped, "Hand me a shirt, will you? I hope—there ought to be one in that pile somewhere."

She found a shirt and handed it to him. "It's kind of wrinkled."

"Yeah, I know. Give me a hand, will you?"

He had one arm in a sleeve. She helped him pull the shirt across his shoulders and locate the other sleeve hole, then tugged and folded the collar into place around his neck. His skin felt smooth and warm and moist, and smelled of something musky and male, and vaguely familiar.

Oh, yes. *His jacket.* She remembered the way he'd dropped it around her shoulders that terrible night after the shooting, remembered the way it smelled—like him, she'd thought then, something uniquely MacDougal—and the way it had made her feel, comforted and safe. A little while ago that same smell had filled her nostrils, the taste and feel of MacDougal had filled all her senses, and feeling safe had been the furthest thing from her mind. . . .

She closed her eyes and clamped down hard with her teeth on her lower lip while her stomach did a flip-flop, as if she were in a boat riding a hard swell.

"That should do it," MacDougal said as he leaned forward in order to pull the shirt down, in the process subtly evading her touch. He threw her a gruff "Thanks," then a grudging look. "You want to stay back there, or get up here in front?"

"I'll get...up there." She didn't add, *With you.* He's angry with me, she thought miserably as she opened her door and dove into the rain—and about half a foot of muddy water that was racing along in the gutter. And who could blame him?

He barely glanced at her when she climbed into the front seat, sniffing and wiping rain from her face. She slammed her door, and he turned on the headlights and put the car in drive. "Buckle up," was all he said as he pulled into the street and headed south, toward Melrose.

There was quite a bit of traffic, considering the weather and the time of night, but then, that was Hollywood. The streets of Hollywood were never quiet, no matter what. Once upon a time, Mary remembered, that had been one of the things she'd liked best about it. *Tinseltown.* But it's all changed, she thought as she watched the gaudy lights dance and shimmer on the wet sidewalks and pavement, reminding her of a movie marquee in a rundown town.

Or maybe it was only she who'd changed. *Maybe this means I've finally grown up.* The thought made her feel indefinably sad.

She looked at MacDougal, watched the lights play across his set features, highlight his grim profile in festive halos of gold and red and green. She could feel the frustration and anger radiating from him in waves that were almost audible—painfully so, like mike feedback. The tension made her jaws ache.

It was certainly unlikely that *he'd* consider her grown up. He knew she'd lied to him about...Belle. He thought she was stubborn and bullheaded and completely irresponsible. And silly, she thought dismally, remembering the business about naming his car, and—oh, Lord, yes—the SaladShooter. Plus there was the fact that she'd pretty much tried to seduce him. And very nearly succeeded.

She cleared her throat and said softly, "I'm sorry."

The look he threw her was dark and preoccupied. They were merging onto the Hollywood Freeway, just then, where the traffic was bumper-to-bumper and creeping along. "What?"

She threw a worried look over her shoulder, hoping to divert him. "Should we be getting into this? I mean—"

"One thing about a snarled freeway," MacDougal said with a dark grin, "is there's no room to maneuver. If we can't go anywhere, neither can they." He wedged the Mercedes skillfully into a center lane, then settled back and gave her a brief, sardonic glance. "Now. What are you sorry about?"

"Oh..." She coughed, then shrugged. "Everything. *You* know—getting you involved." *For lying to you.*

He gave a short bark of laughter. "I was already involved. I've been ten years involved. I'm the cop. I've been looking for *you*, remember?"

"Yeah, but I bet you never expected to get chased out of your house in the pouring rain."

"No." His profile was sharp, his lips a thin, sardonic line. "But then, quite a few things have happened that I never expected."

"I know." Chilled and miserable, Mary looked away, out the window. "I made you compromise your principles."

To her complete surprise, he burst out laughing—real laughter, warm and rueful. "Yeah, well..." He shook his head and said dryly, "The fact is, I've probably got more principles than I know what to do with, anyway. Growing up both Catholic and Presbyterian'll do that to you."

"Both?" She felt shaken by his mood turnabout, off balance and unsure.

MacDougal glanced at her, chuckling at the expression on her face. "Yeah, see, my father is—was—a Scottish Presbyterian cop, probably the only one on the entire Detroit police force. My mom's Irish Catholic, and the daughter of a cop, which is the only way they'd ever have gotten together. So when us kids came along, rather than fight about it they figured, well, the world's a pretty rough place, a double dose of religion couldn't hurt, right? So..." He shrugged. "I got both."

"Wow," said Mary. "Well, at least it doesn't seem to have done you *too* much damage." Aside from those darn principles, of course.

Then it occurred to her that if it hadn't been for those "darn principles," she and MacDougal would probably both be dead. It was a sobering thought.

MacDougal looked over at her in surprise. "Damage? That's kind of a strange thing to say."

She lifted one shoulder and said evasively, "Well, it can, I guess."

"I guess..." He gave a soft, nostalgic laugh and said, "Actually, you know, a lot of it was fun. The Presbyterians had this gigantic pipe organ, I remember. Used to fascinate me when I was little—sounded just like *Phantom of the Opera*. I guess that's where I learned to like Bach. And my Sunday School teacher—she was a kick. She was this little tiny thing with white hair and a sweet little voice, and she used to tell us these flannel-graph stories, you know, where you put cutout pictures on a board covered with flannel? Only most of the time she couldn't make 'em stick, and they'd keep falling off, and we'd all be giggling like crazy.

"And the Catholics—catechism was a blast. The priest wore a robe with rainbows and children embroidered all over it. And a bunch of high school kids with guitars used to come in and teach us songs. And they were always having fund-raisers—carnivals, potluck suppers, things like that. There were always lots of kids—lots of girls. Between those two churches, I had a very active social life."

"You had a happy childhood," Mary said. "Didn't you?" Too late, she heard the wistfulness in her voice.

Unfortunately, MacDougal heard it, too. And since traffic was at a standstill right then, he had time to give her a long, thoughtful look before he murmured, "Yeah, I did."

Rushing to divert him from the inevitable follow-up to that, she blurted, "I thought I wanted to be a Catholic when I was a kid."

"Yeah?" Traffic was moving again. MacDougal nudged the Mercedes forward a few car-lengths before he prompted in an interested tone, "Why was that?"

"I don't know, it just seemed like they had a lot more fun than... than we did. I probably got the idea when I was in junior high. The eighth grade was putting on this condensed version of *The Sound of Music*. I was only in seventh grade, but the teacher in charge asked if I would come and try out, anyway. I thought she meant for one of the children, or a nun, or something like that, you know? Only I got the part of Maria. Omigod, I was so thrilled. I really thought I'd died and gone to heaven. The songs were— I...*loved* the songs." She put her head back against the seat and closed her eyes, swamped with the memory. After a moment she began to sing softly. One of her favorites. But her throat swelled shut and she had to stop.

"Don't stop," MacDougal murmured.

She shook her head and whispered, "I'm sorry." And was ashamed to discover a tear making a cool, tickling trail down one cheek. She brushed at it furiously.

"What happened?" asked MacDougal gently.

"Oh... well." Mary cleared her throat and managed a low, neutral tone of voice. "My parents found out eventually."

"Your parents found out?" He flashed her a surprised frown. "You mean, they didn't want you to be in the play? How come?"

She shrugged. "It was against our—their religion. I knew that, of course. I forged my mother's signature on the permission slip, because I knew they'd never let me do it."

Oh, that's great, Mary, she thought. Let him know what a habitual liar you are....

"But—*The Sound of Music*?" He sounded as if he couldn't fathom it.

"I know. But see, as far as they were concerned, music was only supposed to be for the Lord. Hymns were okay— anything else was a sin. And as for dancing—oh, wow— now, that *was* a bad one." He was silent, apparently speechless, but she'd almost forgotten he was there.

She went on in a faraway voice, half to herself, "When I was in high school, that's when it really got bad. I wasn't supposed to go to dances, or the movies ... or even listen to the radio. The devil was everywhere." She laughed painfully. "And boy, was I full of it. Poor Dad. He tried his best to beat it out of me, and look what happened."

There was a long pause while Mary watched the cars creeping along outside her window. Then she drew an unsteady breath and murmured, "I've wondered, sometimes, if he did the same thing to my sisters...."

MacDougal said quietly, "You told me you didn't have any family."

She turned her head slowly to look at him and after a long moment said in a flat, dull voice, "I lied."

Doug didn't ask her anything more after that, although he knew he could have, and possibly even gotten some information out of her. He wasn't sure why he didn't, except that those two dismal syllables, and the utter hopelessness with which she'd spoken them, had affected him like a blow from a blunt instrument, right to his heart. *I lied....* How could those two simple little words make him feel so sad?

It wasn't the fact that she'd lied to him, not really. He'd known all along she was lying—had even come to expect it. It was what those words, in that particular tone and context, told him about *Joy,* about her family, her past—that was what he found so heartbreaking.

Which was another reason he didn't pursue the subject of her family right then. She'd already given him a lot to think about; he doubted if she even knew how much.

The picture he had in his mind of Joy as a child was becoming amazingly clear and vivid, considering how little she'd actually told him. Mary Jo Delinsky, a child full of mischief and joy, laughter and—most of all—music, whom the angels had somehow sent to the wrong parents. Amazing, how much it hurt to imagine such a child growing up in—what had she called it?—the kind of town everybody leaves, sooner of later. Somewhere in the South, he thought. Maybe Texas. Imagine such a child being raised by parents who would do their best to smother the joy and music in her soul, and when that failed, try to beat it out of her. No wonder she'd left. No wonder she'd never looked back.

But what a miracle she was—like a dandelion, he thought, that keeps getting trampled on and chopped to pieces, and still somehow keeps coming back to make flowers the color of sunshine, and fragile puffs of fun and hope and magic.

His emotions swamped him, making his eyes sting and his throat swell. It went with the territory, he supposed, this vulnerability, this terrible capacity to hurt for—and be hurt by—another person. He wished he'd known how painful it was to love someone…not that it would have done him any good if he had. He'd tried his level best most of his life to avoid finding out, and look where it had got him.

Traffic stayed heavy all the way into downtown, thanks to the usual rash of rain-related fender benders, but once he was headed outbound on Interstate 10, things started flowing more smoothly. By the time they hit Pomona, Joy was asleep. Around Ontario, Doug turned on the radio to catch a weather report, and found out that the forecast was for snow above the five-thousand-foot level. So he pulled off into a truck stop in Fontana to refuel and to pick up a set of tire chains.

That late on a rainy night, the truck stop was beginning to fill up with eighteen-wheelers, and the air throbbed with the muted thunder of idling diesel engines. For those same reasons—the hour and the rain—four-wheeler business was light. Doug filled up at the passenger car diesel pump, then parked near the entrance to the store and left Joy sleeping while he went in to get the chains and pay for the fuel.

While he was at it he bought a few essential grocery items—like orange juice and milk, bread, bacon, eggs, coffee, canned soup and toilet paper. It had been quite a while since he'd been to the cabin, and since he wasn't sure what he was going to find up there, he also bought a five-gallon container of methyl alcohol for his camping stove, some flashlight batteries and a box of matches.

While he was waiting for his total at the cash register, he couldn't help but notice the rack of condoms nearby. When the cashier said, ''Will there be anything else?'' he picked

one at random and tossed it casually onto the counter along
with his credit card.

"Gonna do some skiing?" the cashier inquired in a
friendly way, not even batting an eye.

"Naw," said Doug, "just a little R and R."

"Well," said the cashier, "you have a good eve'nin', now.
Be careful out there."

"Thanks," said Doug dryly. "I mean to do just that."

Joy was awake when he got back to the car with his pur-
chases. While she was using the restroom facilities, he made
a couple of phone calls. Then, since they were both hungry
and Joy couldn't go into the restaurant barefooted, he
bought four hot dogs and two large cups of coffee which
they consumed in the car with the heater on and the rain
drumming on the roof and sluicing in sheets down the windows.

It occurred to Doug that he hadn't eaten so much fast
food since his police academy days, and it came as a surprise to him that a hot dog could taste so good, smothered
in ketchup and mustard and sweet pickle relish. He'd left off
the onions when he'd noticed Joy wasn't having any.

It also came as a surprise to him to realize how pleasur-
able it was to be eating hot dogs with a woman—with this
woman—in a cozy, warm car while the rain poured down
outside and the windows fogged up. As crazy as it seemed,
under the circumstances, he felt good, being there with her.
He felt—rather guiltily—*happy*.

When he thought about it he supposed it wasn't *that*
crazy. He'd seen enough evidence of it in his line of work—
the incredible resilience of the human spirit. Time and time
again he'd seen people laughing in the midst of disaster,
finding comfort and even pleasure in small, simple things.
And what more simple pleasure could there be, he wondered, than watching the woman he loved eat a hot dog, and
laugh when the ketchup oozed out of the bun and dripped
onto her chin.

Especially when *her* laughter was so bright and conta-
gious. "Oops!" she cried, leaning forward just a little too

late. And then, only half chagrined, added, "Oh, man, look—I'm dripping all over your raincoat."

"It'll wash out," he murmured, reaching across the space between them to wipe the dollop of ketchup from her chin with his thumb.

She watched him with dark and luminous eyes as he carried the ketchup-smeared thumb to his mouth and licked it clean. Then she licked her own lips and swallowed, as if the food she'd just eaten hadn't been nearly enough.

With what seemed like a great physical effort she wrenched her eyes away from him and began to gather up their trash. "Well, that was really good," she said with unnatural brightness, taking great care not to look at him. "Okay, so what now? Where are we?"

Doug smiled. "One of the world's garden spots. Fontana." He was wishing it wasn't so dark, because he'd have sworn she was blushing. That thought made him feel young and wicked, alive in ways he thought he'd forgotten about. "It's on the way to San Bernardino. I'm taking you to a cabin I own a piece of up in Big Bear. It should be safe enough, for the time being. I hope," he added grimly as he turned on the Mercedes' ignition and waited for the diesel coil to warm.

"The one in the photograph." Her voice was neutral, so completely without expression that in a contradictory way, it *was* expressive. He looked over at her, but she seemed to be preoccupied with fastening her seat belt, so he couldn't see her face.

"Yeah, that's the one. Four of us went in together and bought it about... oh, five years ago, I guess. We sort of divvy up the year among us. You know how it is. Couple of the guys are really into skiing—it's right near Snow Summit."

"Do you ski?" It was that same polite, almost toneless voice.

"Me? A little, yeah. I'm not that crazy about it, though. Now, Mark Yamamoto and Jim Shannon—they're the nuts for skiing. They usually fight over the winter weekends. Jim can't ski himself, of course, not since he got his knee shot to pieces, but his wife and kids are all gung ho for it. In fact, I just called both Mark and Jim to make sure they weren't going to be heading for the cabin this week. With this storm, there's bound to be some pretty good powder up at the resort levels.''

Joy didn't reply. Doug turned on the headlights, put the Mercedes in drive and headed back out onto the rain-fogged interstate.

Chapter 13

The weather forecast was wrong. Doug noticed the first splotches of snow on the windshield at about 3500 feet, although it didn't begin to thicken up until they were well into the timber. Even then it wasn't sticking to the pavement, and he was beginning to wonder if he'd been premature about buying the chains. By that time, what with the steep climb, the Mercedes' top speed was no more than twenty-five miles an hour, anyway, and in spite of the weather, skiers in a big hurry to get to the slopes for the first snow of the season were whizzing past them as if they were standing still.

"Is she going to make it?" Joy asked at one point, sounding slightly diffident, as if she didn't want to hurt the old car's feelings.

Doug looked at her in surprise; she'd barely spoken a word since they'd left the truck stop. For the last several miles she'd seemed to grow more and more distant, watching the swirling curtain outside the car windows with an expression of wistful longing, as if those incredible luminous eyes of hers could see beyond it into a world of unspeakable beauty.

He answered her with a chuckle. "Old Faithful? Sure, she'll make it. Slow but sure, that's her."

She whispered, "You named her?" He could feel those eyes turning on him now.

He lifted a shoulder, feeling at once eleven feet tall and shaky as a sapling. "Well, not exactly." He cleared his throat. "Turns out she had a name all along. I just never thought to find out what it was."

"And that's it? Old Faithful?" She was smiling, for the first time in what seem like days—just looking and looking at him and smiling that wraparound, megawatt smile.

Hoo-boy, thought Doug. He just hoped to God she never found out what she was capable of doing to him with those eyes and that smile.

Not far beyond that they came to a roadblock with flashing lights and a sign that read Chains Required Beyond this Point. A highway patrolman waved him to the side of the road, then walked over and tapped on the driver's side window. Doug rolled it down, and the patrolman leaned over to get a good look inside the car.

"Sorry, sir, I can't let you go any farther unless you've got some snow chains."

"Right," said Doug. "Got 'em right here."

The officer didn't move away from the door. "Do you live in the area, sir? We're not recommending you go into the area unless you're a local resident. Due to the poor visibility, we are going to be closing the road here very shortly."

"That right?" said Doug. He casually took out his badge and showed it to the officer. "How long do you expect it to stay closed?"

"Depends on the weather conditions. At least until daylight." The patrolman was using his flashlight to take a good long look at Doug's ID. "Is this official business, Sergeant?" He was looking at Joy.

"Yeah, it is," said Doug. He didn't expect to be believed.

"Uh-huh," said the patrolman with an absolutely straight face. "Well, Sergeant MacDougal, if you'll just get those chains on, I guess you can proceed at your own risk. And

you have a nice evening. Drive carefully." He straightened
and went crunching off through the deepening slush to meet
the next set of headlights.

Doug rolled up his window. "Did you hear that? They're
closing the road. At least until daylight."

Joy nodded. They looked at each other for a long time.
Then, like a diver preparing to jump, Doug turned up his
collar, took a breath and murmured, "Well, I guess I'd
better get those chains on. Here goes." He opened the door
and plunged headfirst into the snowstorm.

Until daylight. While she waited for MacDougal to come
back, Mary found herself repeating those words over and
over to herself, like a mantra. Her head was saying, loudly
and insistently, *You have to tell him.* But her heart kept
pleading, *No—oh, no, please...I have until daylight.* Maybe
longer, if it kept snowing, and if the snowplows were late.
But at the very least... until daylight.

"Well—that should do it." MacDougal climbed into the
driver's seat, bringing with him a rush of cold air and scattering snow like a large, exuberant dog. White flakes dusted
his hair and the shoulders of his jacket, and his cheeks and
nose were cold-reddened and glistened with moisture. He
blew on his hands to warm them, then turned to grin at
Mary. Her heart turned over.

When and how, in such a short time, had his face become so familiar and dear to her? How was it even possible? Her throat locked; her fingers tingled with the impulse
to touch him. And in her mind, she did touch him...saw her
hand reaching, felt his cool, wet hair on the tips of her fingers, then his cheek, and the roughness of his jaw...felt his
big, cold hand cover hers, and his breath pool warmth in the
hollow of her palm. Again her stomach lurched and rolled
as if she were standing on the deck of a ship in heavy seas.

"You should have taken the raincoat," she murmured,
feeling too warm in it herself all of a sudden.

"Nah, that's okay. It's just brisk, that's all. It's not that
far to the cabin—we'll get warmed up when we get there."

He started up the car and they moved slowly onto the
road, the chains clanking and jingling with an almost fes-

tive racket. Even MacDougal seemed exhilarated, carefree,
very unlike the MacDougal Mary had come to know. Deep
in her chest her heart began to beat a slow, suspenseful ca-
dence, like a big bass drum.

He'd said it wasn't far to the cabin, but of course distance was a subjective thing in those conditions. It seemed
to take forever to get there. They couldn't go very fast, and
the road twisted and turned through a dizzying swirl of gray
and white that at times seemed to close in on them like a
curtain or a wall, more solid than the ghost-pines that hovered just beyond visibility. Twice they stopped while
MacDougal got out and floundered through the snow to
read a road sign.

Just when Mary was thinking, Oh, God, if we're lost,
we're dead, he turned the Mercedes off the road into a narrow space between towering sentinel pines, and they
crunched through thick, fresh powder to a bumpy stop.

"This is it," he said. "We're here."

And there it was, looming ahead of them, dark in the
snow—the cabin in the photograph. Just about here the
photographer must have stood, to snap that picture of the
four good friends.

Mary shivered suddenly, and MacDougal looked over at
her. "I'm going to leave the motor running while I unlock
and check things out. You stay here, stay warm." He
reached out to touch her cheek in a brief and unexpected
caress. Then he opened the door and once more dived into
the storm.

You have to tell him.

Mary closed her eyes. A shudder rippled through her like
a suppressed sob. No, she cried silently, clenching her jaws
until they hurt. No. Not yet. I still have a few more
hours... until daylight. I'll tell him then. I will. I promise.

She waited for him, her body tense and racked with shivers in spite of the car's efficient heater. It seemed to take him
such a long time, and time was so precious to her now.
When he finally did appear, taking shape like a phantom in
the swirling white, her heart gave a violent surge of relief
and gladness.

Oh, God, she thought, is this what it's like? She'd have walked barefoot through the snowdrifts to go to him, if that was what it took.

She actually had the door open and was preparing to do just that when he stopped her, laughing through a mask of melting snowflakes. "Hey, where do you think you're going? Stay put—I'm going to see if I can find you some boots." He was breathless with cold and exercise, red-cheeked and sparkly-eyed, full of that particular high-octane energy people seem to become infused with when it snows. He slammed her door shut and opened the back one, talking in short bursts as he gathered up the groceries he'd bought at the truck stop. "I've got the pilot lit...and the heater going. At least there's propane—don't know how much, but...we've got the camp stove in case we run out. I'm going to take this stuff in...then come back for you. Okay? Be right back."

The door closed on the cold and the howling wind, and she was left alone with her shivers...and with that very new sensation of *incompleteness*. She decided she didn't like it at all, feeling as if part of herself was missing. She felt naked and vulnerable, and vaguely resentful. She'd been self-sufficient for so long—and she hadn't asked for this! I don't want it, she cried silently. Take it away!

But then MacDougal's big solid form was there beside her once more, blocking out the storm, and she knew that, as terrifying as it was, she wouldn't have traded loving him for anything in the world.

"Couldn't find any boots." His head and shoulders filled the car as he reached across her to turn off the car's engine and remove the key from the ignition. Then it was *his* warmth that enveloped her.

"What are you doing?" she squeaked, grabbing wildly and instinctively for his neck as she felt his arms nudging behind her back and under her knees.

"That's right—put your arms around my neck. Hold on tight—upsy-daisy!"

Mary gave a squawk that was equal parts dismay and giddy delight as she felt herself being lifted bodily, swung upward and hefted like a child, then securely cradled in strong, masculine arms. It was a completely new experience for her. She'd always been a tall, gawky girl—probably hadn't been picked up and carried since she was three years old, if then, since her parents hadn't exactly been known for coddling their children. She found it unnerving, breathtaking, like the very first time on a Ferris wheel. Laughing and speechless, she hid her face against the scratchy wet wool of MacDougal's jacket and hung on for dear life.

It wasn't exactly easy for him, either. The ground was treacherous—snow over pine needles—and she didn't know how he managed to hold on to her *and* keep his footing. Several times it seemed certain they'd both go down in a pile. But then she felt him going up some steps, heard the hollow thump of his footsteps on wood, and she was being bumped up against a door while he groped for the knob.

"Put me...down," she gasped. "I'm okay now. I can make it."

"Shh, I've got it—hold on—*there*." The door gave and burst inward with their combined weight. They stumbled into the cabin in a flurry of wind and snow, half frozen, breathless and laughing.

He lowered her feet to the pinewood floor, but somehow forgot to let go of her. Instead, the arm that had been supporting her legs came up to meet the one that was already around her waist. And she, rather than releasing her hold on his neck, found herself leaning into him, drawn like a magnet to his warmth. She tasted the cold moisture of melting snow on his face, then the cool silk of his lips...the warmth inside...then liquid heat that seemed to pour all through her.

It was probably inevitable, Doug thought later—much later, when he could think again. They were like tinder-dry brush in a Santa Ana wind, just waiting for the spark. He wasn't sure whether he was the arsonist, or she; he only knew he couldn't stop it, even it he'd wanted to.

Wanted? What he wanted right then was simple. He wanted his woman, his mate, wanted to feel her naked skin sliding against his, her body feverish and pliant under him, wanted to bury himself in her softness and feel her heat close around him, and then to move with her to the rhythms of life in a dance as old as humankind. What could be less complicated? What could be more *right?*

Her wants were the same as his, he could tell; her fingers were tangling in his hair, her teeth clashing, tongue battling with his with the same single-minded purpose, as if she'd been hungry—starving—for a very long time. When he drove his tongue deep into her mouth, establishing once and for all his mastery and control, she made a sound low in her throat, a sound of hunger and desire that matched his own.

He felt her knees buckle, heard the throat sounds become little whimpers of need. So it seemed a very natural thing to do, to cast the impeding raincoat to the floor, slide his hands down over her supple waist to the lush swell of her hips, grasp her buttocks and pull her hard against him. Natural, too, that she should come to him with such a perfect fit, and wrap her legs around him.

Holding him in that joyful embrace, she tore her mouth from his and threw her head back, sobbing for breath. With a growl of primitive triumph and dominance he took her bared throat in his open mouth, exerting just enough pressure to elicit a soft moan of surrender before releasing her to rake his teeth along the sensitive cords of her neck. At the join of her shoulder, just above the collarbone, he closed his mouth over her fragile skin and sucked until she gasped and clutched at his shoulders. He could feel her breasts grow hard and tight, her nipples bead against his chest.

He began to think urgently about the need to find a place for this. Standing where they were would have done, but definitely as a last resort. Lying down was preferable, and although the floor wasn't out of the question, in the dim reservoirs of his reason, Doug remembered that they did have access to a bed. And so, without changing much about the position they were in, he began moving in the general direction of one of the bedrooms.

He was totally unprepared when Joy suddenly tore herself free of him and scrambled away across the room as if he'd just sprouted a second head, complete with horns.

"No!" she gasped with her back to him, breathing hard and visibly trembling. "I won't go through this again—don't do this to me again. I can't . . . I can't."

"Joy—" he croaked, cold and thick-witted with shock. "What—if you don't want to, just—"

"Don't want to? Don't *want?* Are you *crazy,* MacDougal, or just *dumb?*" She drove both hands furiously into her hair, then turned to glare at him, and he could see now that her eyes were luminous with unshed tears.

"Then . . . why?" He kept his voice low, treading carefully on unfamiliar ground. "Tell me what's wrong, Joy."

"What's wrong? What's wrong? The same thing that was wrong before, right? What's changed, MacDougal? What were you going to do, take me right to the edge and then leave me there, like you did last time?" She was sobbing in earnest now, dashing angrily at her tears as if they were an affront to her pride—which, he was beginning to understand, was exactly what they were. "Because—" She gulped wretchedly and whispered, "I couldn't take that again. I just couldn't. I thought I was going to die, dammit. It *hurts.*"

For a few moments Doug couldn't say anything. He'd never experienced such a tangle of emotions, and he didn't quite know what to do with them. Finally he cleared his throat and said stiffly, "I wouldn't do that to you again. Or to myself, either, for that matter. The last thing I'd ever want to do is hurt you."

"All right, then, I don't understand." She was hugging herself now, trying to control her violent shivering. He wanted nothing so much as to go to her and wrap her up in his arms, but he wasn't sure enough, yet, of his ground. "What were you thinking of, anyway, MacDougal? You—you're the one with all the principles, remember? The damn B-B-Boy Scout."

He began to chuckle, softly and ruefully. "Well, yeah, I guess I am." He reached inside his coat, searched his pockets until he found the small package he'd tucked away in one of them. He glanced at it, then said, "Here," and tossed it to her.

She caught it, stared down at it, then back at him, saying absolutely nothing while he waited, feeling as vulnerable as he'd ever felt before in his life. Finally, unable to stand the suspense any longer, he shrugged and said diffidently, "That's the Boy Scout motto, by the way. Be Prepared."

Her expression had grown wondering. "You bought these..."

"At the truck stop. Yeah, I did."

He could see her throat working while she studied the package of condoms in her hands. When she looked up at him again she had that wistful, hungry waif look on her face, that big-eyed, crushed-mouth look that always made him feel like he wanted to go to her and wrap his arms around her and keep her warm and safe from all possible harm. He'd gotten that same feeling, he now realized, the very first time he'd ever encountered that look on her face. He just hadn't realized then what it was, or how it was going to affect the course of his life.

He didn't go to her now, though, because he could still sense a certain wariness in her, and knew she wasn't ready to take down the barricades yet.

"I don't understand," she said finally, looking away from him, though not before he saw the bright bloom of color in her cheeks. "I mean, this doesn't really change anything, does it?" She looked back at him, reproachful and accusing. "You're still a cop, and I'm still...whatever it is I am to you. You still...I mean, I don't want to have to feel guilty about...seducing you, or something. What's funny? Why are you laughing?"

"Guilty," he murmured, shaking his head. "Isn't that supposed to be the man's line?" But he really didn't feel like laughing. He was walking slowly toward her now, gaining confidence but keeping his hands in his pockets so he wouldn't reach for her prematurely and ruin everything.

A few feet away from her he stopped. His throat felt clogged with gravel, but he didn't even try to clear it. So his voice came out sounding like a bad George C. Scott imitation. "Yeah, I'm still a cop. But see, what's changed is...what you just said. What you are to me. You're not just a witness in my custody anymore, Joy. I'm not sure you ever were. You're not just...somebody I'm responsible for protecting because that's my job. I..." He took a deep breath. "I care about you."

"You care about me." She said it dully, as if she didn't understand what he was getting at.

He pulled his hands from his pockets and threw them out in a gesture of exasperation and utter helplessness. "Dammit, Joy, I have *feelings* for you."

"Feelings." It was the same flat tone as before, but he could have sworn he saw the shadows of a teasing smile lurking behind the sunshine glow in her eyes. "What kind of feelings, MacDougal? There's all kinds of feelings—good feelings, bad feelings..."

She was right. He was being silly. And a craven coward. What was so hard about saying it? He drew a ragged breath and croaked, "Joy, I'm trying to tell you I've fallen—"

But she winced as if she'd felt a sudden and intense stab of pain, and came into his arms with a cry of what sounded oddly like contrition. "No," she whispered urgently against his mouth, "don't say it. Don't say it. Please—just kiss me. Hold me. I'm sorry. I'm sorry."

He felt rocked and confused, but he gave her what she'd asked for, kissing her long and deeply, until she sagged against him like someone who'd had too much champagne.

"Joy," he breathed fervently into her hair, "I want to make love with you. But only if you want it, too. You understand? No pressure—I'll just hold you, if that's—"

She drew back sharply and mumbled, "How much time do we have?"

"How much *time?*" He frowned at her; it seemed such an odd thing to ask.

She shook her head impatiently. "Until daylight. How long is it until daylight?"

"Uh...I don't know, what time is it now?" He lifted his hand above her shoulder and looked at his watch. "This time of year...probably three more hours, at least. Why?"

"Three hours . . ." Something bleak and desolate flashed across her face, but almost before he could wonder about it, she closed her eyes and swayed toward him, burying her face in the hollow under his jaw as if she were starving, and he a heaven-sent banquet.

"Yes," she whispered. "Oh, yes . . . I do want . . . to make love with you."

Until daylight. Her heart was so full of all that she couldn't say to him—overflowing with it. She felt overwhelmed, almost as if she were drowning in her own emotions.

"I wish we had a fire," said MacDougal, sounding slightly dazed. "I don't want you to be cold." He was holding her close, gently stroking her.

"I wasn't even thinking about that. I don't feel cold at all." She knew what he was doing—deliberately slowing them both down—but she didn't want him to. Time was so very precious.

"Then why are your teeth chattering?"

"Nerves." She gave a small, shaken laugh; she couldn't let him feel her terrible sense of urgency. "I think you're gonna have to calm me down."

"I don't know if I can. I'm in worse shape than you are. Oh, jeez, I just thought of something." He paused, one hand resting lightly on the nape of her neck. "Did you mean it when you said you hadn't . . . since *high school?"* She nodded, rubbing her cheek against the inside of his forearm. "But that's . . . got to be—"

"A long time. I know." She sighed and closed her eyes, smiling. "Hey, listen, don't worry about it, MacDougal. It's not like I'm a virgin. And I've heard it's not something you forget how to do—kind of like swimming, or riding a bike."

"Or singing," MacDougal murmured into her hair. His hands were moving again, stroking along the tendons in her neck. "You sure didn't forget how to do that."

She swayed; her head was beginning to wilt. "Just needed . . . to let it go. You helped me, you know."

"I did?"

She nodded. Her throat was full—those emotions again. Because she couldn't speak, she took his hand in both of hers and laid it against her cheek, then pressed her lips into the warm hollow of his palm.

"Joy..." His voice sounded choked. "I want to see you. But... I don't want you to be cold."

She opened her eyes and looked into his. "I won't be," she said huskily. "You make me feel warm. Always."

She let go of his hand and reached for the buttons on her shirt, but he intercepted her hands and moved them gently aside, and put his there instead. Her eyes clung to his as his fingers moved deftly and surely downward—it was his shirt, after all, they were his buttons, and he'd had some recent practice. Her breathing grew shallow, the barest flutter... not even enough to stir MacDougal's hair when he leaned down to kiss what he'd uncovered.

"I want—" she began, then softly gasped. He'd flicked one of her nipples with his tongue and she'd felt it much farther down, in the very core of her body. She hadn't known... Her voice grew thin and airless. "I want to see you, too, but... you have so many things on."

He reluctantly lifted his head and murmured, "I do, don't I?" He shrugged his shoulders free of his jacket while Mary helped tug it down over his arms, then tossed it over the back of the nearest piece of furniture, a worn, brown plaid couch.

"Your belt," said Mary, letting her hands rest lightly on it, but nothing more.

"Ah." The single syllable was dark and flat. He stepped away from her while he unbuckled it and laid it with care on top of his jacket. When he turned back to her he was unbuttoning his shirt, his expression rueful and uncertain.

Her heart turned over. "Now I am cold," she said in a bumpy voice. "You'll have to warm me up. Hurry—hold me—hold me...."

And then she was in his arms again, enveloped in his warmth, her breasts nestled in his chest hair, her heartbeat bumping frantically against his, and laughing with the exquisite joy of it. He kissed her with a kind of frantic impa-

tience she'd never seen in him before, deep, hard kisses that
left her dizzy and gasping. His hands roamed her body as if
they couldn't get enough of touching her, frustrated where
they met coarse fabric instead of soft, pliant skin.

"Yes," she whispered, "yes..." and clung to his neck
while he dealt with the button, and then the zipper of her
jeans. He pushed them roughly over her hips, then drove his
hands inside, next to her skin, cupping her buttocks briefly
before he shucked everything down and off, taking her
panties along with the rest.

And then she was naked, and felt neither cold nor exposed. She felt no shyness at all. She felt proud and strong,
and intensely feminine. It seemed only natural and right, to
be there with him... with MacDougal. This man was *hers*.
All that she was, everything she had was his, she wanted
nothing hidden from him, no secrets... no secrets.

A stricken cry burst from her throat. Misunderstanding
its source, MacDougal swung her up into his arms. Tears
squeezed from her tightly shut eyes as he carried her, trembling, to the nearest bedroom and laid her gently down.

"The bed's not made up," he whispered, bracing above
her on his arms as he kissed her tears away. And again he
seemed neither touched nor dismayed by them, but simply
accepted them as a natural part of her.

She laughed helplessly and shook her head. The bed
didn't matter; nothing mattered but to be close to him, as
close as two beings could be, for as long a time as she had
left. In a few hours he wasn't going to want her anymore,
and would probably wonder how he ever could have wanted
her. After that, *nothing* mattered. Not even whether she
lived or died.

Doug had forgotten the condoms. He went back for them,
disposing of the rest of his clothes while he was at it, and
even remembering to lock the door and turn off the light.
When he got back to the bedroom, he found that Joy had
already turned on the small lamp beside the bed and was
snuggled under the down comforter that lay on top of it, her
head nested in a pile of caseless pillows. Her eyes were
slumberous and soft, her mouth ripe and full. He won-

dered how it was possible for someone with a haircut like a
small boy's to look so *female* ... so lush ... so sexy.

"I wondered what was taking you so long," she murmured, feasting on him with her eyes and in the process
making him devoutly glad he wasn't prone to blushing. She
threw back the comforter, and he groaned aloud.

"Oh, boy," he said thickly, "you are...so beautiful." He
leaned on his hands and kissed her for a long time and
deeply, swirling his tongue over every inch of her mouth,
inside and out, glazing her with their combined essences,
until she moaned and began to squirm with impatience and
need. He pulled back reluctantly, feeling somewhat light-
headed himself, and sat on the edge of the bed. She reached
for his hand.

"Don't put it on," she pleaded. "Not yet...please, I want
to touch you."

Because there was nothing he could have denied her then,
he summoned all his willpower and lay back on the pillows.
As he stretched himself out beside her, she raised herself on
one elbow and put her hand on his chest, then he avidly
watched as it explored the contours of his chest, seeming to
savor the textures of his hair and skin as a blind person
might, or as if she could taste him with her fingertips. He
held his breath and prayed for self-control when her hand
started downward, following the thick line of hair down the
middle of his torso. But he had only so much control, and
no more.

He did let her put on the condom, though, and watched
her face while she did, taking great pleasure in her sweet in-
eptitude, and frank curiosity.

"Sorry," he groaned, staying her hand finally, putting a
stop to the exquisite torture, "that feels just ... too good."
He raised himself to kiss her, bearing her over onto her
back. "There'll be time for that later," he promised. "All
the time in the world. But for now..." He kissed her again,
deeply, and yet again, deeper still. "Honey, I'm afraid I'm
going to burst. I want to be inside you when I do."

She nodded, licking her lips, and mumbled, "Me, too. I
want you inside me."

He shook his head, rippling deep down in his own chest, wondering how, in such circumstances, she could still make him laugh. "I want ... I need to make you ready for me, sweetheart. I don't want to hurt you."

He could see that that idea had never occurred to her. Her eyes grew dark and liquid, and clung to his with total trust. She didn't say a word, just touched his lips with her fingertips. Her lashes came fluttering down, and she nodded. He wondered if his heart would burst.

Slowly, then, and with all the care and tenderness he possessed, he began to prepare her for his invasion of her body, knowing that, if she wasn't technically a virgin, after so long a time she might as well be. He thought of that, of all she'd missed, of all that she'd come to mean to him and how much he cherished her, and with his heart in his mouth whispered words of love and praise to her as he kissed her. With his soul in his fingers he stroked and caressed her, coaxing fire from the center of her body to its surface until her skin, every centimeter of it, was charged and sensitized.

She writhed and pleaded that she couldn't possibly stand any more, but he gave her more, anyway, using his mouth and fingers to draw liquid heat from deep inside her, until she lay limp and honey-glazed, drunk with desire. "Now ... you're ready," he murmured thickly, intoxicated himself.

Incapable of words, she simply opened her arms to him, and angled her body to make a place for him. He slid up over her, fitted himself to her moistened folds, and with the most exquisite care, eased himself inside her. So heated and ripe was she that she gave only the smallest gasp at the first intrusion, then a long, sweet sigh of fulfillment and pleasure. Her body arched languorously beneath his; her legs came up without his guidance, allowing him the deepest possible penetration.

He couldn't prevent a groan from escaping as he pushed into her body; it felt so good to him, he didn't know how he was going to be able to stand it. Firmly and completely housed, he paused, holding them both still while he counted heartbeats and fought for control. He felt her hands rake down his back and grasp his buttocks, and her body undulate beneath him. He whispered raggedly, "Joy...be still a minute, love...be still."

She nodded, but her body wouldn't obey. Neither would his. The ancient rhythms had taken them both.

"Joy—" he gasped, and then again, cradling her shoulders and head with his forearms and hands as he plunged into her. *"Joy...."*

"Yes...oh, yes—" She was sobbing now, her body rocked by forces absolutely beyond her control. Her face was wet with tears and sweat and the moisture from his kisses.

"Joy..." He whispered it with every kiss, until his jaws cramped with the effort of self-control and words became impossible.

She was breathing in whimpers, already far beyond words. He felt her body buck beneath him, her head and shoulders lift half off the pillows with unbearable tension. He wanted to soothe and encourage her, tell her it was okay and just to let it come, but it was all he could do to stay with her, hold himself together for her sake. And when she finally did cry out and clutch at him like someone tumbling over a precipice, he could only muffle her cries in his own mouth and try his best to hold her together while she shattered.

Then, oh, *then*... how good it felt to finally let go. With a groan he gave himself up to the same undeniable forces that had just claimed her, let them drive him to the same limits of endurance, then pump him dry, leave him limp, euphoric with relief, and utterly drained.

Chapter 14

She was shaking. He couldn't tell, at first, whether it was with laughter or sobs, but when the clouds of passion had parted to allow reason to shine on him again, he saw that it was both. He understood how that could be; he was in much the same shape himself.

"Joy..." He whispered it brokenly, cradling her head in his hands, kissing away the moisture on her cheeks, brushing it away with his thumbs. "Joy..." He murmured it to each eyebrow and eyelid, to the tip of her nose and to the corners of her mouth. And although he'd never been one for poetry, or expressing deep feelings in words of any sort, what he found himself saying to her next, for him amounted to a sonnet. "I know...that's not your real name. But...I think of you that way. I can't help it...because it's what you are. It's what you'll always be to me. You are...my *Joy.*"

She tried to hold back both the sob and the laughter, but it burst forth, anyway, a gasp, a liquid chuckle, a few more tears. She touched his face, gazing at him as if he were the sun itself, and whispered with the solemnity of a vow, "Then that's who I am...who I'll be...as long as I'm with you."

He sighed deeply and kissed her with so much tenderness it made her ache all over. Then he eased himself away from her and went into the bathroom, leaving her shivering and bereft. But in a few minutes he was back, stretching out beside her and pulling her into his arms, covering them both with the comforter. She snuggled into his warmth with a profound sense of *belonging*.

Oh, God, she thought, how I wish I could stay here, just like this, forever.

How easy it would be to pretend that it *was* forever....

She caught herself just as she was sinking into oblivion, and gave her head a sharp shake to wake herself. Mac-Dougal nudged her with his chin and murmured sleepily, "Hey, what's wrong?"

"Nothing," she whispered, squirming a little in the curve of his arm and chest. "I was just dozing off."

"That's okay...go ahead and sleep. I will, too...."

Her hand was resting on his chest. Slowly she drew her fingers through his hair, then tightened them into a fist. "I don't want to sleep. I don't want to lose—" her voice caught "—a single minute."

"Hey..." His fingers stroked her hair, his hand coaxed her face against his shoulder. "You're not going to lose anything. We're gonna have all the time in the world."

Fear settled over her like a heavy, suffocating blanket. She closed her eyes tightly and felt cool moisture seep between her lashes. "I just...don't want this to end. I don't...want to lose you."

She could hear his chuckle, deep down inside his chest. "Honey, you're not going to lose me, that I can promise you." His arms encircled her and tightened, and his voice grew harsh with emotion. "I know this has all been rough on you. But I don't want you to be afraid anymore, okay? I'm not going to let anything bad happen to you, lady. I don't want to lose you, either."

She lay silent, listening to his accelerated heartbeat and wishing with all her heart that she could believe that what he was saying was true.

He began to rub her back with long, soothing strokes, though she could tell by the way he held her that he was calming himself as much as he was her... fighting his own emotions.

After a while he said in a soft, somber voice, "We haven't talked about this thing enough, Joy. That's pretty much my fault. I haven't known quite... *how* to talk to you about it. How to get you to talk to me. And that's kind of funny, you know? Because it's one of the things I'm usually pretty good at. As a cop, that is. But see—that's the problem. I haven't been able to deal with you like a cop would. I realize that now. Right from the beginning of this, from the first moment I met you, I knew I didn't want to force you, or use pressure to get you to tell me what you knew. What I wanted—I kept hoping you'd eventually trust me enough to talk to me on your own. And the more I got to know you, the more feelings I had for you, the more frustrating it got that you couldn't seem to do that. Do you understand?"

Again his arms tightened around her; she could feel him quivering with the power of what was inside him, and what it was costing him to hold it back. "Can you understand how much it hurts to want so badly to help you...and know that you can't trust me enough to let me? God...Joy..."

She pressed her knuckles against her mouth and drew a ragged breath, balancing her voice on a fragile bubble of air. "It's not that I don't trust you. I want to tell you. I do."

"Then for God's sake, tell me. Just...*tell* me, Joy. Please. Let's put this nightmare behind us."

The entreaty in his voice pierced her like a knife. She pulled away from him and sat up, drawing her knees to her chest and wrapping her arms around them. Her voice came out through her tightly clenched teeth sounding low and sad and even, though inside she was screaming with pain.

"That's where you're wrong, MacDougal. You have this idea everything's going to be all right as soon as I tell you who killed Belle, right? But it won't be." She began to rock herself back and forth with a small, jerky motion. *"It won't be."*

Doug watched her in silence for a few moments, aching for her, for the struggle he knew she must be going through, the betrayal she must have felt. Her shoulders looked hunched and defensive, as if she expected blows; when he touched her, she actually flinched.

He began to rub her back again, gently massaging, while in a voice filled with gravel he said, "Joy, I know why you think that, but it's not true." Beneath his hand, her body had gone very still. He kept rubbing, stroking her with his love and reassurance. "Honey, I know why you don't want to tell me."

She turned her head to look at him over her shoulder. He saw her swallow hard before she whispered, "You do?"

"Yeah, I think I do. Come on, baby, I'll make it easier for you." His voice got rougher, rockier, but he forced the words out. "It's a cop, isn't it?"

For a fraction of a second her body seemed to turn to stone beneath his hand. He'd have sworn her heart, her breathing, all her life signs, simply... stopped. Then he felt her relax, grow warm and vital again. She let go of her knees and turned half-around so he could see her eyes, her lush and vulnerable mouth. She looked at him for a long time, while he held his breath. Then she smiled, a tremulous ghost of her usual radiance.

"Yeah," she said on an exhalation, closing her eyes as if in great relief, "You're right. It was a cop."

He should have felt a sense of triumph... of victory. But he didn't. Something wasn't right. He knew it. He could feel it... *hear* it. He was used to hearing what people tried not to say, listening to their slightest inflections, reading their eyes, their gestures, their body language, learning more from their silences than from their words. He was good at it, like a piano master with perfect pitch. He was hearing a sour note now, and it sent a cold chill down his spine.

He let go of the breath he'd been holding and swore quietly under his breath. Then he sat up and swung his legs over the side of the bed.

In an airless, frightened voice, Joy said, "Where are you going?" She was sitting up very straight with her legs tucked under her. He could see that her nipples were tight-budded and erect with cold.

He pulled the comforter up and tucked it around her, then kissed her and said gently, "It's getting light. I'm going to put on some coffee. Stay warm. I'll be right back."

"G-getting light?" She scrambled nimbly off the bed and came after him, wrapped like an Indian chief in the comforter and shivering violently in spite of it. "I g-guess that means they'll be opening up the roads, huh?"

He was rummaging in the closet for the sweats he usually kept there; he waited until he'd located a pair of bottoms without too many holes and pulled them on before he answered her.

"Oh, I doubt it—it's still pretty much blizzard conditions out there. I don't think they'd try to open the roads until it stops." He looked at her suddenly and frowned. She was dangerously pale.

"Hey," he murmured, reaching for her, "what are you worried about, hmm?" He opened the comforter and pulled her arms around his neck so that the comforter enfolded the two of them, and he could put his arms inside it and bring her soft and naked body against his. "You've got nothing to be afraid of. Don't you know that? You're safe now... here with me. We just have to figure out exactly where we take things from here, that's all. But first—" He kissed her and put her reluctantly aside. "First, I'm going to make us some coffee and something to eat. Okay?"

It wasn't okay, and they both knew it. He was talking to her the way he would to a distraught victim. He could feel the tension in her—tension and fear. Something... *something* was still eating Joy alive.

He didn't understand it. He tried his best to put it out of his mind, at least for the moment, but he knew he wasn't through with this thing. Not yet. It wasn't over.

It was much warmer in the main part of the cabin, thanks to the propane wall heater in the living room. He left Joy curled up on the couch, cocooned in the comforter, while he filled the coffee maker, put a couple of slices of bread in the toaster oven and broke eggs into a frying pan. He was layering bacon on paper towels to go in the microwave when he heard Joy's throaty chuckle.

"Boy, you guys really rough it up here, don't you?"

"Hey," said Doug, tossing a severe look her way, "if God had intended man to live without electricity, he'd never have invented lightning—right? And life's sure as hell too short to spend it chopping wood. Besides—" he popped the bacon into the microwave and punched buttons with a flourish "—fires are pretty much a no-no up here, anyway. Too dangerous. Hey, how do you like your eggs?"

For the next few minutes he was busy buttering toast and tending the frying pan, filling two red plastic picnic plates, looking for the checkered napkins and plastic-handled silverware that matched the plates. When he set everything down on the coffee table, Joy lifted her eyebrows and made an appreciative little murmur.

"This is a really nice cabin," she said, looking around, taking in the glowing knotty pine and ruffled window curtains. "Pretty, you know? Who fixed it up—you guys? You . . . cops?"

Doug laughed at the expression of total disbelief on her face. "No, not us. Carol Shannon did most of it, I guess. Jim's wife—you'd like her."

He went to get the coffee. When he came back, Joy was sitting exactly as he'd left her, regarding the plate he'd given her with all the enthusiasm she might have shown for a bowlful of kibble. Well, he thought, who could blame her? She had a lot on her mind.

"Hey . . ." he said softly, picking up a piece of bacon and passing it temptingly over her lips. "Eat. You gotta keep up your strength. Open up . . . here comes the birdie." She smiled and accepted the offering. He leaned over and kissed her.

"Mmm," she murmured, licking her lips, "I'll have some more of *that*."

"Later," he said sternly. "Food first. Then we talk."

She nodded reluctantly. He supervised her while she ate, making sure she polished off every last bite. Then he carried the plates to the sink and refilled the coffee mugs. He handed one to Joy, then sat himself down on the edge of the coffee table, thinking maybe that way he wouldn't be so apt to get sidetracked by thoughts of that gorgeous body of hers, separated from him only by a couple of inches of down comforter....

He leaned forward, holding the steaming mug between his knees, cleared his throat and in his most calming, take-charge manner said, "Now...Joy, I want you to tell me what happened. After you left Belle's apartment. Can you do that?"

Her eyes met his across the rim of her red plastic coffee mug with a look of such despair, such utter hopelessness, that he thought he might explode with fury and frustration.

Why? That was what he kept asking himself. What was it she was still keeping back, that was causing her so much misery? He wanted to take hold of her, shake it out of her—but he forced himself to remain silent...and waited.

She cast one terrible look toward the windows, as if she expected to see the Four Horsemen themselves come riding through the blizzard, then closed her eyes and sagged back into her cocoon.

"Well...okay," she said in a rusty-sounding voice, then cleared it purposefully and began. "At first, I guess I just ran. I was sure he'd come after me, and he did."

"You did see him, then?"

She cleared her throat again. "Yes, I saw him. He looked right at me. We both sort of froze, and then...I ran. I could hear him coming after me. I made it to the car—I had Belle's car, you know, because she'd been...when she left the club she was supposed to meet someone. Anyway, I got the car started and was backing out of the parking space, and he was right there. He...grabbed the door handle and tried to open it. I was terrified—I hit the lock and just kept going, and he, um...he pounded on the window. I could see him yelling at me through the glass. Then...he had to let go."

"Easy." Doug gently removed the coffee from her hands, which were shaking so badly he was afraid she might scald herself. He enfolded them between both of his and murmured soothingly, "So you got away. What then? Did you know then that he was a cop?"

She shook her head. "He was just...a guy. He wasn't wearing a uniform or anything, just a suit and a topcoat, you know? Anyway, I drove around for a long time—I don't have any idea where. I just know that when morning came I was down in Santa Monica, on the Palisades—you know, where the homeless people hang out? I didn't know what to do. I knew Belle was dead, and I had to call the police. I remember I had trouble finding a phone booth that wasn't out of order. Then, when I called, they already knew about it— I guess one of the neighbors must have heard the commotion and called them. I told them I...had information about what happened, but I was too afraid to move. I kept seeing that guy *everywhere,* you know? They said to sit tight, they'd send a car for me.

"So...I was sitting there on a bench on the Palisades, just looking at the ocean, and there was this homeless lady feeding the birds nearby. I remember hearing a noise, and all of a sudden the birds just...took off. Something hit the bench—it felt just like somebody'd kicked it hard. I sort of got up, I think, turned around...and I saw this car, and then I saw the *gun.* I couldn't believe it—I don't know what told me to do it, but I just dropped down flat, and I heard that noise again—kind of a *zing,* and then I heard tires squealing, and...the car drove away."

"*God.* So that was what happened." Doug let go of her hands abruptly and sat back, propping his elbows on his knees. He laced his fingers together, pressed his thumbs against his lips and frowned at nothing, concentrating hard. Something was hovering, just out of conscious reach...if only he could focus on it.

"You called again, didn't you?" he prompted her at last, giving up on it for the time being. "What was it, a day or so later?"

She nodded, then shrugged and looked away. He could see her throat working as she struggled to get the words out. "But first, I, um...I went to the police station."

"You did?" He sat up straight, staring at her. "When? You mean the Hollywood station?"

Again she nodded, her eyes dark and faintly accusing. "I wasn't sure what to do—I'd never been in a police station before, so I told the guy at the front counter I wanted to talk to somebody about a murder. He told me to sit down, and he'd call a detective to come out and talk to me. But I was kind of nervous, you know, so I didn't sit down, I was kind of pacing around and reading the signs and posters and stuff on the walls, getting a drink from the drinking fountain— you know how you do. And..." Her eyes slid away. "That's when I saw him."

"Him? You mean...the *guy?* The man you saw in Belle's apartment—he was *there?*" He felt cold...sick inside. So it was true. Someone he'd known, worked with, saw every day...someone he trusted.... "Who was it?" he demanded in a hard, flat voice. "Do you know his name? Would you know him if you saw him again?"

"I—" Her mouth snapped shut, just as it had done that very first night, the very first time he'd questioned her. She seemed to shrink from him, like an animal in a trap.

"*Dammit,* Joy!" His frustration boiled up and over. He flung himself away from her, hardening himself to the way she flinched when he did, as if he'd actually struck her. "I thought we'd gone beyond this, you and I. I thought we..."

He paced to the windows, rubbing with utter futility at the back of his neck. Of course she'd know the bastard if she saw him again—that was what this was all about, wasn't it? Somebody was very determined to make sure she never got that chance. Right now it looked as though he was the only one standing between Joy and that somebody, and he was fighting blindfolded. He didn't like the feeling.

Without turning or bothering to soften the edge in his voice, he said, "Okay, tell me what happened after you went to the station. You called again, didn't you?"

"Yeah." The word had a liquid sound. "I, um...asked to speak to the officer in charge of the investigation, but they said he wasn't available."

"That was Jim Shannon. He was out sick. You talked to me." God . . . who had he told about that meeting? Jim, of course—he'd asked to be notified of any and all developments in the case. *Who else had known?* He couldn't think. Dammit, he couldn't *remember.*

He didn't know how long he stood there at the window. It was a very small sound—a muffled sniff—that brought him back to the cabin, to the blizzard howling outside and the quiet desolation within. He turned and saw that Joy was crying without making a sound, the tears simply pouring down her cheeks, silently and unchecked. He wasn't usually affected much by women's tears, but these burned in his throat like acid. He gave a harsh, guttural cry, and in the next instant was beside her on the couch, gathering her close so that his chest, his hands and arms, his neck and even his face, were wet from her tears.

She kept trying to dry him off with a corner of the comforter, and saying "I'm sorry" over and over again—he couldn't quite fathom whether for soaking him or for something else entirely.

The first kisses were salty and wet and pretty much hit and miss, aimed at whatever part of the other's anatomy they happened to be within range of. But they rapidly narrowed in both focus and intent, so that when their mouths finally came together it was with little cries of relief and gladness, as if they'd been wandering, lost, and had at last found their way home.

Doug lay back on the couch and pulled her with him. Joy opened the comforter wide and let it drift down over them both, and in a matter of seconds her sniffles had become little snuffles of laughter, chuckles of anticipation, soft moans of pleasure and passion.

Amazing, he thought as she lay naked and full-length on top of him—though he'd seen it many times before—how thin the line was between such vastly different emotions . . . love and hate, fear and anger, desire and despair. Amazing how quickly one could become the other . . .

She wriggled downward under the comforter, hooking her fingers under the waistband of his sweatpants and skinning them off as she went, kissing him everywhere she could reach along the way, nuzzling in his chest hair, pausing to explore a flat, pebbly nipple with her tongue. He groaned and tried to halt her progress, but his protests, halfhearted to begin with, grew increasingly feeble as she came closer to her intended goal. By the time he felt her lips and warm breath stirring in the thicket of hair below his belly he was weak as a kitten, barely able to touch her hair and wheeze, "Joy... what do you think you're doing?"

She muttered something without raising her head, which he couldn't hear a word of, but which had a remarkable effect on him nonetheless. He threw back the comforter and croaked, "What?"

She looked up at him, shamelessly smiling. "You said I could, later. This is *later.*"

He lay back, swearing and muttering under his breath. And then it was her turn to say, "What?"

"I said, the damn condoms are in the other room!"

She tilted her head and inquired drolly, "How come there's never a condom around when you need one?"

It was, for Doug, a totally new experience—to be *giggling* at a time like that! Only with Joy, he thought, could such a thing be possible.

"All right—that's it," he growled, and hauled her up and over his body to where he could get his arms around her again. "A man can take just so much of *that.*" She was laughing and breathless and totally unsuspecting. Before she had any idea in the world what he was about to do, he had her over his shoulder in the classic fireman's carry and was striding with her into the bedroom.

After the first squawks of surprise and outrage, she remarked, "This isn't very dignified, you know."

He chuckled. "Yeah, well... neither is sex."

He was sure it wouldn't ever be with Joy. He knew that beyond a shadow of a doubt. It would be... fun. It would be wild, a whole kaleidoscope of emotions and sensations from the most deeply touching to the almost terrifying. It might be a kittenish romp through sunshine meadows, or a dizzying midnight ride on a roller coaster, or anything at all in between. The possibilities seemed limitless, and Doug knew he'd never wanted anything more than to spend the rest of his life exploring every single one of them.

She was so wonderfully uninhibited—that was what he found so extraordinary and delightful about her. Nothing dismayed or embarrassed her, which of course freed him of those handicaps, as well. Having decided to give herself to him, she simply gave it all, holding absolutely nothing back—in that respect, at least. For Doug, her physical and emotional openness made the contrast with that part of her she couldn't—or wouldn't—share with him all the more frustrating. It was a dull pain, like a toothache that he could just about manage to forget... for a little while.

To forget... for a little while. That was all she wanted. The blizzard outside—the whistling wind and swirling white—seemed to Joy like a curtain God had drawn between now and forever. As long as it raged, she didn't have to think about what lay ahead. She knew there might not even be a tomorrow for her, or any future for the two of them, but for now, for this moment, at least, they were together, and that was all that mattered. She wanted not to have to think, only to laugh; not to talk, simply to love. But of course, nothing about it was simple, and there was an underlying despair in both her laughter and her loving, as in those who dance and make merry on the eve of battle.

"Make love to me," she demanded fiercely as he laid her down, reaching greedily for him when he straightened and pulled away from her momentarily. She gazed at him from beneath passion-weighted eyelids, drinking in the sight of him as he towered above her, one knee braced on the mattress between her open thighs. He seemed huge... overwhelmingly masculine. Desire curled and knotted in her belly; reason went up in smoke, obliterated by the primal fires that burned inside her. She watched him put on the condom in a state of seething impatience, resenting it with a passion that was almost personal, as if it were a third person standing between her and the man she craved.

But then... Still kneeling over her, he hooked his arms under her knees, lifted and spread her legs wide so that she was completely open to him, then drove into her with one powerful, joining thrust. She arched and cried out, not in protest, but in gladness, in welcome, in praise.

She felt herself engulfed and enfolded, overwhelmed by his warmth and strength, his life's force, all that he was and that had attracted her to him from the first moment—only now it was so much *more*. Now there was the raw sexuality, the pure animal magnetism of male to female. And still more. Because now he—this man, this MacDougal—was *hers*.

He let go of her legs and laced his fingers through hers, pressing her hands into the pillows so that there was nothing to hold him back, nothing to impede his movement. She felt the gathering power in his muscles, the surging strength, and his quivering efforts to hold it back as he drove himself deep, deep inside her.

Her instinct was to close her eyes, but instead she opened them and looked straight into his, defying the raging fires she saw burning there. His features were suffused with passion, dark and fierce and unfamiliar to her, but she wasn't afraid. Something dark and fierce and wild within her recognized, answered and rushed to meet it, passion for passion, fire with fire. She felt herself calling to him from the midst of the flames, from the deepest part of her being, telling him with her eyes what she couldn't with words: *Oh, MacDougal, how I do love you!*

But . . . her eyes *would* close, and her body begin to throb and swell, and then to quake and tremble. She tightened her fingers convulsively around his and gasped, "Please . . . don't . . . let me—" But the rest was only sobs.

Dimly she heard him groan, felt him arch backward for a tense, suspenseful moment, then drive himself home, deep into her pulsing body, filling her up, completing her . . . at last.

I love you . . . I love you.

"Shh . . . I know, I know . . ."

Had she said it out loud? She'd hadn't thought so, hadn't meant to, but he was looking at her as if he knew, as if he'd heard her somehow. He was kissing her eyes, her mouth, her cheeks, her throat, and then his arms were around her and they were rolling over and holding on to each other, and laughing in sheer relief.

"Oh, man," MacDougal said a long time later, still sounding dazed. "You are really something, you know that?"

"So are you..." She felt groggy, utterly sated.

But he shook his head. "I'm nothin' special. But you... God, when I think about what you've been through..." His arms tightened around her. "What you've survived..." He nudged her head with his chin. "How did you, by the way? That's something I've been really curious about. What in the world did you do, all those years? How did you manage to drop off the face of the earth like that? I'm a pretty good detective, lady, and I mean to tell you, I tried *real* hard to find you."

She drew a long, shaky breath, then laughed softly. "Well, of course, the first thing I did—after I got shot at the second time—was... I had to find some clothes."

"Clothes?" He lifted his head off the pillows in order to look at her.

To make it easier for him, she raised herself on one elbow. "Think about it, MacDougal. I was pretty conspicuous at that point. I was wearing a dress with *sequins,* for Pete's sake."

"Sequins?" His body shook with laughter. "No kidding?"

"I'd been singing at the club, remember? And I couldn't very well go back to the apartment after... what happened." She paused. "Do you really want to know what I did?"

"Yeah," he said, "I do."

She snuggled back down in the circle of his arm. "Well, okay. After I got shot at the second time, I kind of got mad—"

"That," said MacDougal with a wry chuckle, "I can believe."

"Hey—be quiet. Anyway, I knew I had to get rid of the car, so I drove down to the garment district and parked it, and left the keys in it—stop laughing, MacDougal. That's what I did, okay? Then I bought some clothes at the Alley—you know that place where all the junk that nobody wants winds up? Just a pair of jeans and a couple of shirts, some shoes and underthings. After that I didn't have much money left, but I wanted to get as far from L.A. as I could, so I walked to the Greyhound bus station and bought a ticket to Oxnard."

"Oxnard? Why Oxnard?"

She shrugged. "It was one of the next buses leaving, and I didn't have enough money to go to Bakersfield, I guess. Anyway, it turned out that almost everybody on the bus spoke Spanish—they were all Mexican migrant workers—probably half of them illegals. It was February. They were all going to Oxnard to pick strawberries."

"Ah . . ." said MacDougal on a long exhalation. "Strawberries."

"Yeah. Well, that's what gave me the idea. I had a pair of nail scissors in my purse, and . . . when I got off the bus, the first thing I did was, I went into the restroom and cut all my hair off."

"God . . ."

She smiled. "All that Hollywood hair." She was silent for a little while.

Then she raised herself on her elbow again and looked somberly down at him. "So that's how I did it, MacDougal. I became an illegal—an undocumented worker. There's a whole subculture of them in this country, you know. Back then it was fairly easy to find work. I picked strawberries, lettuce, celery—you name it. I also worked as a domestic, when I could. Every time it looked as though the INS was about to close in, I'd move on. The last time it happened was about three years ago, down in San Diego. I almost got caught in an INS raid, and I thought, it had been such a long time, you know—and I'd saved up some money. So I took a chance and applied for a name change on my social security card, got a driver's license, got the job at Saint Vincent's . . . rented the duplex, bought the Bronco. Even got a cat."

She sighed and lay back down, this time with her head on MacDougal's chest. "For a while it seemed like . . . life was almost normal."

"Normal!" He snorted, and for a moment she thought he must be angry. "Why didn't you ever try to contact us again? For God's sake, Joy, you saw someone kill your friend. How could you stay silent all those years? That's what I can't understand. I know it must have been a shock, finding out the killer was a cop, but—"

"But they said I did it! It was in all the newspapers, on TV, *everywhere*. Who was going to believe *me*? It was my word against a cop's. Who would believe a cocktail waitress, huh? *You* tell me, MacDougal—who would you believe?"

He didn't say anything, but after a while began stroking her hair again, combing it gently away from her face with his fingers. Finally he drew a long, uneven breath and asked softly, "What about your family?"

"My family?" She said it on a bright little hiccup of unexpected pain.

"Yeah—you never went to them for help?" She shook her head and went on shaking it while he asked the other questions. "Never even called them? They never knew what was happening to you? Jeez, Joy, why not? I can't believe—"

"What I said to you was true." She pulled away from him and sat up, drawing in her knees as she had before, hugging them against the aching place in her heart. "I don't have a family. Not anymore."

"What the hell are you talking about? Did something—"

She gave her head a shake and looked back at him across her shoulder, trying her best to smile. "No, nothing happened to them, MacDougal. They just decided they didn't want me, that's all. Finally got fed up with their black sheep, I guess. Kicked me out of the family—end of story. When I left home, my daddy told me I couldn't come back, and he meant what he said. I called a few times, after I got to California, but they'd just hang up on me. Then one day, my little sister answered the phone. The oldest of the little ones—Sarah. I think she was...let's see, she would have been twelve at the time. And she, um...." She tried to laugh, but it just wouldn't come. After so long, she was amazed at how much it still hurt. She turned quickly away from the dark compassion in MacDougal's gaze and finished in a whisper. "She told me she didn't have a sister named Mary anymore. I pretty much got the message then, you know?"

MacDougal was muttering to himself, quietly and vehemently swearing. She straightened her back and drew a short, calming breath before she looked at him again. She even managed to smile.

"That's okay. It is, you know. In a way, I guess it was a good experience for me. I had to grow up pretty fast, and I really did learn a lot from the homeless people, the illegals. About...*you* know, survival. And about what's really important."

"And?" he murmured. "What's that?"

"Oh, food, shelter—that has to come first. That's just pure instinct—survival, you know? You can't deny your basic needs. Then...friends, I guess, people who care about you. And after that, a lot of little things. You appreciate things like sunshine. Flowers. Kindness. Babies. A nice shady tree."

"What about love?" MacDougal's voice was gravelly. "That's not important?"

She shook her head somberly. "That's a luxury—the man-woman kind, anyway. The other kind, though—the friendship kind—I guess you can't survive very long without that. Passion, romantic love—that you can't depend on. It sometimes goes away, you know? Lovers will let you down. Friends never..." Her voice broke unexpectedly. She rolled away from him and fled to the bathroom.

"Preacher," yelled Daisy, "what are you doin' in there? Come on outta the kitchen."

Preacher's voice floated back to her, suspicious in its innocence. "Just checking, Mrs. Pepper...just checking. Our

Mary's policeman friend does seem to keep a well-stocked larder... including a goodly supply of nice cold—"

"You ain't drinkin' the cop's beer. Now get your rosy nose outta that icebox. We agreed on it—we don't touch nothin' unless it's absolutely necessary."

"I'm gettin' hungry," said JoJo. He was lying flat on the floor with the Siamese cat recumbent on his chest, posed like a sphinx.

"Eating is a necessary function," Preacher pointed out, coming to stand in the kitchen doorway. "We've already disposed of everything we brought from the car. I don't think Mary would want us to starve while we're sitting here waiting for her to come back."

"Well... all right," said Daisy grudgingly, "I guess it's okay if we eat. But *no beer*." She was eying the cat, who was staring fixedly at the mynah bird in its cage. Every once in a while his tail would jerk and twitch, swiping JoJo across the face. "I think we better feed that cat, too, while we're at it. Maybe you shouldn't'a let him out, JoJo. I don't like the way he's lookin' at that ugly bird."

"Yeah, but he was makin' a lot of noise," said JoJo, looking worried. "I don't think he liked it, bein' all locked up like that."

"Yeah, well, *we* ain't gonna like bein' locked up much, either," said Daisy morosely. "We gotta be crazy, breakin' into a cop's house."

"We didn't break in, the other guy did," Preacher reminded her. "We're just... taking care of the place until Mary comes back, that's all. Kind of like baby-sitting." He cocked his head, pleased with the sound of that. "Yeah, that's it. We're *house*-sitting."

"Right," said Daisy. "Tell that to the cop." She took off her baseball cap and slapped it restlessly against her leg.

"What would you have had us do?" Preacher inquired matter-of-factly. "Wait in the driveway? It's raining out there."

"Yeah, I know. I just wish we hadn't had to go off and leave Mary's car like that."

"The car will be okay," Preacher said comfortingly. "The authorities have no doubt towed it off somewhere. I'm sure the officer will know right where to find it." He paused, rubbing at his beard. "I must confess, though, I am a bit worried about Mary. I fear she may be in serious danger."

"Yeah," said Daisy grimly, "No foolin'. And there's nothin' we can do except sit here and *wait.*"

"But she's with the cop, ain't she?" said JoJo, sitting up suddenly and looking from Daisy to Preacher and back again. "And he's a good guy, right? He's gonna take care of her, don't worry."

He smiled, which was probably what caused the mynah bird to go fluttering into a corner of his cage, yelling, *"Help! Help!"*

"He ain't gonna let nothin' bad happen to our Mary."

"I hope you're right," said Preacher fervently. "I do hope you're right."

Chapter 15

Doug woke Joy as gently as he knew how, brushing a kiss on her sweet, vulnerable mouth. And when she smiled and reached for him without opening her eyes, he chuckled and kissed her again, then told her the news.

"Hey, it's stopped snowing. Looks like they'll be opening the roads soon."

She opened her eyes and took her arms from around his neck. "It's stopped?" she croaked, already scrambling out from under the covers. "How—how long...?"

"Hey, take it easy," he soothed, laughing at her as she stood swaying tipsily, groping for support. "There's no hurry—it'll take the snowplows a while to get around to the side roads, anyway. Hey—come here, there's something I want you to see."

He wrapped her like a mummy in the comforter and walked her into the cabin's main room and across it to the front door. When he opened it, the cold made her gasp. He put his arms around her, enfolding her from behind, lowered his face to hers and murmured, "Now, look at that...did you ever see anything so beautiful in your life?"

She shook her head, saying nothing.

He filled his lungs with the sharp, clear air and sighed, "Ah...yes. I'm a Michigan boy, and I don't really miss the cold winters, but every now and then I do miss the snow. Especially when it's like this, all new and untouched." He nudged her head with his chin. "Did you have snow where you grew up?"

Again she shook her head. "Not like this." Her voice sounded rusty. The sound of snow falling from a weighted branch with a soft, plopping sound made her start as if she'd heard gunshots.

Realizing belatedly that she was shivering even in the down comforter, Doug drew her back and closed the door. He kissed her neck noisily and said, "Why don't you get in the shower and warm up while I fix us something to eat? I've had mine, but there should be plenty of hot water. Go on— I'll find you some warm clothes to put on. Not that I don't approve of what you're wearing, but..."

But she wouldn't respond, either to his teasing or the nuzzling that went with it. She seemed...mechanical, almost numb, he thought, as if she'd shut the vital, feeling part of herself away somewhere he couldn't reach.

So instead he found himself responding to *her* mood. Feeling increasingly chilled and uneasy, he guided her to the bathroom and went off to look for something for her to wear. He was already fully dressed, himself, in thermals and jeans and even an old pair of basketball shoes he'd found. He managed to scrounge up another pair of thermals that looked as if they'd fit Joy, and a sweatshirt to go over them, along with her jeans. Shoes were still going to be a problem, but he figured he'd fix lunch first and tackle that one later.

He was in the kitchen opening cans of clam chowder when he heard the scuff and thump of someone climbing the steps to the cabin's front deck.

He uttered a single, sibilant swear word and dropped both can and opener in the sink, crossed the cabin in an instant, pausing only long enough to slip his weapon from the gun belt he'd left lying over the back of the couch. Flattened against the wall next to a window, he fingered back the curtain the barest fraction of an inch and looked out. Then he said the same word again, this time along with a bit of wry laughter.

Feeling more than a bit foolish, he reached behind him and tucked the gun into the waistband of his jeans and pulled his sweatshirt down over it. Then he stepped over to the door and opened it wide.

"W-h-hell, hey there, buddy," he said as Jim Shannon stepped across the threshold, "what in the hell are you doing here? Didn't you get my message?"

"Message?" Shannon was smiling, but the smile seemed odd, somehow—stretched and frozen. He had both hands in his pockets and his shoulders were hunched, as if he was feeling the cold.

Doug closed the door behind him. "I called late last night. Wanted to make sure you weren't going to be using the cabin this weekend. Carol told me you were in Palm Springs."

"Yeah, I talked to her this morning. . . ." Shannon's eyes were restless, darting around the cabin. He shifted them back to Doug. "So—where is she? The Donnelly woman— I know you brought her here."

He was still smiling that fixed, frozen smile. Doug felt the first little frisson of warning go slithering down his spine. *Something isn't right here.*

He began to feel a peculiar sense of unreality, as if he were watching himself and Jim through one-way glass, watching them say all the right things, go through all the motions of normalcy, when he knew things were *not* normal. He just couldn't make contact with what it was that was so wrong.

He clapped Jim on the shoulder, laughed and shook his head. "What are you worrying about that for? Didn't they tell you? The first thing you've got to learn about being a chief is, you let the Indians do all the work. Hey, how 'bout some lunch—I was just about to warm up some soup. You look about frozen, buddy. How'd you get here, by the way? I didn't hear your car. They got the roads plowed already?"

Shannon shook his head. "I left it a ways back." His roving glance flicked at the door to the smaller bedroom, the one they hadn't used. Then it shifted to the other door, which was partly open. He indicated it with a nod. "She in there?"

"Come on," Doug said softly, almost pleading, "leave it alone, Jim. You don't want to get involved in this."

The smile stretched a fraction of a centimeter wider. "I *am* involved—you know that." His eyes suddenly narrowed and slid past Doug to focus on something behind him.

Doug turned, still with that strange sense of detachment, of make-believe, as if everything was perfectly all right. He saw Joy standing there in the doorway, wearing her jeans and a too-big sweatshirt, with a towel wrapped around her head like a turban, and he heard himself say, "Joy, there you are. Hey, here's somebody I want you to meet."

But he could see from the look on her face that she and Jim Shannon had met before.

The funny thing was, he felt almost no real sense of surprise. Only self-disgust, foolishness and utter failure. He wondered how long his guts had known the truth, and why in the hell it had taken his head so long to figure it out. Because it made such perfect sense, filled in all the blanks, answered all the questions. Why Joy had been acting so strangely, why she hadn't wanted to tell him . . .

Oh, God, he thought, how she must have felt when she realized *who* . . . so alone and helpless. He felt a terrible, crushing weight in his chest when he thought about all the times she'd looked at him with anguish in her eyes. *Who would believe me?*

Between a rock and a hard place—hadn't he said that to her, a long, long time ago?

And then he thought, but . . . it *was* a long time ago, dammit. They'd come a long way since then. Things had changed between them, hadn't they? After everything that had just happened, how could she not have trusted him to believe her? She had to know he loved her, didn't she? And she'd all but told him she felt the same about him. How, then, could she still not trust him?

The weight in his chest grew heavier. He knew that what he was feeling most was betrayal. But not by his ex-partner. Not then.

Damn you, Joy. You should have trusted me.

He held her eyes for one brief, agonizing moment, while all those things danced like lightning through his brain. Then he turned back to Shannon. Somehow he wasn't surprised to see the gun in his hand.

He even laughed. "I feel like I ought to say, '*Et tu, Brute?*' Jeez, Jim, what the hell *do* I say?" He lifted his hand to rub the back of his neck, but froze when the gun jerked and zeroed in on his belt buckle.

"Keep your hands where I can see them," Shannon said in the calm, expressionless voice of the top-notch street cop he'd once been. He nodded toward the belt on the back of the couch. "That yours?"

Doug nodded. "It's empty."

"Where's your weapon?"

"In there. Beside the bed."

"Good place for it." For the first time Shannon seemed to relax a little, smiling ruefully and with even a ghost of his customary charm. "I hope you know, buddy—I never meant to involve you in . . . my little problem. The last thing I ever wanted to do was hurt you. I tried my damnedest to get you out of the way."

He jerked his head toward Joy without looking at her, an almost negligent motion that chilled Doug to the bone, because he knew that in Jim Shannon's mind she'd ceased to exist as a person at all, if she ever had. She was just . . . his "little problem."

Shannon's smile suddenly twisted and became ugly. "It was supposed to have been taken care of down in San Diego—dammit, it should have been. I hired the best available. I still don't know how they missed. Then yesterday—you were supposed to be out on a case, man. I was monitoring the calls, I heard you and Burnside get the Mulholland Drive homicide. What in the hell happened? You weren't supposed to be there!'' His face was a study in anguish. For a moment Doug almost felt sorry for him.

He shrugged and said dryly, "The body got dumped on the wrong side of Mulholland. I left Burnside looking after things and came home early. Sorry."

Shannon puffed out air and shook his head, making an obvious effort to get himself under control. "Not half as sorry as I am, my friend. This really makes things hard. But I don't have any choice, you can see that, can't you?"

Very softly, Doug said, "Why, Jim?"

"Why?" The question seemed to enrage him. "How can you even ask me that? You said it yourself—I have too much at stake, too much to lose. You expect me—"

"No, I mean, why did you do it? Why'd you kill her?"

"Belle?" Shannon ran a hand over his thick, silvering hair, his eyes shifting away from Doug for the first time since he'd brought out the gun. He seemed almost...bewildered, as if he couldn't quite understand it, either. "Why did I kill her?"

"Yeah—was she blackmailing you? Was that it? God, Jim—I'd have sworn you were the cleanest cop that ever carried a badge. I'd have staked my life on it. What could she have had on you that you had to kill her?"

"Had on me? You think..." His face crumpled, and he began, horribly and painfully, to laugh. "No, no—you don't understand. *I loved her.* I mean, I really loved her, you know? Oh, man, I'd never thought I could feel like that, the way she made me feel. It was...all the poetry and popular songs ever written. I felt like a damn kid...."

"Then, why—"

He swiped his free hand furiously across his face and again seemed to pull himself together. "Because she was going to tell Carol, that's why. She wanted me to leave Carol and marry her."

"But if you loved her so much..."

Shannon looked at him as if he'd lost his mind. "I couldn't do that—are you kidding? Belle was...incredible, but she was hardly the ideal wife and mother type, if you know what I mean. Carol was the perfect wife for me, for my career—I knew that. Plus, she was—is—a terrific mother. You know what I think of her and the kids. I couldn't throw all that away, risk my whole future. I tried to explain that to Belle, but she wouldn't listen to reason. She insisted that if I didn't tell Carol about us, she would." He sniffed like a small child. "I couldn't let that happen. I couldn't."

There was a tense pause. Doug could see that Shannon was struggling for composure. He was conscious of Joy there behind him like a pale, silent wraith, and of the hard press of gunmetal, a reassuring weight against his backbone. But something told him it wasn't the right time—not yet. Not yet . . .

"It should have been so easy, so clean," Shannon said, sounding almost wistful. "I'd been careful, there wasn't anything to connect me with Belle. Nothing. Her body wasn't ever supposed to be found—I'd made arrangements for that. She was just going to . . . disappear. There'd have been a few postcards. She'd gone off with a lover, of course. No one would ever have known. But then, *she* came back." Again, chillingly, he didn't even look at Joy. "She saw me. Obviously I had to go after her, try to stop her. So I couldn't get rid of the body, couldn't even clean up the scene. After that, it was all I could do just to try to keep one jump ahead of the investigation. And all the time, I knew there was an eyewitness out there somewhere, just waiting for the chance to ID me." He ran his hand distractedly over his hair. "God, it's been hell—just *hell*."

"Bummer," said Joy.

She wasn't sure why she took such a foolish risk. She almost couldn't believe what she was hearing. She'd been standing there like a block of wood listening to this guy, this man she'd been so terrified of for so long, and she'd just realized something. She wasn't afraid of him any longer.

Maybe, she thought, that was what happened when your worst nightmares came true. There just wasn't anything left to fear. Or to lose.

In any case, the word just slipped out, in a voice that wasn't familiar to her. It sounded dry and derisive, and, judging from the expressions on the two men's faces, as shocking as if it had been the couch that had spoken.

She shook her head and made a soft, sarcastic clicking sound with her tongue. "Yeah, must have been rough, all right."

"Joy..."

She ignored MacDougal's hiss of warning, didn't even glance his way. She couldn't bear to look at his face, see that stark betrayal in his eyes. She'd expected it, of course, but nothing in the world could have prepared her for the pain.

She moved her cold lips into the shape of a smile. "I guess that's why Belle's dead, huh? And you're about to be Chief of Police."

"That's right. And I will be," said Shannon. He'd taken a step to one side in order to see past MacDougal, and to train the gun on her, now, and she could see that his eyes were hard and as cold as she felt inside. "That's why I have to do this. Doug, I'm sorry, I really am...."

Joy's heart stopped. MacDougal moved slightly, positioning himself once more between her and Shannon's gun. He spoke quietly, calmly. "Jim, it's too late. It's over."

"What the hell do you mean, it's too late? It's not too late, man, I've worked everything—"

"Lieutenant Mabry knows, Jim."

"Knows..." The gun in Shannon's hand jerked; Joy saw it appear, then disappear again behind MacDougal's baby-blue UCLA sweatshirt. Then he laughed. "You're lying. You didn't have a clue, you know you didn't. So how could you tell Mabry?"

"She knows it's a cop, one of the investigation team. The two of us turn up dead, you think she won't put two and two together? Think about it, man—don't make things worse than they already are. It's *over*."

"No—no," Shannon was shaking his head, still smiling and sure of himself. "No, see, you don't understand. I've got this all set up. I have an airtight alibi. Right now I'm in Palm Springs. And when they find you two, both shot with your weapon—"

"Won't work," said MacDougal. "Why would I kill the witness if I'm gonna kill myself, anyway? Come on, you can do better than that."

Shannon shrugged. "Love makes people do some pretty terrible things—ask me, I know. Hey—it's common knowledge you've been obsessed with the Donnelly woman since day one. I can certainly testify to that."

He was looking thoughtfully around the room. "You know, you're right, though. I think I can do better."

Come on, now! Joy directed the thought like a laser beam at the back of MacDougal's head. What was the matter with him? Why wasn't he going for it while he had a ghost of a chance?

Then the truth hit her. He was afraid to risk it because of *her.* She felt clammy and sick with unspent adrenaline.

"You!" The gun was waggling again, pointed at Joy. "Over here, Donnelly. Doug, don't do anything stupid. I *will* shoot you if I have to, you know I will."

Joy edged into the room, slipping past MacDougal, close enough to feel the power and tension radiating from his body in almost visible waves, like heat. She was careful not to look at him. She didn't dare look at him, especially not his face... his dear, open face and dark, intelligent eyes, composed now of granite and steel....

"All right," Shannon barked at Joy, still looking at Doug, "now, pick up the can." He grinned. "Good for you, partner, you remembered to bring alcohol for the backup heater. You really came prepared, didn't you?"

"That's me," said Doug. "A regular Boy Scout." If he hadn't been watching Joy so intently he might not have seen the tiny movement she made—just the smallest flinch, the slightest change in the angle of her head. She'd heard him, he was sure of it. Heard his message—*Be Prepared.* Be prepared for his signal. God, he thought—prayed—I hope I'm not wrong.

Look at me, Joy. Please. Look at me.

But she didn't. In an agony of suspense he watched her unscrew the cap to the can of alcohol and begin sprinkling it over the couch, the rug, the floor, following Shannon's instructions like an automaton. Had he been wrong, after all? Maybe she hadn't understood. And he was running out of time!

He watched her move closer and closer to the propane heater, the clear alcohol pumping out of the can with soft gulping noises, some of it splashing over her bare feet. Then all at once she looked up, turned her head and looked straight at him. And he knew what she meant to do.

His whole body, his brain, his very *soul* turned cold. For the first time in his life he knew what absolute fear was. How could she know, she couldn't *possibly* know, how dangerous it was—what she was going to do—the terrible risk she'd be taking. And he couldn't warn her. Couldn't so much as shake his head or move his eyes, anything that might alert Shannon to her intentions. Because Shannon's eyes—and the gun—were riveted on Doug. Any signal from him and he and Joy would both be dead. All he could do was look at her and send the message with every fiber of his being, with all the force of his love for her behind it.

Don't do it! For God's sake, Joy—leave it to me. Please... no!

His heartbeat was a drum that resounded through his brain, deafening him. He couldn't think, couldn't breathe!

And then it happened. With a dancer's grace, Joy whirled and threw the last splash of alcohol onto the propane heater's gently flickering flame. There was only a soft *poof* of sound. The can dropped from Joy's hands with a clatter, and then she began to scream.

Doug struck out blindly, instinctively aiming for Shannon's gun hand even as he was pulling his own weapon from its hiding place. There was a bellow of surprise, outrage and pain. As Shannon's gun hit the floor, Doug kicked it as hard as he could toward the far end of the room, where the alcohol burned with its insidious and invisible blue fire. He thrust his gun straight into Shannon's face and yelled at him to get out, out of the cabin. Then all he thought about was Joy.

He lunged for her, caught her around the waist with one arm and lifted her clear off the floor. Shannon was already

at the cabin door. Doug all but tackled him, bulldozed him
through it and out onto the deck, hauling Joy with him.

"Out!" he screamed at Shannon. "Down the steps—
move!"

He couldn't see the flames, couldn't even tell what part of
her was burning! He half slid, half fell, with her down the
steps, pushed Shannon out of the way and dropped her into
the deep, wet snow, tumbling her over and over in it until she
struggled and flailed at him with her arms, yelling at him
that she was all right, except that he was smothering her to
death.

He rolled off her then, and turned his attention—and his
gun—back to Shannon. Propping himself on one elbow in
the snow, he managed to croak, "Don't...move."

His former partner was leaning against the side of the
Mercedes, staring at the cabin and swaying like a punch-
drunk fighter. Doug jerked his head around to see what was
happening. Breathing hard and covered with snow, he
watched the flames flicker and dance behind the window-
panes, a gleeful orange now that they'd found an abun-
dance of varnished wood and cloth fiber for fuel. Black
smoke was already beginning to billow from the open
doorway.

Shannon looked over at Doug and shrugged. "Sorry,
man." His smile was crooked. "We had some good times
here, didn't we?"

He pushed himself away from the car and began to walk
slowly toward the cabin, limping badly.

Doug shouted at him from his prone position, "Hey,
where do you think you're going? Get back here—come
on."

Shannon looked at him, almost in surprise. "What, you
don't think I'm going back with you, do you? Face all
that...face Carol...the kids? Uh-uh—no way, man. Can't
do it." He started walking again, almost dragging his bad
leg, slipping a little in the trampled snow.

"Jim—for God's sake, what are you doing? Are you
crazy?" Doug was struggling to sit up. In spite of the gun in
his hand he felt helpless. His throat felt raw.

Again his ex-partner paused to look back, this time smiling that lopsided, rueful smile. "I guess I have been, haven't I? But I'm not now. In fact, this is probably the sanest thing I've done in a long time." He turned once more toward the burning cabin.

Doug lurched to his feet, feeling as if his whole body had turned to lead. "Get back here, Shannon!" he yelled. "I'm not going to let you do it. You know I can't!"

By that time Shannon had almost reached the steps. He was shaking his head and laughing like his old, charming, handsome self. "What are you going to do, partner? Shoot me?"

"I will if I have to!"

He heard Shannon chuckle softly. "You couldn't shoot me, my friend. You haven't got it in you."

"I don't have to kill you to stop you," Doug grated between clenched teeth. He started forward, head down, like a bull charging.

Shannon backed away from him, moving up the steps, holding out his hand like a traffic cop. "Stop right there! I mean it—you can't stop me, Doug, don't even try!"

Doug stopped. He didn't say a word, just cocked his weapon, steadied it with both hands and took aim. Dimly, he heard Joy gasp.

Then Shannon spoke again in a soft, cracking voice. Pleading. "Hey, Doug—I took a bullet for you. For God's sake, you owe me your *life*. Please—do this for me. It's the best thing for everybody." His face contorted. He ended in a whisper, "Don't let Carol know...."

Doug's voice failed him. His body felt numb, boneless. He shook his head and managed an agonized groan. "I can't do it, Jim—please don't ask me! Please—"

He started toward him once more, slipped and went down on one knee in the melting snow. He scrambled desperately to his feet, his heart almost bursting his chest, just in time to see Shannon plunge through the cabin door, straight into the inferno.

"*Jim!*" The cry tore through his throat.

He lunged forward, but something grabbed his leg and held on, dragging him back. He yanked and pulled, but it wouldn't let go. Half blind with fury, he looked down and saw Joy clinging to his leg with both her arms as if her very life depended on it, breathing in frantic sobs.

He struck out at her, struggling to break free, yelling hoarsely, "Let go—I have to get Jim! Let me *go*, dammit!"

"No!" she screamed. "You can't—it's too late. Let him go! He's gone, can't you see that? Let him go!"

For a few moments more he fought her while she pulled at him with all her strength and will. But he could see that she was right, that it was too late. The cabin was fully engulfed; the heat from it scorched his face and turned the snow around him to slush that gleamed in the hellish light of the fire like molten gold.

He felt his knees buckle. The next thing he knew he was on the cold, soggy ground, and Joy's arms were wrapped around him, holding him so tightly he could barely breathe, and she was sobbing and whispering, *"It's over. It's over. Let him go . . . let him go."*

It had been a picture postcard day in Los Angeles. After washing the basin clean of smog the storm front had moved east, leaving the mountains unshrouded, for once, the better to show off their gorgeous, new snowy-white caps. All over the southland photographers were out in droves, taking advantage of the brilliant skies and unpolluted vistas, while at the higher elevations ski resort operators were busy counting their blessings and cash receipts.

Joy had spent most of the day in a hospital in Redlands, mostly for observation, after being treated for hypothermia, shock and second-degree burns to her hands and feet.

Doug, after being assured that Joy was in good hands and resting comfortably, spent the day in conferences with various law enforcement agencies and news media. Ironically, the press conference called to report the death of Assistant Chief of Police Jim Shannon in a tragic fire that destroyed his vacation cabin near Big Bear came only hours after the one announcing his selection as the new head of the Los Angeles Police Department.

There hadn't been any reference at all to the infamous "Rhinestone Collar" murder case. Eventually, Doug knew, he and Lieutenant Mabry were going to have to decide just exactly how they were going to handle the reappearance of the key witness in the case. It was clear that the murder itself couldn't remain forever officially "unsolved."

Now it was evening, and Doug and Joy were in the white Mercedes heading home, straight into the setting sun. They hadn't done much talking on the way into L.A. Doug had the radio on, tuned to the Dodgers' pregame show, which was leading up to the postponed second game of the National League Championship Series. But when the headline news came on, he switched it off.

In the droning silence that fell then, he heard Joy clear her throat, swallow and say gruffly, "It's okay to grieve, you know. He was your friend."

Grieve? He wasn't sure he even knew how to grieve for Jim Shannon. He didn't know what to feel. He knew that the pain inside him was still sharp and bitter.

After a moment he nodded, frowning fiercely into the sun. "More than a friend. He saved my life, you know." He laughed painfully. "And my ass more than once. He was...more like a brother."

Joy nodded and looked away, out the side window. God only knew what *she* must be feeling.

She gave a liquid little laugh and said, "I guess I sure was wrong about that one, wasn't I?"

"Wrong?" He took a deep breath and made an effort to pull his thoughts together. There was so much he wanted—needed—to say to her. "Wrong about what?"

"What I said about lovers...friends. I guess both can let you down, huh?"

"Oh. Yeah..." He thought about it, then said softly, "Well, people do, you know—they just aren't always perfect, or even the way we'd like them to be."

He felt her flinch at the irony in his voice and knew she'd misunderstood. He was sorry he wasn't saying it very well.

He wasn't very good at this sort of thing, and he wasn't even sure he had it all sorted out in his own mind yet. Too much had happened in a very short time. He felt shaky, as if he were the one who had just been released from a hospital.

Joy whispered to the window glass, "Yeah...guess you can't really count on anybody."

She wondered why he didn't turn the baseball game back on. He didn't seem to be in the mood to talk, and anything, she thought, would be better than the silence.

But then he began to speak in a slow, cautious way, as if he had something to say that was going to be very difficult for him. Something painful. Oh, God, she thought, here it comes. Her stomach knotted and grew cold with dread.

He said, "I've been thinking...you know, about what you said? About there being two different kinds of love—friendship and passionate? And it's true, I guess, they'll both let you down. But what I've decided, is, there's other kinds of love you didn't mention. The kind I'm talking about, I don't think... I'm not sure I can explain it—at least, not very well—but what it is, is...something that happens when you have both of those, plus this..." He struggled with it, bringing his hand up to his chest, clenched tightly in a fist. "Part of it, I guess, is something that just happens, like with wild geese and wolves, you know? But the other part is more like...it's a choice. You make a decision."

"A commitment," said Joy, watching him now with breath suspended.

He threw her a distracted frown. "Yeah, I guess. You decide that this is the person you're going to spend your life with, and you choose to accept that person—all of that person, along with whatever faults and imperfections she might have, and you dump all your faults and imperfections on her because you trust her to accept and love you in spite of them. Is that what you call commitment?"

"I think so," said Joy, air-starved and shaking.

"I think so, too," said Doug, and fell into an exhausted silence.

She wanted very much to strangle him. When the suspense had become unbearable, she forced her constricted throat to swallow and muttered, "What are you trying to say, MacDougal?" It came out sounding bumpy and uneven, as if she were riding in a wagon on a rough and rocky road.

"What am I trying to say? What do you *think* I'm trying to say?" He threw her another look, distraught and angry. "I'm saying how I feel about *you*, dammit!"

"Well, *excuse me*," she flung right back at him, "but this isn't quite how I thought it would be to have somebody declare eternal love for me!" It was a relief to be yelling. "And if you don't mind my saying so, you don't seem very happy about it!"

"I'm not!" he shouted back. "How can I be happy when I don't know what in the world I'm going to do about it? I'm a cop, dammit—I don't know how to *be* anything else."

"Why in the world *should* you be anything else?"

"Because—I told you. Cops make lousy husbands."

"Oh, for heaven's sake, MacDougal! Sure, some do. Some doctors, plumbers, accountants and farmers make lousy husbands, too."

Silence fell, charged with emotion and filled with the sounds of agitated breathing. Then Joy drew a quivering breath and said quietly, "Tell me something, MacDougal. Was your dad a lousy husband?"

"What?" Doug threw her a look, wondering what she was getting at. "I don't know, sometimes I think he was, yeah."

"What about your mother? Did you ever ask her how *she* felt about it?"

Doug couldn't explain it, the way that quiet question hit him. He only knew that all of a sudden all the pain he was feeling seemed to be concentrated in his chest and throat. He felt himself flashing back once more to that cemetery in the rain, watching his father weep . . . only this time it was his mother's face he was seeing. For the first time in his memory he saw the look of love on his mother's face, the look of fierce and protective devotion. And he saw something else.

He saw that his father's arm was around his wife's shoulders, and that he was holding on to her as if she were the only thing keeping him from falling. Leaning on her strength. Drawing comfort from the absolute certainty of her love.

And he didn't say anything at all. He couldn't.

Joy watched MacDougal's profile, his solid-as-a-rock, strong, dependable profile, blurred now by vulnerability and uncertainty. Her heart swelled and quivered with tenderness. Yes, she thought. Oh, yes... with all his faults and imperfections...

"Hey," she squeaked, "where are you going?"

She clutched at the dash with a bandaged hand as MacDougal suddenly made a left turn onto Vine, heading south toward Melrose instead of north, toward his place.

"MacDougal," she murmured a short time later, laughing nervously, "what are we doing here? Are you out of your mind? Put me down!"

She was in MacDougal's arms. He was carrying her because of her bandaged feet, and they were standing smack in the middle of the landscaped strip that runs down the center of Highland Avenue. The long line of towering palm trees were silhouettes against a sky of gaudy coral and salmon. The light was a golden wash, the color of fantasy.... Pure Hollywood.

"Hush," said MacDougal, turning with her in a slow circle. "Tell me what you see."

"Uh...palm trees. Great, big, gorgeous houses."

He shook his head, impatient with her. "What did you see ten years ago? When you asked that gardener to snap your picture...."

"Oh, that," she whispered. "That was just make-believe. Dreams. Impossible dreams."

"*No*—not impossible." He lowered her bandaged feet carefully to the damp grass and caught her to him, capturing her face with one hand, the gentleness in it in sharp contrast to the fervor in his voice. "Joy—those dreams are still there, I know they are. You can still have them. You can have it all."

She was shaking her head, holding his face between her
hands. "No—no—it was a long time ago. It doesn't matter
now. I told you—I've grown up. I've changed a lot. I know
what's important now."

"But that's just it," said MacDougal. "It does matter.
Dreams are important. Don't you know that? Maybe even
the most important things of all, because it's what makes us
more than just animals, bent on surviving. You *need* those
dreams. Just like you need love."

"But," she whispered, "that's all I want. For you ... to
love me."

He smiled at her with so much tenderness she began to
cry, tears welling up and pouring down her cheeks, wetting
his fingers. "Honey, you already have me. Where's the
challenge in that?"

She drew a trembling breath and let it go with laughter.

"Promise me," he said hoarsely, bending his forehead to
hers. "Swear a solemn vow on this palm tree right here ...
that if you marry me—"

"*If* I marry you!"

"—You won't give up on your dreams. *Promise.*"

"I promise," she sobbed, and he sealed it with his kiss.

A little while later, while they were crawling up the steep,
winding road to Doug's house in Old Faithful, he said,
"About marrying me..."

"Anytime," she murmured. "My calendar is clear. And
I'm pretty much unencumbered with relatives and such."

"Well, actually ... that's what I wanted to know. About
your family. Don't you want them to be here? Have you
thought about trying to get in touch with them again?"

She took a deep breath and huffed it out, then laughed in
a tight, fragile way. "Oh, boy. I don't know. I think I'd like
to find my little sisters someday, but not now. Not for this.
It's too much, you know what I mean? I think I'd like it to
be just us, if that's okay. Oh—of course, and *your* family."

Doug chuckled ominously. "You don't know what you're
asking for." And then, very gently, he said, "No family, no
friends at all? You're sure?"

"Yeah—oh, well...actually, you know, there are some people I'd really like to have there, but I don't know how you'd feel about it." She colored slightly, looking almost apologetic. "They're from Saint Vincent's...homeless, you know?"

"Saint Vincent's, huh?" He paused. "They, um... wouldn't happen to include a little tiny feisty lady—wears a baseball cap—and a tall, skinny white-haired guy who looks like Charlton Heston, and a great big slow-moving black kid, would they?"

"How did you know?" Joy asked, staring at him with those great, luminous eyes of hers, smiling that wrap-around smile.

"Oh," he said dryly, "we've met. Plus...right now they just happen to be sitting up there on my front steps. And believe it or not, the black guy seems to be wearing your cat around his neck—kind of like one of those fox stoles from the 1930s."

"Omigod," she gasped. "How—"

He pulled the white Mercedes into his driveway and shut off the motor. He looked at the woman beside him and felt laughter welling up inside him...laughter and sunshine. And Joy.

And who in this world, he thought, grateful for a wisdom far greater than his own, needs laughter, sunshine and joy in his life more than a cop?

Epilogue

A couple of years later...

Preacher shot his tuxedo sleeves, peeled back the edge of his white glove and peered for the seventh or eighth time at his watch.

"What," he muttered, "can be keeping that woman? All she had to do was wash and fill up the car. Here it's almost time to go and she's not back yet. Sometimes I—oh for heaven's sake, JoJo, come here and let me fix that. I told you to stop fiddling with it, didn't I? A tie is not a plaything!"

"It feels funny," said JoJo, looking mulish. "I don't like it."

"You want our Mary to be proud of us, don't you? The Music Center is a nice place. Therefore, *we* must look nice as well. Chin up...there. That's better."

"Do I look nice now?" JoJo sounded doubtful.

"Like a prince," Preacher assured him. "Like a prince. Now—do you remember what you're supposed to do?"

JoJo nodded, smiling happily. "I'm the bodyguard. I walk right behind Mary and watch out for her so nobody can't hurt her."

"That's right. Only not *too* close—don't step on her heels. And for heaven's sake, *don't smile.* We don't want to cause a panic."

"Don't smile," repeated JoJo, trying his best not to.

Preacher sighed. "Don't worry, as her manager I'll be right there beside you. We must try not to—oh, thank God."

"Here comes Daisy," said JoJo helpfully, as the white Mercedes chugged slowly into view up the narrow, winding street.

"Mrs. Pepper, what in the world kept you?" scolded Preacher as Daisy stepped out of the car, tugging at the cuffs of her brand new chauffeur's uniform. "It's time we were leaving. We can't be late—not on opening night!"

"Quit fussing," snapped Daisy. "I was just having a few words with that bozo at the gas station about his dirty diesel, is all. Told him if he didn't clean up his act we was gonna take Sergeant MacDougal's business elsewhere." She gave a lofty sniff.

"Huh," said Preacher. "You know the man won't hear of that. When it comes to his hard-luck cases—"

"Here they come," said JoJo. His voice sounded unusually hushed as he shifted excitedly from one foot to the other.

As the door at the top of the stairs opened they could hear Maurice yelling, "Hey, baby...*shake it, baby!*" Then Mary stepped into view, wearing a coat of soft blue brocade, with rhinestones winking at the base of her throat. The cop followed, wearing a tuxedo just like Preacher's and JoJo's. He pulled the door shut, cutting off Maurice's exhortations in mid-syllable, then offered Mary his arm. Smiling at one another, they started down the long flight of steps, which Daisy had spent the afternoon sweeping clean of bougainvillea blossoms.

"Ah," said Daisy, beaming like a doting mama, "don't she look pretty, though?"

"They do make a handsome couple," agreed Preacher. "I told you that policeman was going to turn out all right. He does seem to make our Mary happy."

"Well," said Daisy with a sniff, "I don't know. I'm gonna wait and see what kind of daddy he makes. *Then* I let you know."

"Mrs. Pepper!" Preacher grabbed her excitedly by the arm and spoke in a hoarse whisper. "Then it's definite? When did she find out? Did she tell you?"

"Men," scoffed Daisy as she shook herself loose. "She don't have to tell me a thing. All you gotta do is look at her. She's got that *glow.*"

"What glow?" said JoJo, looking bewildered.

"Hush!" said Daisy out of one side of her mouth, as Mary and the cop arrived at the bottom of the steps. She reached grandly to open the back door of the Mercedes, then snapped smartly to attention.

"Oh, you guys," said Mary, breaking into a nervous giggle.

The cop handed her into the back seat with a care that warmed Preacher's heart clear to its core. Before he got in beside her, though, he straightened up and said, "You guys going to be okay in the Bronco?"

"We'll be right behind you," Preacher assured him, beaming. His new driver's license was in his wallet, right there in his hip pocket. The feel of it, just thinking about it, made him proud.

Daisy was sitting in the driver's seat waiting for the diesel coil to warm up. When the engine fired, she slammed her door and yelled, "See you guys later!" The Mercedes backed slowly out of the driveway.

"All the way..." murmured Preacher. When the car had disappeared from view he pulled a handkerchief out of his pocket, surreptitiously dabbed at his eyes and then loudly blew his nose.

In the back seat of the Mercedes, Joy took a deep breath, huffed it out and said, "Hoo boy!"

"Nervous?" asked Doug tenderly, reaching for her hand.

She gave him the look he hadn't seen in a long time, the crushed-mouth, luminous eyes...the scared, vulnerable waif look. "God, yes. Oh man, MacDougal, the *Music Center*. And Andrew Lloyd Webber! I can't believe I'm actually going to be on a stage singing *that song*. I mean, *Streisand* sings that song. Who do I think I am? Oh, God, I'm going to be sick."

"Sweetheart," said Doug fervently, "if anybody can do that song justice, it's you. You've been there. You know what it's like. Just sing like you always do, my love—from your heart and soul. And nobody in this world can touch you—*including* Streisand!"

Joy studied him for a moment, then leaned over and gravely kissed him. But the waif-look remained.

"Now what?" Doug asked, his voice gentle.

She swallowed audibly. "MacDougal, I'm scared. Not about tonight. About...what comes after. I mean, what if..."

Doug shrugged, all his love for her in his eyes...and clogging up his throat. "It happens sometimes, love. Dreams do come true."

"Yes, but...I already have everything I want." Her voice was hushed, frightened. "I don't want to lose it."

"What do you think you're going to lose, huh? Me? Listen, lady, I'll be the big burly cop standing in the wings beaming so hard with pride they'll have to throw a tarp over me to shut off the glow. Don't you know that? Silly..."

A ghost, just a ghost of her megawatt smile appeared. "I know. I guess...I'm just afraid I...don't deserve so much happiness."

"Nobody," growled Doug, doing his George C. Scott impression, "deserves it more than you do. By God, you've *earned* it. And there's more where that came from, believe me. A whole lifetime's worth. I intend to make damn sure of that."

Her smile began to bloom in earnest, then, but she caught it back, pressing her fingertips to her lips. "Omigod—that reminds me. I have something important to tell you. Something really, really..."

A few moments later, up in the driver's seat, Daisy heard the cop give a shout of pure delight. "He said it's for sure? *When?* Hey—you...come here and let me..."

Daisy looked in the rear-view mirror and smiled. Then, with what was for her the most unwonted and unprecedented tact, she turned the mirror aside.

* * * * *

And now for something completely different....

SPELLBOUND
R O M A N C E

**In January, look for
SAM'S WORLD (IM #615)
by Ann Williams**

Contemporary Woman: Marina Ross had landed in the strangest of worlds: the future. And her only ally was the man responsible for bringing her there.

Future Man: Sam's world was one without emotion or passion, one he was desperately trying to save—even as he himself felt the first stirrings of desire....

**Don't miss SAM'S WORLD,
by Ann Williams, available this January,
only from**

INTIMATE MOMENTS®
Silhouette®

SPELL6

HUSBAND: SOME ASSEMBLY REQUIRED
Marie Ferrarella
(SE #931, January)

Murphy Pendleton's act of bravery landed him in the
hospital—and right back in Shawna Saunders's life.
She'd lost her heart to him before—and now this dashing real-life hero was just too tempting to resist. He
could be the Mr. Right Shawna was waiting for....

Don't miss
HUSBAND: SOME ASSEMBLY REQUIRED,
by Marie Ferrarella,
available in January!

She's friend, wife, mother—she's you! And beside
each Special Woman stands a wonderfully
special man. It's a celebration of our heroines—
and the men who become part of their lives.

EXTRA! EXTRA! READ ALL ABOUT...
MORE ROMANCE
MORE SUSPENSE
MORE INTIMATE MOMENTS

Join us in February 1995 when Silhouette Intimate Moments introduces the first title in a whole new program: INTIMATE MOMENTS EXTRA. These break-through, innovative novels by your favorite category writers will come out every few months, beginning with Karen Leabo's *Into Thin Air*, IM #619.

Pregnant teenagers had been disappearing without a trace, and Detectives Caroline Triece and Austin Lomax were called in for heavy-duty damage control...because now the missing girls were turning up dead.

In May, Merline Lovelace offers *Night of the Jaguar*, and other INTIMATE MOMENTS EXTRA novels will follow throughout 1995, only in—